W9-DED-535

search history

search history

/ A NOVEL /

amy taylor

THE DIAL PRESS
NEW YORK

Published in the United States by The Dial Press, an imprint of Random House, a division of Penguin Random House LLC, New York.

THE DIAL PRESS is a registered trademark and the colophon is a trademark of Penguin Random House LLC.

Originally published in Australia by Allen & Unwin.

LIBRARY OF CONGRESS CATALOGING-IN-PUBLICATION DATA
Names: Taylor, Amy.
Title: Search history: a novel / Amy Taylor.
Description: First edition. | New York: The Dial Press [2023] | Originally published in Australia by Allen & Unwin.
Identifiers: LCCN 2023007453 (print) | LCCN 2023007454 (ebook) | ISBN 9780593595572 (hardcover; acid-free paper) | ISBN 9780593595589 (ebook)
Subjects: LCGFT: Romance fiction. | Novels.
Classification: LCC PR9619.4.T34 S43 2023 (print) | LCC PR9619.4.T34 (ebook) | DDC 823/.92--dc23/eng/20230524
LC record available at https://lccn.loc.gov/2023007453
LC ebook record available at https://lccn.loc.gov/2023007454

PRINTED IN CANADA ON ACID-FREE PAPER

randomhousebooks.com

2 4 6 8 9 7 5 3 1

First U.S. Edition

For C&L, of course.

search history

CHAPTER
one

At some point after a breakup, the desire to sleep with someone else arrives. There is no universal timeline for how long this takes. On one occasion the desire showed up almost immediately, winking seductively at me from a doorway. On another, I'd tried to force its appearance, placing the cart before the horse, only to find myself weeping in the limp arms of a disappointed and horny stranger. This time, when my ex and I broke up, it took a few months; a period I spent busying myself with logistical distractions—moving out of the house we shared, and, later, packing up my halved possessions and fleeing across the country. Then, when the desire did eventually turn up, I did what was expected of me: I selected someone from an app.

The man I chose told me he worked as a chef at a wine bar in Fitzroy, so I looked it up online. On the bar's account I was able to find photos of him that weren't included in his sparse dating app profile. In one photo he wore a navy apron and held out a plate of food for the camera: a chunk of charred meat floating in a thick beige sauce. His face held a sly grin. I found him handsome. I liked his smiling green eyes and the evidence of a sense of humor in the arrangement of his features. I spent an unreasonable amount of time zoomed in on his hands. They were pale, freckled, and a little rough. They made my stomach flutter. I've always been attracted to a man's hands; I love the way they look, and I love what they can do to me.

Even though we'd never met, The Chef and I fell quickly into the habit of messaging each other every day. He was consistently quick to respond and, to me, this felt strange, as if he lived behind the screen of my phone and waited to be summoned. After four days of unbroken dialogue, I woke up to a message that read:

Sleep well? :) x

That's when I wondered if I'd done something wrong. Maybe I'd forgotten to signal early on that I didn't want a date, only the part that comes after. I wasn't interested in receiving good morning messages. I was still enjoying the pang of loss I felt when I woke up alone. I didn't want his intrusion, but I also didn't want to hurt his feelings. I frowned at my phone and began to workshop ways to subtly set expectations.

That night, apropos of nothing, he sent me a photo of his dick captioned: *Free tonight?* and I laughed at myself.

//

While I waited for him to arrive, I changed my outfit four times. Then I walked around my apartment, simultaneously tidying and disguising any evidence of effort. Eventually I sat down on the couch and messaged my friend Beverly to let her know he was coming over. I included a screenshot of his account.

Be safe!!! she replied and sent a string of pink love hearts.

He showed up just after eleven, a wine bottle in hand.

"Here, this is for us. It's French, from Beaujolais," he said, placing the bottle down on the kitchen counter and taking his jacket off. "I stole it from the bar."

"Thanks," I said, unsure of how to respond to any part of that sentence.

I was surprised by his size; he was tall and broad and when he opened his arms to hug me, he entirely absorbed me. He smelled like grease and charcoal. I tried to imagine myself turning up to have sex with someone after working a ten-hour shift and not showering, but I couldn't. I'd showered and shaved. I'd put on makeup. I'd tidied my apartment and lit a candle.

He draped his jacket over the back of my couch, before wandering across the room. It occurred to me then that he was the first visitor I'd had since I moved to Melbourne after the breakup, and I realized that by being the only person who had stepped foot in my apartment, I had imbued it with a particular and very personal energy. I felt his energy spreading around, muddying the room as if he were literally tracking a pair of dirty boots across my floor. I wondered then if I genuinely wanted to do this, or if I had just relented to the pressure of this seemingly expected act of moving on. Was I exercising my freedoms as a sexually liberated fourth-wave feminist by sleeping with a stranger I'd met online? Or was I betraying my freedom by choosing to engage in a sexual experience that I was feeling increasingly apprehensive of?

I wondered what he was thinking.

I opened the bottle of wine and watched him casually consider the collection of books I'd stacked on the floor. I felt exposed. The same way I felt as a teenager, my stomach in knots, as I watched the first boy I'd ever had in my bedroom browse my CD collection.

"You have lots of books," he said, holding one in his hand. With an ache I thought of all the books I'd left abandoned in the house my ex and I had shared back in Perth. When I fled shortly after our separation, many of my belongings (my coffee machine, my couch) were sacrificed.

"Do you read much?" I asked.

"Nah," he said, putting the book back down.

That was probably strike three, but I'd already lost count.

It was evident from his unfocused gaze and clunky movements that he was not sober but that didn't bother me. I only hoped to yield momentarily to a blinding and deafening diversion, that elevated form of release that you can't give to yourself. I wanted to lose myself, even for a second, against an unfamiliar body, and then I wanted to sit on a stranger's face until my body felt like it belonged to me again.

We drank the wine and made an earnest effort at conversation, fumbling through some small talk about his shift. When enough conversation had passed, I moved toward him and kissed him. He seemed a little surprised that I'd made the first move and it was awkward for a few beats, our mouths moving at different speeds, our teeth overly present. Then he took control and guided me across the short distance between my kitchen and the bedroom. He pulled at my jumper, my favorite jumper, and I took it off myself so he wouldn't stretch out the neckline. Then I helped him remove his T-shirt. He was so different from my ex, so much bigger. This was an immediate relief; I needed someone completely unrecognizable. I didn't want to feel any hipbones pressing into me. I specifically required someone who wasn't going to arrive wearing a threadbare hooded jumper and a pair of jeans held up by an old shoelace.

When we reached my bed, he pushed me down onto it and something inside me lit up. He stared at me and took his pants off slowly without breaking eye contact. Then he said, "You want it so bad, don't you?" And something inside me switched back off.

I allowed him to continue to lead, though it became obvious that he was performing a method he had most likely perfected in his last long-term relationship and now applied like a template to all his sexual encounters. His exploration of my body felt like an uninteresting task he was required to complete for a reward. He ran his hands over me with impatience, like he was keen to move on. He swooped his head down to kiss me, his technique all exhale and tongue. Then he pulled away and smiled as if to tease me, before swooping once again. All of this was accompanied by a surprising level of confidence. He seemed sure that he knew what I wanted and didn't need to ask me or read any nonverbal cues. I could have told him what I wanted, but I didn't. I couldn't find the right words; the ones that wouldn't wound him and instantly halt the momentum, leaving us stranded somewhere. Instead, I sent him body language signals, slowing my movements down and shifting his searching fingers to the left by moving my hips. I made affirming noises when he got closer to the right speed, location, and pressure. He bulldozed blindly through these cues. Whether this was because they didn't land or because he thought himself in possession of a better idea, I wasn't sure.

Then he was on his knees, guiding himself inside me. I sucked air through my teeth as he entered me, my own body not quite ready. The first few thrusts hurt, but I moaned anyway. The futility of the situation was becoming apparent, but I felt the weight of the unspoken commitment made in these kinds of situations. A line that, once crossed, signaled it was too late to back out. In this case, a line established because: (1) He caught an Uber from Fitzroy to Brunswick for me. (2) He stole us a bottle of wine. (3) He might not like being told no.

I attempted to engineer a change of position so I could be on top of him, a final effort to gain back some control, but it was ignored. He placed one hand on the wall behind my bed and his other hand around my neck. I surmised then that his last girlfriend was probably into being choked and he'd assumed I would be too. The alternative to this theory was that it was for his own pleasure that he choked women, a problematic distinction. I could breathe fine and so I didn't bother to move his hand.

By this stage, his pounding rhythm had bored me, and I'd begun to detach from my body. I sank into numbness and the climax I'd been working toward left the room entirely. Soon his rhythm became faster and less conscious, which told me that he was getting close. I participated by gripping his body with my legs and moaning, engaging my pelvic floor and running my nails over his back, performing a sort of exorcism to speed things up. He didn't make any noise besides breathing heavily and aerobically. His grip on my neck tightened. Blurry shadows scattered across my vision, and I wondered if I should say something. Maybe if I hadn't retreated so far away and didn't feel so much like a spectator, I would have. Instead, I simply watched him with detached curiosity as black seeped into my vision, first from the outer corners and then moving inward to the center.

//

The first thing I saw when I opened my eyes was The Chef crouching over me, naked, ghostly white and terrified. He was shaking me by the shoulders.

"Fuck. Fuck. Fuck," he was repeating in a panicked voice. His flaccid dick swung back and forth, tapping against my thigh. I groaned.

"Holy shit, Ana, are you okay?" he asked, letting go of me.

"Yeah, I'm okay," I replied, surprised at the smallness of my voice.

When I sat up, I noticed my hands were trembling.

"Oh my god." He sighed with relief and sat down on the bed next to me. "*Jesus*—that was scary. What happened? Are you sure you're okay?"

I suddenly, urgently, wanted him out of my apartment.

"I'm fine," I answered. "Sorry, could you please just leave? I'm okay."

He seemed torn by my request: Did it imply I was angry at him? Would there be consequences if I was? Who was in the wrong here?

"Why didn't you say anything?" he asked.

There it was: my part of the blame stated out loud to remind me that this wasn't his fault entirely.

"Please just go. I'm fine."

"Okay, okay," he said, his hands held up in defeat.

He pulled his pants on, followed by his T-shirt, and finally his boots. I sat and watched from the bed, not yet ready to move. Once his jacket was on, he hovered awkwardly by the front door.

"Are you sure you're okay?" he asked for the third time.

"I'm *fine*."

"Okay, well . . ." He looked down at his phone and then back at me. "Bye, I guess."

He pulled the door shut behind him, and in the silence that followed, I realized I could hear myself breathing. I lay back down on my bed, closed my eyes, and focused on slowing my breath down. Then I made my way slowly to the bathroom. In the shower, I rocked side to side, rolling the stream of water from shoulder to shoulder until the hot ran out. I pulled on a pair of trackpants and a jumper and watched in the mirror as the bruising around my neck grew darker and darker.

An hour or so after he left, he sent me a message:

Hey Ana, that was really messed
up. I didn't realize what was
happening, you should have said
something. I hope you're okay.

I closed the message and held my finger over the dating app icon until it began to tremble nervously, then I deleted it.

CHAPTER
two

A week later I was on the tram to work when I noticed the woman in the row of seats in front of mine was crafting a message. It seemed like she was having some difficulty. I leaned forward so I could see the whole thread. The message she was responding to read:

Friday night was fun, are you free
for a drink this weekend? x

So far, she had drafted:

Hey, I had fun too. I'm really sorry,
but I just don't think

Uh oh, I thought, here comes the soft letdown. She paused and then deleted *think*, replacing it with *feel*. I saw what she did there. *Feel* has more conviction; it's harder to argue with. A good tactic. She chewed her thumbnail as she turned to look out the window, and my eyes followed hers. It was a grim, cold morning and the sky was a consistent shade of gray, unmarked by the blemish of a single cloud; it looked flat and vaguely unreal. I watched as two droplets of water raced each other down the window, leaving trails of moisture behind them. The carriage was full of other blank-faced morning commuters, all of us looking presentable but lacking in some vital force, like clothing hung in a wardrobe. When I looked back at the woman's phone, I saw she'd finished the message.

Hey, I had fun too. I'm really sorry, but I just don't feel like there was real chemistry between us. It was nice to meet you though :)

She placed one hand on the pole next to her and, without taking her eyes from the message, she pressed the bell for her stop. Then she reread the message a few more times and hit send. A response came back suspiciously quickly:

No worries. Thanks.

Another message swiftly followed:

You shouldn't have let me pay for the second bottle if you weren't interested.

The tram rattled to a stop, and she pulled her bag over her shoulder, leaving her seat to stand by the door. Her eyes flicked toward me, and I quickly glanced back out the window. The doors clanged open and cold air rushed into the tram as she left. I watched her cross the street, intently looking at her phone once again, her fingers typing. The tram crawled on and I turned my attention to my own phone, specifically to the vacant space that had been previously occupied. Over the last few weeks, I'd grown accustomed to daily conversations with men who wanted to sleep with me. Now, with the app deleted, it seemed that I had unknowingly become reliant on that attention, and the sudden absence of it left me in my own company for periods of time when I'd otherwise have been blissfully distracted. I knew that other unexamined habits had a way of imposing themselves quickly on newly vacated space, and I watched as my fingers moved of their own accord, navigating a well-worn path that led me straight to my ex's Instagram account.

My ex had unfollowed me a few weeks after we broke up and, reactively, I'd decided to permanently delete my account. This, on reflection, was a desperate clamber for higher ground, but at the time it felt strategic and powerful; a checkmate. I regretted the decision now. The option of simply unfollowing him back had felt at the time like the equivalent of shouting: "No, fuck *you!*" An admission of hurt I was not willing to make. But I'd overlooked the option of doing nothing; I could have allowed my account's presence in his follower list to remain as a constant reminder of my maturity. I would have appeared nonchalant, or even entirely oblivious to his passive aggression. Now I was certain that would have been more satisfying. But instead, I'd deleted my account altogether.

In the days after that act, it was as though I'd stumbled upon the not-so-secret secret to happiness. I felt clearheaded and liberated, my mind no longer clouded with the irrelevant details of other people's lives. I was excited by the abundance of spare time and the dizzying potential it held. I watched TV series and movies with a new heightened focus, appreciating the physical acting and following the plotlines with ease. In moments of stillness, when I'd usually mindlessly scroll, I opted instead to stare out of windows or to close my eyes. I went for slow, meandering walks, stopping to touch the trunks of trees, or to marvel at dew-covered leaves, or to smile directly into the faces of flowers. I was unbearably smug. Then, on the morning of day eight, I created a ghost account and visited my ex's profile, and I'd logged on nearly every day since.

Now I was a silent observer. As well as my ex, I began haunting the profiles of all the friends I'd left behind in Perth. I read the comments they left on each other's posts, as if I were grinning and laughing along with them, only from the bushes outside their window. Mostly I enjoyed having no identity. I liked the way the algorithm was perplexed by me; it kept offering up random content in a desperate attempt to figure out what I wanted, so I could be lured back into the fold, but I followed no one, I liked nothing, and I never posted. What was I looking for?

Recently, one of my ex's friends had posted a photo of him mid goofy laugh with all his crooked teeth on display. When I saw it I felt a rush of superiority. Here it is, I thought. This was what I was looking for: an unflattering photo to as- suage my tender ego. But I didn't enjoy the feeling for long before I chastised myself for using something as superficial as appearance to dictate worth. There was also the fact that my ex's crooked teeth and stupid laugh were some of the things I'd loved the most about him.

Now, when his account loaded, I saw that he'd posted a new photo. This was unusual. It was a vinyl purchase, a col- lector's edition Black Flag album, with a mug of black coffee next to it. I saw Larry, my monstera plant, forlorn and droop- ing in the top right corner of the shot. Then I noticed a second mug of coffee on the far right of the coffee table. There was a small hand clasped around the mug, and the small hand had pastel blue painted nails.

Who was she? With the limited facts at my disposal immediately exhausted, I employed my imagination. He would have met her at the bar where she worked. After she cleared the glasses from his table, he would have watched her walk away, a bar towel swinging from the back pocket of her black jeans. Then he would have glanced at her every so often, deliberately getting caught in the act so he could lead her to believe she had the upper hand. Eventually, at the end of the night, he would have asked for her number, and she would have smiled coyly and given it to him, flattered that he had chosen her when he appeared to choose so few. Then, after a date or two, she would have begun to interpret his delayed and short message replies as sudden disinterest and, without realizing it, she would have embarked on the never-ending journey of desperately trying to win back the initial high of his approval. That's why she would have continued to sleep with him, even though she was probably far more attractive than he was.

There were no comments, and the post had collected only thirteen likes, all of which I recognized as his friends. There was nothing to direct me further. I locked my phone and looked back out of the window, but my eyes slid across a gray blur of unrecognizable buildings. I'd missed my stop.

three

"What's stopping you?" the voice asked. "Time? Money? Discipline?"

A montage of black-and-white movie clips, most likely pirated, transitioned across the projector screen. Dramatic music rallied toward a crescendo.

"You have a choice. You can sit there and let the world stop you or you can fight back," the voice continued.

A gymnast spun in the air before landing triumphantly on both feet. A boxer stared into her own eyes in a mirror, beads of sweat dripping down her forehead. A clip from *The Pursuit of Happyness* was shown for the second time.

"Because nothing can stop you unless you let it. You only have one life to live."

At Gro this was known as the Monday Motivation Meeting. It involved my boss, Paul, playing an inspirational video he had found on YouTube to the entire team.

I looked across the ping-pong table at Paul. The images on the screen were reflected in his glasses. It was obvious from the small, unconscious nodding movements he was making that he was completely invested in the video. Paul was a silver fox; the type of man whose well-placed wrinkles made him more attractive. He was quintessentially corporate. His personality could be described as *professional*. He probably exited the womb with a full set of veneers and a meeting to get to.

I returned my eyes to the screen. The scenes transitioned faster. A woman collapsed in tears of joy after running through the tape at a finish line. A ballerina grimaced as she rubbed her bruised and bleeding feet. Steve Jobs presented the iPhone to a cheering audience.

I assumed Paul hoped these videos would stoke the flames of ambition in the pits of our stomachs and send us back to our desks with a renewed motivation, as if the secret to increasing employee productivity could be unlocked by watching old videos of Michael Jordan dunking.

"Only you can let yourself be stopped. So, will you be stopped? You have to make that choice."

I glanced around the room and wondered whether the furrowed brows or vacant expressions on the faces of my colleagues told me I was not the only one who didn't enjoy being forced to grapple with the purpose of my existence at eight-thirty on a Monday morning.

I found Soph and tried to catch her eye. She wore her blond hair loosely tied so that it trailed down the back of her white shirt. As always, she had the luminous, dewy glow of a person who can somehow wear multiple layers of makeup while also concealing any evidence of its application. She looked back at me, smirked, and rolled her eyes. We would mock this video later. We would send each other funny GIFs and I would feel better.

"Don't be stopped. It's that simple. Just don't stop," the

voice concluded. The music faded out and the screen went black. I tugged at the collar of my turtleneck sweater to try to let some air in; it was far too muggy in the office to be dressed like this, but I didn't want to take the sweater off and expose my bruises. Even though they were over a week old, they still bloomed across my neck, only now in a disturbingly jaundiced color. Paul switched the office lights back on and I took a sip of my coffee.

When I first interviewed at Gro for the position of user experience designer, Paul had sat across the table from me, one of his legs slung over the other and one loafered foot jigging as if pulled by a string. He explained that Gro's purpose was to "demystify investing and empower our clients to build wealth." I learned a lot during that meeting, like, for example, that Gro was no different from a traditional hedge fund except it had an aesthetically designed app and an office located in a renovated warehouse filled with plants. Paul dressed the story of Gro up in a philanthropic idealism ("helping, empowering"), which felt odd considering the company offered a straightforward exchange of service for payment. It wasn't even a particularly affordable service.

"So, Ana, why do you want to work here at Gro?" Paul had asked, and I'd resisted the urge to start listing Maslow's physiological needs: food, water, shelter—all of which required money. Then I remembered the magic word: "culture."

"From what I've seen," I said, aiming for sincerity, "Gro has an incredible culture."

Paul leaned back in his chair, absolutely chuffed. "I'm so glad you said that. We've worked hard to create a culture here at Gro that we can all be proud of."

"I can see that." I smiled, pretending that earlier, when I'd used the bathroom, I hadn't heard someone sobbing in the stall next to mine.

The fact was that I needed a job and he was offering me one. The only other interview I'd managed to get was at a female-only rideshare start-up called She Moves. During that interview, one of the CEO's official interview questions was: "What's your star sign?" When I told her I was a Scorpio she pulled a *yikes* face and by the time I'd reached my tram stop I had a *We regret to inform you . . .* email sitting in my inbox. *ChauffHer was the obvious choice,* I wanted to reply.

Fair to say I had needed little encouragement to accept Paul's offer, and when I saw that my desk would be in an isolated corner, far from the ping-pong table, I smiled and shook his hand.

According to Soph, Paul started the Monday Motivation Meeting around two months ago, which made me wonder how many more videos he had. A quick search on YouTube had revealed the number of motivational montage videos to be practically infinite.

Nobody openly mocked the Monday Motivation Meeting, because the office was Paul's world and we just worked in it. For the same reason, nobody mocked the motivational quote calendar stuck to the fridge in the kitchen. When I started at Gro, the quote on the calendar read: *If you don't chase your dreams, someone will employ you to chase theirs.*

The irony of the quote had at first been hilarious to me, but as the days wore on, the humor wore off and the words began to taunt me. I soon found that whenever I was in the kitchen I would begin to wonder if there was a dream of mine I'd left neglected somewhere while I wasted my life performing the uninspiring task of being employed. But the more I thought about it, the more I realized that nothing had ever called to me. Maybe I just wasn't listening hard enough.

When someone had finally flipped the page over to July, I felt a surprising amount of relief. The quote now read: *To get ahead, you must start.*

"All right, gang, who kicked some goals last week?" Paul asked now that the video had concluded.

"Ah." Dave from customer experience cleared his throat. "I managed to save two clients from canceling their accounts."

"Yes, buddy! That's a goal!" Paul exclaimed. We all clapped.

"Hayley and I managed to fix the bug that was logging users out," said Greg, one of the app developers. We all clapped.

"Ana showed me the prototype for the new app update. It's incredible," Soph said to the team before smiling directly at me.

Soph had recently made a pledge to "lift up" the other women in the office and, in a well-meaning effort to make good on the promise, she had begun to aggressively advocate on my behalf. This meant she often handballed conversational control to me by saying things like: "Actually, Ana had a really great idea," before smiling at me encouragingly, both inflating my skills and thrusting me into the spotlight unrehearsed and doomed to disappoint. Her energy was less supportive solidarity and more overly zealous pageant mum. At times like this I found Soph annoying, in an almost endearing way, but she also frequently made me laugh. When you spend over forty hours a week in an office, finding someone who can make you laugh is a gift; you become willing to accommodate their flaws, like you would a neurotic roommate who also had a predisposition for stress cleaning.

"That's great, Ana. Send it around once you're back at your desk," Paul said, as everyone clapped for me.

The prototype was not finished. I had anticipated having three more days to work on it before I would reveal the final product. I nodded at Paul and smiled back at Soph as gratefully as I could manage.

"Anyone else?" Paul asked. Nobody said anything.

"Great, well, let's get out there and get to work," he concluded, beaming professionally, all blinding porcelain teeth and clasped hands. "And don't forget: Just don't stop!"

Back at my desk I opened the visuals, assessed how unfinished they were, and began picking at my cuticles. Soph sent me a message:

Did you download Hinge again yet?

I replied: *Nope. Day 9 . . .*

Her response came through quickly: *You're mental. No idea how you do it.*

I typed *vibrator* into the GIF library and was surprised to find six options. I sent Soph a dildo flying through outer space, closed the chat, and opened my ex's Instagram account.

CHAPTER
four

When I arrived back at my apartment after a run, my body humming with endorphins, and climbed the flight of concrete stairs to the second floor, I saw that Maria had left another plate of food wrapped in aluminum foil on my doorstep. She did that every Saturday—homemade dolmades, spanakopita, baklava, and once, to my disappointment, a bag of lemons.

On the gray and windswept June morning when I'd moved into the apartment, Maria had watched me through her front window from across the building's courtyard with a frown on her face. I was already familiar with this manner of apartment-renter archetype: the building management's trusted informant; a sort of grown-up version of a teacher's pet. I assumed she'd be the complainant if I ever received a sternly worded email reminding me of correct communal clothesline use, or rubbish disposal etiquette. But then she knocked on my flyscreen with a custard-filled pastry and introduced herself, and I realized that she was just a sweet woman of few words and many baked goods.

I was yet to see plates of food left on anyone else's doormat, and so my assumption was that Maria did this as a show of solidarity; two women living alone needed to look out for each other. Or perhaps she had sensed some sort of orphan-like energy emanating from me and had decided to bring me into her familial embrace. Either way, I found it both concerning and touching that she was determined to climb the stairs to my floor. I'd watched from my kitchen window as she hung her laundry out on the clothesline; she moved in difficult, shuffling steps. It must take her half an hour to get to my door. The apartment building's stairs had only a decrepit metal railing that wobbled and shed rusty psoriatic flakes. The idea of Maria crouched over, climbing stair after treacherous stair to my floor, made me anxious. I imagined coming home one day to the grim news that Maria had fallen down a flight of stairs while trying to deliver me some spiced walnut cake.

I picked up the plate and leaned over the balustrade to look at Maria's front window. Her lace curtains were pulled shut, which I knew meant she was asleep or not home.

My one-bedroom apartment was small with exposed brick walls, linoleum floors and surfaces, and an old four-burner stove. When I viewed the apartment, the property manager had followed me around wringing her hands. She sighed disapprovingly as she tried to open one of the blinds and found she needed to pull at the cord with all her strength. She flattened a corner of peeling lino with her foot and asked me if I could push a little higher with my budget. Then, she explained, I could find something more modern. I found myself sticking up for the apartment. Our roles reversed: Where she pointed out dampness, poor ventilation, and impenetrable mustiness, I mentioned affordability and character. I suggested a yearlong lease and she approved it immediately.

Living alone had required an adjustment. I played music constantly to drown out the silence or the sound of the family upstairs using the bathroom. Whenever they flushed, there was a *whoosh* as the water ran down a pipe located somewhere in my bedroom wall. The upstairs bathroom was used multiple times a night so my dreams were frequently water-themed: tidal waves and rough seas.

The apartment was still relatively empty. In the first week after I moved into it, I bought a mattress and a bed frame. Then I found a secondhand couch, a dark green two-seater that only smelled very faintly of cigarettes and weed. Since then, I hadn't accumulated much else, except another monstera, Larry II.

I liked living in Brunswick. I was now accustomed to the sound of the train boom gate ringing in the distance. At times it would cut through my thoughts, reminding me that there was a world outside of my brain and that it was progressing along as usual despite all of my worries; a comforting feeling.

I'd formed a routine of running around Princes Park, under the golden leaves the elm trees discarded like litter. I liked sharing the muddy dirt path with other runners. All of us forcing our bodies through the movements, just to experience the sweet relief of stopping.

I now had a favorite coffee shop, a converted mechanic's warehouse filled with old, mismatched furniture. On Saturday mornings I took a book and sat happily among the stowed bikes and whimpering greyhounds, waiting for the barista to call my name. I listened vicariously to the love-life gossip of the other customers, smiling indulgently to myself at the drama of it all, as if I were some old spinster who lived a quiet, calm existence. The vastness of Melbourne allowed me to be anonymous but not alone, and that's exactly what I wanted.

//

I put Maria's plate down on the kitchen counter and drank a glass of water by the sink. I was refilling my glass when my phone pulsed on the table. It was my dad was calling for one of our spontaneous, poorly connected catch-ups, which tended to happen once every few months.

When I was fifteen my parents got divorced. A year or so after that, my dad sold his bricklaying business, along with most of his belongings, and moved to Uluwatu in Bali. He started a new business teaching tourists how to surf and he'd lived there ever since. Our conversations usually followed a pattern: I would tell him about my life, and he would tell me about his, and then he would impart some nonspecific, intangible life advice. This advice was normally repurposed from whatever book he was reading at the time, and therefore almost always irrelevant to me, but I knew that it was important to him that he give me guidance. My gift to him in return was my acceptance of it. This dynamic was one of the supporting structures of our relationship, and I knew that such structures were important when our relationship was conducted almost exclusively through a screen.

"Hey, Dad," I said, mentally tracking back to the last conversation we'd had. I'd still been living in Perth.

My father appeared on the screen and froze. I waited patiently. His blurry face slowly became clear but remained frozen in a confused look. His gray hair was tied back and he was wearing a faded blue singlet. There was an aura of gray fuzz around his tanned shoulders. Behind him I could see rattan, bamboo, and greenery; he was at a café. Eventually he moved.

"Don't know what happened there, think your connection's not so good," he said. I let the comment pass.

"How are you?" I asked.

"Good, yeah, good." He squinted as if looking past me. "Where are you? That doesn't look like your place."

"It's not." I sighed, rubbing a hand over my face. I told him about the last couple of months: my breakup and the lead-up to it; the logistics and the splitting of possessions; the stages of grief, all of which can be passed through in the span of a single argument; the emotional outbursts and the quiet, resentful passive aggression. I summarized it all neatly as if I was reciting a plotline.

"I'm sorry to hear that, Ana."

"It happened back in May. I'm fine."

He nodded, smiling with his lips curled in, making a *that's a real bummer* face.

"You know these things have a way of happening for a reason," he offered, sagely.

"Yeah, I know—"

"One day you'll look back and realize everything was unfolding exactly as it was meant to. Everything that is meant for you will find its way to you eventually. The universe is just clearing the way for you to find your divine path. Hey—did you end up finding some breath work classes?"

My father and his partner, Elke, had been paying someone to teach them how to breathe very loudly and they'd been trying to convince me to do it too.

"Oh, no—not yet. I've been really busy," I lied.

"You really should find some. You know, it's just incredible how focusing on your breath can take you out of your own thoughts," he continued. "It really gives you perspective. We're all so obsessed with our own pain and suffering. I'm telling you, breathing, like *really* breathing, takes you right back into the present moment like that." He clicked his fingers. "Powerful stuff."

"I'll look into it—"

"It's so important to remind ourselves that we can choose not to connect with our suffering," he resumed, now speaking and gesturing as if addressing an auditorium of people. "We can't always control the outside world, but we can choose to not listen to the voice in our head that tells us to be scared."

No one spiritually bypasses quite like my father. He chastises negativity and flat-out refuses to acknowledge unhappiness. He often wields his inherent contentment, or at least his ability to fake it consistently, like a weapon against people who admit their disappointment with life. To him dissatisfaction and discontent are the traits of the greedy and ungrateful.

"How's Elke?" I attempted to change the subject.

He didn't hear me. "So where are ya? Have you got a new place?"

"Well, actually, that's the next piece of news. I moved to Melbourne."

"Wow, a change of scenery. Nice!" he said. "How is it?"

"It's great so far." I thought about the time recently when I laughed out loud at a TV show I was watching and then realized that was the first time I'd made a sound in nearly two days. "I'm really liking it."

He smiled and nodded knowingly back at me. "Good for you, bug. I remember when I moved to Bali all those years ago." He gazed wistfully beyond the top left corner of the camera, before looking back at me. "The moment I stepped off the plane, I knew I'd made the right decision. I think we all belong somewhere, but sometimes it's just not where we were born . . ." He paused as if building up to something. "But,

Ana, you also have to let yourself be happy. I've been meditating on this lately, and I realized I made that mistake a lot when I was your age. I always found a reason why I couldn't be happy *yet*. There was always something that needed to be achieved or figured out or bought or fixed."

For a moment the wisdom of his words reached me, like a beam of sunlight reaching out from in between two passing trees. Then a disembodied arm entered the screen and placed a coffee down on the table in front of him.

"Oh, *Kasih*. Thank you," he said, putting his palms together in prayer hands and nodding to the waitress. When I visited my dad in Bali a year after he had moved, I'd noticed this new habit of his. I remember how strange it was to watch my father put his palms together and bow like a monk. This was, after all, the same man who would shout "HORSE-SHIT!" at the TV so loudly while watching football that our neighbors would complain. At first he did this new bowing gesture at the beginning and end of yoga class. Now he did it all the time.

"Are you at a café?" I asked.

"Yeah, internet at the bungalow isn't working at the moment," he said, frowning, a hint of annoyance in his voice. "Anyway, how did ya mum take the news about you moving?"

"Not well. She hasn't returned any of my calls or messages since I left Perth."

He sighed, *tsked,* and shook his head in a disapproving way.

"Ros is a proud woman, you know that. She's never taken too kindly to people leaving her. She still has a lot of work to do on herself."

I immediately imagined my mum looking at me from across the room; her arms crossed, and her eyes narrowed beneath the feathery fringe she's loyally back-combed every morning since the early nineties. My mother is petite, but fiery and surprisingly intimidating, like a Pomeranian with a mean look in its eye. She's always taken up a space far beyond her size; in part because of an echo of the strong Italian women that colored our lineage, a temperament that was noticeably diluted by the time it reached me. My mother's dark, serious eyes have a tendency to narrow accusingly when she's listening, an expression often read as skepticism by those who don't know her well. As someone with the exact same eyes, I know it as a look of concentration.

At twenty-eight years of age, I still felt like I was betraying my parents when I listened to them vaguely criticize each other, something they often did; my father usually denouncing what he thought was my mother's spiritual immaturity and my mother usually denouncing what she thought was my father's general immaturity. It was a strange concept to have your DNA split evenly between two people who despise each other; sometimes I wondered if *I* should be offended by their criticisms.

"She'll get tired of herself and come back around. She always does aaaaa"—my dad had frozen again, briefly becoming a cubist rendition of himself before coming back into focus—"it's all part of being in the life of someone like your mother. You gotta bless them, send them love, and let it go—" His voice became robotic—half man, half printer—before the video cut out altogether.

"Dad, your connection is really bad."

"Yeah, can you hear me?"

"Yep," I replied, lifting the foil on the plate Maria had left me to reveal some kind of delicious-looking spinach and feta pastry.

"Are you still there, Ana? I can't—"

"Yeah, I can hear you."

"I can't hear—" His voice became distant, scrambled somewhere out in space. "Hang on. I'll—"

The call cut out. I put my phone down, pulled a piece of pastry off, and placed it in my mouth. It was perfectly warm, oily and salty. A message from my dad lit up my phone screen.

Some drongo in the cafe is
downloading a movie. I'll call back
later.

I knew he wouldn't call back today. I stared at my phone as I swayed between the conflicting voices of pride and reason. Then I resigned, sighing and tapping the icon to call my mother. The call continued to ring until it reached the point at which it was obvious she was not going to pick up. I remained stubbornly waiting; having given up on her answering, I was now hoping that the sound of her ringtone was at least placing some guilt-induced image of me into her mind. Eventually the call rang out.

I pulled my jumper and tank top off and went to have a shower.

chapter five

That Friday, the whole office had gathered at the type of bar that is popular only at the end of the workweek: overpriced and understaffed. The bartenders rushed up and down the length of the bar, seemingly surprised that once again—at the same time, on the same day of the week—the venue had filled up with workers from the surrounding offices, mismatched collections of people who would, after the boss left with the corporate card, want nothing to do with each other until Monday morning. The air was filled with the general buzz of celebration, whether due to reaching key performance measures or just another week survived.

I was sitting next to Soph and Dave from customer experience.

"I don't know, obviously what happened to her is a horrible tragedy," Dave said. "But I mean, would you walk along *that* bike path alone at night?" The question, in reference to the recent murder of a woman who had been walking home at night, was directed at Soph, though he didn't pause to let her answer.

"And anyway, the whole thing has been really taken out of context and made into this feminist issue. Men are actually far more likely to be the victims of violence, statistically speaking." He lifted his pint to his lips.

"Yeah, but the ones committing the violent crimes in either situation are most likely men, *statistically speaking*. The fact is, I should be able to walk home at night without being attacked by a man," Soph responded, her cheeks flushed with frustration. The conversation had been cycling for a while now.

"See!" Dave exclaimed triumphantly, placing the beer back down. "That's such a generalization. Yes, you should be able to walk home at night, but it's not only men who commit these crimes and it's not only women who are victims. That kind of language just antagonizes people."

I was unable to bear the gulf of misunderstanding between them any longer, and I was sick of hearing about a woman's responsibility to not be murdered. The abrupt sound of my chair scraping across the wooden floor jarred them both into silence, and they looked at me.

"I'm going to get another drink," I explained, leaving them to argue.

It was seven-thirty, and the bar was at capacity. I searched for where two backs met and then slid between them to navigate through the crowd. The energy in the room was high, voices blended and emerged raucously. I sidestepped to avoid a collision with a woman who had suddenly leaned back and cackled, obliviously sloshing her white wine. I noticed a man who was carving a path to the bar and took the opportunity to follow in his wake. He was tall; my cheek lined up with his shoulder. I could smell his cologne, it was smoky like incense.

When he reached the bar, I stood in the space next to him

and turned to catch a glimpse of his face. He had a balanced profile and well-groomed dark stubble. His hands were authoritative and confident. I imagined them on me. When I looked away, I felt him gaze in my direction and linger. The flustered bartender came over to take his order and the man signaled to me.

"She was first, mate."

I wasn't. He knew this. I knew this. He was being charming.

"Oh," I responded, "thanks."

I ordered and the bartender turned away.

"Work drinks?" the man then asked.

"Yep."

"Same."

I paid for my drink and the bartender took the man's order. It was now my turn to say something, to show mutual enthusiasm in continuing the conversation, or to take my drink and leave. Either was acceptable. Standing there in silence and staring at him with my pint in my hand was not. I made a decision.

"What do you do?" I asked.

He turned to look at me. I had declared interest and in response he smiled, revealing two slightly pointed canines that gave him a roguish smile; the sexiest teeth I'd ever seen.

We moved away from the bar and he introduced himself as Evan. He told me about his job in finance, specifically risk advisory. I told him about my recent move from Perth and my new job in user experience design. The conversation a vessel for us to pass both information about ourselves and flirtatious eye contact back and forth. Evan was fit-looking, tidy, and smart, an aberration from my usual type: tortured artist; tortured stoner; tortured audio technician. He looked and spoke like he had his life together. Even the well-fitted suit jacket he wore was impressive to me. He had a wallet that wasn't attached to his pants by a chain. It was all so different.

"So, do you like your job?" I asked.

"Wow, that's a serious question. Does anyone actually like their job?" he remarked. "Do *you* like your job?"

"Well, my job basically amounts to figuring out how many pop-ups I can force on a person before they leave a webpage so, yes, it's what I was put on this earth to do. It's my divine path."

Evan laughed. The sound caught me by surprise. I realized I had expected to hear my ex's breathy laugh. Evan's mouth didn't open and the top row of his teeth didn't jut out the way my ex's did, his Adam's apple bobbing along. When Evan laughed it was subtle. He smiled, but the *haha* was only visible in the vibration of his shoulders and chest. He kept his eyes locked on mine. My attraction to him was disconcerting, requiring me to exercise conscious control over my facial expressions.

"Well, my job basically amounts to helping huge, wealthy companies make even more money so . . . ."

"On some level isn't that pretty much every job?"

"Yeah, I guess so," he conceded.

"Don't worry, robots will take all of our jobs soon," I said.

"Can't wait." He sighed with mock relief. "I can finally paint all day."

"Oh, you paint?"

"No." He grinned.

I laughed, both confused and delighted by his sense of humor.

I watched his hand as he took a sip of beer. His nails were

trimmed and clean and his fingers were long and thin, a little bony. Clearly my experience with The Chef had not affected my attraction to a man's hands.

My brief reverie was broken when a man grabbed Evan in a bear hug around his midsection, causing them both to lurch toward me. I took a step back, shielding my beer as Evan gave me an apologetic look. The man let Evan go but slung a meaty arm over his shoulder and shouted drunkenly into his ear, "They're asking where you got to."

"I'll be back in a bit, mate," Evan replied, clapping the man on the shoulder. "I think you need another beer."

"Too right!" the man slurred, red-faced and shiny. He released Evan and staggered toward the bar.

"I should go before he comes back," Evan said as he watched the man. "Believe it or not, that's actually my boss."

"Well, looks like now would be a good time to get him to sign off on that pay increase," I joked.

"Honestly, he's always like this. He's a high-functioning alcoholic."

" 'High' seems complimentary."

Evan smiled at me. Then, as if deliberating, he rubbed his hand over his chin. "Would you want to get a drink with me sometime?" he asked. "Somewhere else? Anywhere other than here?"

"Yeah, I'd like that," I replied, fighting the corners of my mouth in an effort to keep my smile an appropriate size.

//

I arrived back at the table to find Soph alone scrolling on her phone and Dave deep in conversation with someone else.

"I just met a guy," I told her.

She looked up from her phone and stared at me with a skeptical look on her face. "What? Here?"

"Yeah, just at the bar, he asked for my number."

Soph's eyes were now darting around the room, as if it had only just occurred to her that there were other people here and that meeting someone was a possibility.

"He just came up to you?" she asked.

"Yeah, well, he asked me if I was here for work drinks and then we started chatting."

"*Bizarre,*" Soph concluded suspiciously before looking back down at her phone. "I'm meeting up with this guy tonight."

She showed me a photo of a headless but impressively rippled torso.

//

I caught the tram home, but in light of the recent murder of a woman in this exact neighborhood, the short walk from the stop to my apartment felt charged with danger. To distract myself, I called Beverly.

Beverly was my closest friend. We met in our first year of high school because our parents both dropped us at school half an hour early every day so they could get to work on time. On the first morning we sat on separate metal benches in silence. On the second morning she walked straight up to me and offered me a copy of the previous month's *Dolly* magazine. Her parents ran a news agency in our local shopping center and she would steal old magazines before they were destroyed. Sometimes she would gift me a glitter pen or a scented highlighter, which meant a lot in year seven, when the contents of your pencil case represented your social status and a scented highlighter was the sort of leverage that could make you the most interesting person in class for a short time. I couldn't really offer her anything in return, except my constant companionship, but she seemed satisfied with the deal and by the end of the year we were best friends.

It was during our early twenties that we became completely inseparable; there was something about the turbulence of those years (bad jobs, exams, financial instability, infinite identity crises) that made us cling to each other for comfort. Beverly studied nursing, fashioning her innate compassion into a useful offering for society, and going out into the world with a solid sense of humanitarian purpose. I studied graphic design and spent my time in a glare of blue light, toiling with the ambiguities of color, line, and contrast. Upon graduation, all I had to offer society was my angsty Tumblr blog.

During those years, Beverly and I were entirely codependent. We went out drinking every weekend and when we weren't sleeping in someone else's bed, we slept in each other's. We even had matching fringes, which we would often trim for each other at the bathroom sink before a night out. For a couple of years neither of us dated anyone for longer than a month. It wasn't a conscious decision, we just lived in a self-sustaining ecosystem. Spending those years together allowed us to build a stable foundation for our friendship. We'd made it through the dramatic years and now our relationship was calm, without ever feeling perfunctory.

When the video call connected I saw Beverly was wearing gym gear, her hair tied up on the top of her head. I remembered that I now lived a few hours into the future and it was still only 8 P.M. in Perth.

"The gym on a Friday night?" I asked, aghast.

"Me and Matt went indoor rock climbing."

Beverly and her boyfriend, Matt, were always starting new hobbies. They were obsessed with self-improvement and newness. Beverly was especially good at picking up a trend early. If she told me she really wanted to go to Oaxaca, or that her cocktail of choice was now a Paloma, I knew it was destined to be popular in the next couple of months. These talents of hers were wasted on her job as a nurse.

"What are you doing?" she asked, pulling her hair tie out and shaking out her long dark hair.

"I had work drinks and now I'm walking home."

"I heard what happened to that woman. Be careful."

"Yeah." I frowned, leaving out how close the bike path was to my apartment.

"By the way, guess who I saw," she said, alluding to my ex.

"Oh—really?"

"Yep," she said, nodding. "Looks like he's got a new girlfriend. I saw him with her last night at the pub."

"Poor girl," I said, pretending that I hadn't already deduced this information from the presence of one-eighth of a coffee mug and one-fifth of her small hand in the bottom right-hand corner of his latest photo.

"She has pink hair," Beverly continued, now walking down the hallway and carrying me along, her nose crinkled in disgust. Pink hair was obviously now passé.

"I swear to you, I was so close to walking up to him and pouring my drink over his head. Can you imagine?"

I forced out a halfhearted laugh, not quite nailing the delivery.

Beverly picked up on my change of tone and frowned at me. "I'm sorry, I didn't really think about how that news might still hurt to hear. Are you okay?"

"I'm fine," I said, waving her concern away. "I'm actually doing really well. Oh—and I met someone tonight."

"What, at the bar?"

"Yeah."

"He just came up to you?"

She was performing an impressive impersonation of Soph.

"Yes," I replied. "Why? Is that strange?"

"I didn't know people still met like that." She shrugged. "Was he handsome?"

I thought about his hands, his dark eyes, and his teeth.

"He's really handsome." I recalled myself laughing at something he had said. "And funny too."

"Dreamy. Did he ask for your number?"

She turned her head away from the screen and I could hear Matt saying something in the distance.

"YEP, OKAY!" she shouted, before turning back to me.

"Sorry—our Spanish lesson starts in five."

"It's eight o'clock on a Friday night. Why are you doing Spanish lessons now?"

"It's the only time we had free around my shifts."

Matt shouted again in the distance, more urgently this time.

She sighed. "I have to go."

"Okay, well, give me a call soon," I said, trying not to sound desperate or sad.

"Of course. I miss you. Bye!"

"Adiós," I said, but she'd already hung up on me.

I continued down the street with a smile on my face, enjoying the cool night air and the peaceful silence. I looked up at the stars, appreciating their indifference, something I was in the habit of doing when things in my life were going well. At those times, it's possible to believe that I'm completely safe in the universe's capable yet impartial hands; that I'm too insignificant to warrant malicious intervention from some greater force, and for a moment I can find comfort in the idea of my meaninglessness.

That was until my thoughts were interrupted as someone lunged out of the shadows to my left.

"NO!" I shrieked, breaking into a sprint before stealing a panicked glance back. The shadow was only a cat jumping onto a letter box. I still ran the rest of the way home.

CHAPTER
six

I woke up the next morning to a headache and a text message from Evan.

Did you enjoy the rest of your night?

I got up slowly, draining the last of the water I'd left by my bed and wriggling my feet into my slippers. I took my robe off the back of the door and wrapped it around me, before moving around the apartment, pulling the blinds open to let the light in. I left coffee to steep in the French press while I ran through some potential responses.

Sorry, who's this?

A joke. Though, a risky one.

I left straight after. How was yours?

Straightforward, but boring. Nothing to be misunderstood there, but at the same time I wasn't really selling myself. A lost opportunity.

*Hey :) not really I left pretty
quickly after we chatted. I did enjoy
meeting you though.*

Flirty, but too much. I decided to drop the smiley face.

*Hey, not really I left pretty quickly
after we chatted. I did enjoy
meeting you though.*

Now I sounded depressed.

*Hey, it was okay. I did enjoy
meeting you though . . .*

A little saucy. When used correctly, an ellipsis can basically be a proposition for sex. I sent it. He replied in four minutes.

*Meeting you was the highlight of
my night.*

Proposition accepted.

//

I spent the morning making an orange and almond Ottolenghi cake for Maria, pausing at intervals to read Evan's responses from my home screen, through the increasing blur of flour, butter, and sugar. I juiced oranges and grated the rind with infinite patience, while my mind happily wandered from flashbacks of meeting Evan to his messages in the present and projections of a future in which I saw him again. Evan's responses to my texts were fast, which suggested confidence, interest, and quick wit. All promising signs.

I put the cake in the oven, set the timer, and left the orange syrup to cool on the stove as I carefully crafted another reply. Evan and I were now discussing books. He appeared to be exclusively interested in nonfiction: finance, self-development, and gratuitous biographies of men who had forced themselves upon Mount Everest and lost a couple of toes in the process. Still, it was refreshing that Evan liked to read at all. My ex had owned books, a handful of pristine Penguin Classics dying to have their spines cracked, but in the four years we dated, I never saw him pick one up.

I still didn't know much about Evan, and the conversation, though entertaining, was providing little concrete information. Each response was beginning to feel like a blind bet. I knew the solution was simple: I could find him online.

My fingers itched to put his name into the search bar. I didn't have his surname, so it wouldn't be easy, but I was confident. Once I found him, I'd have the cheat sheet. As I strategized, I forced myself to acknowledge that looking people up online is a shortcut I utilize to learn about someone without the pressure of being face-to-face, and of having to react and respond in real time. I knew it wasn't healthy to use what I would learn to decide which parts of myself to reveal and which to hide from Evan. I knew that a social media account is a form of performance; a profile, feed, or grid can't contain all the nuances of a personality. I also knew that I had a tendency to extract what I could and then fill in the gaps with my own fantasies. Later I am often left having to deconstruct the version I'd created of someone in order to make room for the version that actually exists. I'm often disappointed. I'm sure we all are.

I resolved to not look him up. I wanted Evan to reveal himself to me piece by piece in real life, unburdened by my preconceived assumptions, which meant I needed to resist the temptation to gather intel. I would not create Evan out of insufficient data.

//

After the cake had cooled, I poured the orange syrup over it and decorated it with the rind. I went outside and checked from the balustrade in front of my door that Maria's curtains were open, then I covered the plate in foil and walked down the steps to her apartment.

My plan was to leave the cake on her doormat, so I didn't impose. But as I placed it down, Maria opened the door, and I quickly picked the plate back up. She peered through the flyscreen cautiously before recognizing me and pushing the screen open.

"Ana," she said in her thick Greek accent. "Come in."

She smiled and then turned her back on me, shuffling toward the kitchen. I followed her awkwardly.

Her apartment was the same as mine, only it was north facing and filled with decades of accumulated belongings. All of Maria's furniture matched. It was heavy and made of dark wood, more suited to a larger home. It gave the apartment a cramped feeling. In the center of the lounge room, in lieu of a sofa, sat a circular dining table, which was covered in a piece of lace with a transparent plastic tablecloth protectively laid over it. I noticed a shrine on top of a cabinet in the corner of the room, where a small flame flickered in a tumbler filled with red liquid. Organized neatly around the candle was a collection of statues featuring baby Jesus and the Virgin Mary, and behind that, an audience of framed saints I didn't recognize, most of whom were wearing pained expressions and rolling their eyes up to the ceiling as if they'd just stubbed their toe. The apartment smelled of roses on the verge of decay, and I spied the offending vase of wilted flowers in another corner of the room.

"I made you a cake to say thank you for all the food," I said.

We'd reached the kitchen and Maria was pulling two mugs from a cupboard. "My husband and I ran a bakery. I still like to bake," she said matter-of-factly.

I was suddenly reminded that I hadn't tasted the cake. I looked down at it nervously, imagining myself diligently measuring out one and a half cups of salt instead of sugar. "It's nothing special though, just orange and almond."

She thanked me, smiled, and took the cake, rubbing my arm with a hand covered in gold rings.

"Now sit, sit," she said, ushering me out of the kitchen. I retraced my steps, taking a seat at the squeaky, plastic-covered dining table.

She spoke to me about the weather as she moved around her kitchen. She wore a long skirt, sheer stockings, and sensible-looking black shoes; the kind they sell in pharmacies. I admired her, the way I often did when I watched an elderly woman going about her day; a silent acknowledgment of all the horrors I assumed she would have experienced on account of the year she was born and her gender; a bitter recognition of all the things she could have been prevented from doing. There was something about watching a woman like Maria alone in her apartment, now living life for herself, that demanded reverence. It made me want to stand and clap, or maybe weep.

There was no doubt that Maria had spent many years of her life pregnant and rearing children. I saw at least one framed family photo on every surface of the apartment. Some were black-and-white photos, small and weathered. Others were more modern. One appeared to be a Snapchat selfie of two teenage girls, which had somehow been printed and then framed. The subjects of the photos ranged from crying babies in christening gowns to rosy-cheeked children smiling proudly in school uniforms, and all the way through to grown-up milestones: graduations, weddings, and holiday photos.

I had a misplaced sense of nostalgia for a childhood I never had. I'd never met my grandmother, Nonna Giulia, who had stopped speaking to my mother after she fell pregnant with me at seventeen.

In an alternate version of reality, in which my nonna had been capable of forgiveness, and in which my mother hadn't inherited the same fiery stubborn streak, I would probably have memories of visiting my nonna in an apartment not too different from Maria's. Maybe there would have been framed photos of me on a doily-covered cabinet. Giulia passed away years ago, and when my mother told me the news of her passing, she'd shrugged, sighed, and said, "Bitterness makes life short." The irony was lost on her, but not on me.

Maria's kettle whistled, and soon she shuffled back across the room carrying a tray with a teapot, two mugs, and the cake. Her thin arms were working hard.

"Here, let me help you." I stood, leaning over the table to help her, but I ended up uselessly hovering my hands near the tray as she confidently lowered it onto the table.

She cut us both a slice of the cake, her movements slow and calm. The silence she left was comfortable. She poured us chamomile tea, and then eased herself down into the chair slowly with a slight grimace on her face. "My knees are bad," she explained.

I made a sympathetic sound.

"You have a beautiful family," I said, pointing to the collection of photo frames closest to me. She smiled and gestured toward a black-and-white photo on the cabinet to my right.

"My husband," she said. "That was taken on our wedding day."

The photo showed a dark, serious-faced man, far older than the bright, round-faced woman by his side. In the photo, Maria wore a heavy-looking lace wedding dress with long sleeves and a high neckline. Slung over the picture frame was what looked like a string of beads.

"He passed away a long time ago."

"I'm sorry," I said uselessly. "He looks like he was much older than you in that photo."

"Yes." She clucked knowingly. "Twenty-three years. He was forty-one and I was eighteen."

At eighteen I spent my weekends at grimy basement gigs, usually drunk and high on pills. I was obsessed with glimpsing the chemically induced oblivion that would take me out of the uncomfortable space of my own brain. I tried to imagine that angsty version of myself getting married, but it was impossible. I wondered if getting married and having children so young would have stripped me of the luxury of my own self-loathing, of all the time I had selfishly spent wallowing in my own privileged paralysis. Maybe it would have given me something outside of myself to focus on. Then I wondered if that was a naïve and ungrateful thought.

Maria took a bite of the cake and I followed her lead. I was relieved to find that it tasted good.

"How many grandchildren do you have?" I asked. She beamed with pride and I knew I'd asked the right question.

"Sixteen."

"Wow, Maria. That's a lot of birthdays to remember."

She laughed and I took a sip of tea.

"Where is your family?" she asked.

"Oh, my mother's in Perth and my father's in Bali. I have a much smaller family."

"You live alone. You're not married?"

I laughed. But Maria did not.

"No." I shook my head.

"No boyfriend?"

"No, I'm single. Recently single, actually."

Maria stood and shuffled over to a small lampstand. She picked up a photo and brought it back to the table. The photo was of an angsty teenager, probably about fourteen. He wore a My Chemical Romance T-shirt and had his dark hair pulled down the side of his face. He frowned slightly, clearly not happy to have his photo taken.

"Alexander, my grandson," she explained as she gave me the photo. "He lives in London now." I took the photo from her, a little confused as to why she was giving it to me, and tried to think of an appropriate reaction. "You must be very proud of your family," I said, handing it back to her.

She looked at it for a moment with a smile on her face, before putting it back in its place. We finished our cake and tea and then discussed where in Brunswick had the best fresh produce. Maria informed me that I was being ripped off and gave me the names of a few grocers to visit. When she eventually stood, signaling the visit had come to an end, I helped her carry the tray back to the kitchen. I thanked her again for the food and said goodbye.

//

I spent the rest of the afternoon at the laundromat, responding to Evan and reading, while I waited for my washing to dry. We had officially messaged each other all day, but there still hadn't been any mention of meeting for a drink, even though Evan had declared that he wanted to get a drink with me before he'd asked for my number. I knew I could just ask him out, but I didn't. The fear that he might turn around and reject me lingered. To be safe I decided to wait for an invitation.

What are you up to tonight? he asked.

Huge night of staying in. You? I replied.

Heading out for drinks with a couple of friends.

Things were getting tricky to navigate. The *haha*s had stopped. We were inching toward the point where one of us was going to have to ask the other if they wanted to meet up, and like a game of musical chairs, we had been circling for a suspiciously long time. His apparent reluctance to proactively suggest a date ate away at the little confidence I had.

Enjoy! I replied and shoved my phone in my back pocket.

CHAPTER
seven

The next day Evan texted me:

Get a drink with me next weekend x

The way he had posed this as an order rather than a question could have seemed arrogant to me, but with the context I already had of him—that he was politically progressive; self-deprecating; sweet—it was endearing. The message arrived as I was standing in the health food shop, deciding between two boxes of tea. Suddenly the decision of whether to buy "Calm" tea or "Relax" tea was completely unimportant. I grabbed a box and headed to the counter, skipping my usual browse through the rows of vague and expensive supplements; a habit that often resulted in me leaving the store poorer and not entirely sure of how reishi mushroom powder was going to find a place in my life. I paid for the tea and smiled as I read the message from my lock screen. I would open it later when I'd already decided on how to respond.

I walked up Sydney Road, past the windows of headless

mannequin brides and the bolts of fabric that hung ghost-like behind glass, and my afternoon transformed. A new sense of excitement made the air feel fresh rather than cold; it made having to wait behind the train track boom gate more of an adventure and less of an inconvenience; it changed the color of the sky from gray to silver; it made people inherently good again. I found myself smiling without even trying.

When I got home, I put on a podcast about love languages and leisurely made myself a couscous salad for dinner. I sat on the couch and ate, contemplating how to respond to Evan. After multiple revisions, I sent:

Okay, you've convinced me :)

An hour of not receiving a response passed, followed by another, and I worried that Evan's silence was due specifically to the words I'd chosen. I should have asked where he wanted to get a drink. Or, I could have been more useful by suggesting a place. I knew for certain that I should have dropped the juvenile smiley face, which now, on reflection, looked ridiculous. It also occurred to me that, through my stubborn refusal to ask Evan out on a date, I had starved our conversation and left him with no choice but to once again bravely declare his interest. Even so, Evan had swallowed his pride in a way that I was incapable of, and then doubled down by adding an *x*. Which I hadn't reciprocated. Instead I'd just callously smiled back at him, like an absolute sociopath. I'd given him nothing but lukewarm waters to test and I concluded that if he never messaged me again, it would be a completely fair reaction, and one I deserved for refusing to give him even the smallest glimpse of my cold, dark heart. I pushed my phone down to the end of the couch with my foot and tried to focus on the TV show I was watching.

//

Later when I got into bed, I had a notification. Evan had sent me a friend request. This was surprising given he still hadn't responded to my last message, but also because I hadn't received a friend request in years. I wondered if he'd been forced to go to Facebook after being unable to locate me anywhere else. Of course, I hadn't forgotten that I'd recently made the very mature decision to not research Evan online before getting to know him in person. I contemplated ignoring the request; if need be I could claim that I didn't use my account. But the fact that he hadn't responded to my message made me think I was not handling these early conversations as well as I could be and some support would be helpful. I freed my phone from the charger and rolled over in bed to make myself more comfortable. Then I accepted the request.

Evan's profile picture was six months old. It was a film photo of him and a friend sitting side by side on the grass at a picnic. Other people could be seen half in and half out of the shot. Evan had a beer in his hand. His sunglasses were being pushed up his face by his grin and smile lines creased the corners of his eyes. He looked good.

The next photo was from over a year ago, Evan was sitting on a mustard couch on the front porch of an old terrace house. He was grinning again, this time with one arm wrapped around the shoulders of the girl seated next to him. The girl's name was Emily, as I learned from a comment she'd left on the photo:

You're ugly x

Love you x, he'd responded.

My suspicion that I'd found Evan's ex was confirmed

when I walked further back in time to the next profile photo and saw Emily again. This time the two of them were guests at a wedding. Evan's eyes, which I thought were brown, revealed themselves as dark green. It was a piece of information I should have learned the first time I saw his eyes catch sunlight, not through a screen. These little moments of discovery were being stripped away from us by our online presences, but I accepted that they were a sacrifice; a necessary loss in order to gain useful information.

Emily was stunning in a conventional and indisputable way; tanned and thin with a grown-out blond fringe that was parted in the middle and framed her heart-shaped face perfectly. I couldn't help but find her presence in his photos disappointing.

When my ex and I broke up, before I deleted my account for good, I performed a cleanse and removed every picture of him. The choice to do that was not motivated by anger or pettiness, nor was it an attempt to elicit a response from him. It was more like a digital sage burning exercise.

I wished Evan had performed a similar ritual. It wasn't pleasant to see images of him, someone I was actively interested in, with his ex. Even the most platonic photo dripped with imagined sexual tension. The image might not have captured it, but my mind had no issue imagining all the sex they would have had before the photo was taken, after the photo was taken, in between.

Of course, I immediately wondered what went wrong between Evan and Emily. But the presence of the photos implied that the dissolution of their relationship couldn't possibly have been dramatic. Were they still close friends? Was that worse? I clicked on Emily's name.

In her profile picture she was sitting on the beach, smiling and sun-drenched and unfairly photogenic. Her knees were hugged into her chest and her chin tilted up toward the camera. Two dimples that never seemed to fully actualize were hinted at on either side of her smiling mouth. A bucket hat covered her long blond hair and she wore white-rimmed cat-eye sunglasses. The image stirred in me an indefinable feeling, a little like envy, a little like guilt, and a lot like bitterness. She looked uninhibited and effortless; a cool girl who is masterful at covering up the effort and the level of curation required to appear so nonchalantly aesthetic. On top of that, the image had nearly three hundred comments, a ridiculously high number for a pedestrian profile photo. So, she was popular as well. I clicked on the comments.

The first one said:

Miss you Em x

The second:

RIP Emily. Miss you every day.

CHAPTER
eight

Over the next few days, I examined Emily's social media accounts with the deliberation an archeologist might give to an old and precious object they'd dug from the ground. I did this on the tram to work in the morning, or in stolen moments at my desk. Mostly though, I visited them in bed, occasionally shifting my position to ease my stiff neck. At first, I let myself be drawn to whatever captured my attention, usually photos that contained Evan, but soon I desired a more linear understanding. I began to approach her Instagram grid methodically, scrolling backward so I could start the story from the beginning of their relationship. Evan's account, which I found through hers, was of no help; it was a desolate screen of negative space, broken only by one caption-less photo of a sunset, which he'd posted six years ago. Emily's, on the other hand, had 428 images and, to a trained eye like mine, each of them was rich with detail.

This was not the first time I had stalked a partner's ex on social media. When I first started dating my ex, his dismissive, perpetually unimpressed nature had made me so insecure that, in an effort to understand what he liked and who he wanted me to be—so that I could avoid the sting of his disapproval—I'd created a fake account and added Mei, the recent ex who broke his heart. I wanted to find out more about her. I wanted to know what she did to make him so utterly smitten by her, while she, by his telling, had remained detached and ultimately disinterested. I wanted to embody a little of whatever it was that drove him wild, so that I too might access its power. Mei was petite, with long black hair and clear skin the color of milk. Most devastatingly of all, she could play the guitar.

I tortured myself with her updates for over a year. I was both addicted to seeing what she was up to and entirely mortified by this strange desire. One day, Mei announced she was moving to Berlin and then deleted her account. I was forced to give her up and it was only after that happened that I realized how much better off I was.

I knew that observing Emily's account was likely to create those same conflicting feelings, but the fact that she had died was too sad, too *fascinating*. It was like driving past a car crash. I couldn't look away.

Emily's passing revealed how needlessly cruel the permanency of social media accounts could be: an incessant reminder of the horrifying abruptness of death and its disregard for plans or potential. When I looked at a photo Emily had posted of a coffee mug on a wooden table at a café in Fitzroy, I imagined that even a bland image like that must pierce Evan like a knife. I was sure that he would experience a fresh heartbreak every time he was exposed to words she had written and photos she had taken. Another photo, an artful selfie Emily had posted (white singlet, mirror, film camera), would present a different kind of pain, one I couldn't even begin to understand. I learned that she'd died in early November, less than a year ago. This was a troubling discovery given that this was not a lot of time to grieve.

The beginning of their relationship presented itself in the form of a photo of Evan sitting on a crate against a brick wall, a coffee in his hand and an expression of postcoital satisfaction worn plainly on his face, or at least that's what I assumed. From the image's time stamp I was able to figure out they had been dating for five years when she died.

I winced a little every time I saw Evan in Emily's feed. His presence was an abrupt reminder that I was deep in a time capsule from when they were blissfully in love. Even though the photos were posted years ago, it hurt as if their story were unfolding in real time, an unusual feeling.

I watched Emily and Evan travel to Italy and eat pasta with the hills of Umbria behind them; Emily vibrant and beautiful in a white linen dress, and Evan tanned and handsome. They shared pistachio gelato in Rome and visited the Uffizi Galleries in Florence; Emily posted a terrible photo she'd taken of *The Birth of Venus*, its colors and dimension flattened and its proportions skewed. She posted a photo of Evan on a beach in Cefalù. He had a book in one hand and was reclining on a striped towel wearing only a pair of black shorts. I stared at the photo, surprised to realize that I was turned on. I briefly imagined myself climbing on top of this version of Evan, straddling him, taking the book out of his hand, and licking salt off his skin. I felt an unwelcome and irrational annoyance at the fact that if Evan and I were to go to Italy, he would undoubtedly think of Emily the whole time; recalling the way the pink Umbrian sunset lent her skin its rose gold glow; the way the salty Cefalù water dried in white tendrils across her skin. He'd probably think about how our bodies differed, or how they were the same. In this way, I would always hold second place. I would always have come *after,* earning my position by default. I supposed that was not so different from dating someone after their heart had been broken, except that being discarded usually led to a resentment or dislike toward one's ex. The difference here was the sense that if Evan and Emily had had any control over the situation, I assumed they would have chosen to return to each other. I imagined, fifteen years into the future, on a dark and stormy night, a violent banging on the door while Evan and I huddled with our terrified children on the couch; outside was Emily, coming to claim what had been hers all along.

The photos on my screen soon returned geographically to Melbourne and I continued to collect information. I learned that Emily's coffee order had been an oat milk latte; she had taught yoga at a studio in East Brunswick called Bend; and she could do the splits, which was both impressive and intimidating, as if it directly translated to some sort of acrobatic skill in the bedroom. Emily's beauty was definitive. I selfishly hunted for an unflattering angle, or the hint of a poorly concealed flaw, but I found nothing and was forced to conclude that she was perfect.

On Wednesday, as I stood in the kitchen at work microwaving my leftovers and reading an article about the global food crisis on my phone, Evan sent me a link to a wine bar on Lygon Street.

Here? Friday 6:30?

CHAPTER
nine

"I mean, what does that even mean?" Soph was holding her phone out in front of my face. The text read:

Hey, really busy this weekend.
Maybe next weekend?

"Is there a possibility that he's actually busy? And the text means exactly what it says?" I was only being nice, as the guy in question seemed to have zero interest in Soph beyond the late-night visits he'd been making to her apartment every second weekend. I'd counseled her for weeks, attempting to subtly tell her to move on. "What about that other guy? What was his name? Tom?"

She wrinkled her nose and frowned at her phone.

"He's okay. I'm just not that keen. He wants to catch up for drinks again." She sighed. "I'll just keep telling him I've got plans until he takes the hint."

It was Friday afternoon and Paul had left the office to "meet a client" an hour ago. We all knew this meant he would not be returning until Monday morning. His departure caused an immediate deflation of energy; shoulders dropped, key-board clicking slowed, and everyone seemed to slouch in their chairs. Some of the team now milled around in the kitchen, beers in hand, the pretense of working entirely abandoned. I was meeting Evan tonight for our first date. On Wednesday afternoon, I'd responded to his time and location suggestion with:

Sounds good x

To which he responded:

See you then

Leaving a seemingly deliberate blank space instead of an *x,* which was probably fair punishment for when I had not reciprocated his *x* days before.

"Anyway, your hair looks great today," Soph continued, still hovering by my shoulder and now playing with my hair like a hairdresser.

I'd blow-dried and styled my hair in the morning before work, mostly because images of Emily with her perfect grown-out fringe were still imprinted on the inside of my eyelids. They revisited me in the morning as I stood in front of the mirror and washed my face. In a burst of inspiration, I'd pulled my neglected hair dryer out of the cupboard.

As I spent the slow hours staring at a screen, my date with Evan drew closer and I started to question whether I even liked what I'd done to my hair. It felt weirdly competitive and I didn't want to enter into a competition, especially not with Emily, who appeared to have been flawless and would forever remain that way. I also didn't want to set a standard for my appearance that would require me to keep blow-drying my hair; it had taken me a whole hour. I now touched it self-consciously, feeling the sleek straightness instead of its usual curls.

"Thanks. I'm not sure I like it."

Soph looked at me in a perplexed but amused way. "Well, I think it looks nice, you weirdo. Ciao!"

She turned and made her way to Dave's desk, holding her phone out in front of her. "*Daaave,* what do you think this message *actually* means?"

I went to the bathroom immediately and splashed water on my hair, before attempting to dry it by crouching underneath the hand dryer.

"What the fuck am I doing?" I asked of my damp-haired reflection.

Earlier that morning, when Soph asked me what I had planned for the weekend, I'd told her I was going on a date and her reaction had been one of concern.

"The guy from the bar?" she had asked, wheeling around in her chair to face me.

"Yeah, we've been messaging each other."

"You'll be careful, right?" Worry creased her brow.

I wondered if her concern was in response to the woman murdered on the bike path, or more specifically because she considered meeting a man in real life to be more dangerous than first meeting him online.

"Of course. I don't think there is anything to worry about," I said, attempting to assuage her apprehension. "He seems nice."

"I'm sure he is," she replied, with the air of being considerate to a small child who was talking about their imaginary friend. "Have you found him online yet?"

"Yeah."

"Oh, good." She sighed with genuine relief. "So, he is who he says he is?"

"Well, yeah."

"At least there's that," she concluded knowingly.

//

I slipped out of the office undetected at five-thirty, motivated by avoiding another stranger danger talk with Soph. On the way to the bar, I sat on the tram listening to music, picking my cuticles, and watching as my knee bounced nervously of its own accord. When I arrived at the bar I spied Evan through the window. His suit jacket was hung over the stool next to him and he was scrolling on his phone. His knee was bouncing nervously as if of its own accord.

When I approached him, he looked up at me and smiled, causing my heart to rattle violently in my chest. We hugged and he moved his jacket so I could take a seat next to him.

"This place is cool," I ventured conversationally.

"Yeah, it's a favorite of mine," Evan replied, looking around the room.

Favorite of mine. Immediately I wondered if this was somewhere he and Emily had come together. Maybe this had been her favorite place too. Strange then that he would bring me here or that he would want to come here at all. I imagined that he would see her in my place, smiling back at him with that dimpled smile and wearing the vintage suede jacket that had clearly been her favorite. I wondered if, in a small way, his heart would break over and over, every single time he saw me instead. On the other hand, he couldn't be expected to avoid every place where memories of her may lie waiting to

ambush him. I decided that it was brave of him to commit
to eclipsing old memories with the creation of new ones, and
to take back the city that had taken something from him.

"Oh, so you've been here a few times?" I asked.

"Yeah." He nodded. "They only opened a couple of
months ago, but I've come here three times already."

His words broke the cycle of thought in the back of my
mind and all trace of Emily disappeared. I looked around the
room with a new sense of confidence, now seeing it as an un-
charted land. Free of accumulated history.

It was a small bar with a mirrored wall of countless bottles and vinyl sleeves which covered the entire right side of the
room. At the back of the room there was an exposed kitchen,
like a stainless-steel fish tank. I saw a commis chef preparing
something, his hands moving quickly between two metal con-
tainers. As I watched him, his hands seemed to grow more
and more familiar. My mind was transforming them and I
was suddenly transported back to my bed. I saw The Chef on
top of me, thrusting and breathing heavily, one of his hands
around my neck. For a split second Evan's voice sank away
and became a murmur through a wall. Then it was over, and
I was back in the room. I realized I was holding my breath
and subtly released it. Evan didn't seem to notice.

"Should we get a bottle and something to eat?" he asked.

I nodded and made myself smile. He passed me the menu
and I stared at it, trying to remember how to read.

"I have a serious question to ask you," Evan said.

I looked over the menu at him. "What?" I asked with a
vague sense of dread.

"I need to know before we go any further," he continued,
a small smile struggling its way onto his face and giving away
that the question was not in fact a serious one.

"What?" I laughed.

"Are you one of those people who takes photos of your food at restaurants?"

"No." I laughed again. "Are you?"

Of course, I already knew he wasn't.

His smile dropped away briefly, shifting his face almost imperceptibly. He shook his head. "Nah, I don't really use my account."

"Me neither," I lied. "I deleted it a couple of months ago, actually."

"Really?"

He seemed impressed and I nodded, enjoying the feeling of holding his approval.

"Why did you get rid of it?" he asked.

"I didn't want to know what everyone was doing all the time," I lied, again. "What about you? Why don't you use it?"

"I just got sick of it," he said. "Everyone just pretends to be some perfected version of themselves. Or they use it ironically. I'm not sure which is worse."

The waiter arrived and, as we ordered, Evan's phone lit up on the table, revealing an email notification and his phone's wallpaper. I recognized the scene by the deck chairs and striped umbrellas, the blue ocean and the row of slanted buildings piled directly on the seawall. Cefalù. A photo from his trip with Emily. I wondered then if he'd grown so accustomed to his phone's wallpaper that he no longer saw it; in the same way that art hung on walls or postcards on a fridge eventually stop capturing the eye in any meaningful way. Or maybe, I thought, he kept the photo as his wallpaper in a conscious effort not to forget her.

As we ate and drank, the conversation didn't even brush

against the topic of exes. I felt a strange mixture of relief and disappointment. Emily remained shrouded in mystery, and because of this, my knowledge of her required conscious maneuvering. At times, I wondered if I was smiling at Evan like someone might smile during a wake. Was I betraying my attempts to hide the sympathy I felt toward him? I tried not to reduce him to an individual who had experienced an insurmountable tragedy, and I was conscious not to treat him differently because of it, but it was difficult. I wanted to return to ignorance but it was too late for that. The only reassurance I had was the assumption that, at some stage, he would share Emily with me and then I would no longer need to double-check every word before it left my mouth.

Soon most of the bottle was finished, we relaxed in each other's company and grew brave. We'd shifted toward each other, our bodies becoming invitational. I knew I should call it a night. The temptation to invite him back to my apartment was strong, but I wanted to try to do things differently. Slowly.

"So, what brought on your move to Melbourne?" Evan asked.

"I just needed a change," I answered, pausing to choose my next words carefully. "I arrived at a point where there wasn't much to keep me in Perth and an opportunity presented itself so I took it."

"Yeah, that makes sense," he replied.

"My ex and I broke up and it was his name on the rental lease, most of our stuff was his, most of my friends were his," I confidently continued. "It was kind of like a forced fresh start."

"A fresh start is a good way to move on," Evan agreed.

"Sounds like you've gone through one of those breakups too," I said, surprised by my own cunning.

"Not really," he replied, giving away no hint of emotion. "Not quite like that."

I was unsure of what to say next. It felt as if I'd been led into a labyrinth; I'd followed Evan's voice, taking turn after turn, and now I found myself at a dead end. Evan changed the subject.

"So tell me, how many pop-ups can you force on a person before they leave a webpage?" he asked, pouring the last of the wine into each of our glasses.

//

Evan asked where I lived and offered to walk me home. It wasn't raining but the air outside was cold and we kept our hands hidden in our pockets for warmth. We passed large old terrace houses and picket fences and our conversation continued.

"Where do you live?" I asked.

"East Brunswick, near Lygon actually."

I stopped walking.

"Wait, you're walking in the complete opposite direction. Why didn't you say something? I could have ordered a car."

"*Shhh*," Evan whispered. "I'm having fun."

I laughed, turning to continue our walk, but Evan stayed where he was, a grin stretched across his face. When I realized he hadn't moved I turned back to him.

"What?" I asked.

"It's your laugh," he said.

I put a hand over my mouth. I'd always been self-conscious of my laugh; it had an uncontrollable way of exploding out of me with surprising volume, entirely at odds with my speaking voice. Evan stepped toward me and pulled my hand away.

"No—don't," he said. "I like it."

Then his lips were on mine with the perfect amount of polite assertiveness. I was caught by surprise and for a moment I saw the slope of his cheekbone as if through a microscope, then I closed my eyes.

The rest of the walk home was broken intermittently by more kissing and in between we laughed guiltily. We kissed one last time at the front of my building before saying good night. I drank a glass of water over my kitchen sink and went to bed.

CHAPTER
ten

It was Sunday night and I was making a futile attempt to seduce myself. In fact, I had not been able to successfully masturbate ever since my experience with The Chef. This was a concerning development. I've always regarded my ability to orgasm as the truest marker of my health: a reliable and reassuring confirmation that my body is working fine, despite whatever state my mind might be in. And now it was gone.

Whenever I began to enjoy myself, The Chef appeared. Whatever scene I had conjured would drop away and there he was on top of me. I would sense the weight of him, then I would smell his skin, and when I felt his hands around my neck I knew it was over. My body would shift into a stress response, sending cortisol flooding through my system, raising my heart rate, and shattering any hope of climax. I would roll over and groan into my pillow.

I sought the advice of the internet, which recommended I treat my body more romantically. It suggested a series of six steps, which included: lighting candles, playing music, and giving yourself a massage. I don't usually have the patience or desire for any of that, but I'd grown desperate. As step four recommended, I'd spent the last minute caressing my own nipples, but I'd felt nothing. I gave up, retreating to my own tried and tested methods. I closed my eyes and began to search my mind for a fantasy, which is a lot like searching for a TV show to watch. I have favorites, some of them formed way back in high school, reliable fantasies that lead me down well-trodden neural pathways. If I was feeling lazy I'd choose one of those. They had simple plotlines and were usually quick and efficient.

I trialed a few fantasies, waiting for a physical reaction of encouragement, but soon I had explored my entire library, testing all the different versions of the same fervid eagerness that usually excited me. Nothing worked.

Recently, I'd even tried watching porn again, something I'd given up on a long time ago. I thought that maybe if someone else took the wheel I could relax a little, but it was too contrived and overacted. The women whined like they were in pain and the men grunted like they enjoyed the sound of pain. Porn had nothing on the power of my imagination and the level of nuance I could infuse into a scene. It occurred to me then that I could create a new fantasy: Evan in Cefalù.

I grabbed my phone and opened Emily's Instagram, scrolling back until I found the photo, and sliding my hand between my legs, I began to build a scene. First I recalled Evan and me kissing, taking the elements I could remember into the fantasy: the slope of his cheekbone, one of his hands under my chin, the feeling of his body pressed against mine. I imagined us post-swim, our skin still holding the lingering cool of the ocean. Then I imagined us fucking under the afternoon sun, our bodies sleepy and relaxed but still moving in an urgent way. I felt a flicker of something, a sign of life. I opened my eyes in surprise. Then I closed them again and played out the rest of the scene; directing and editing to move the plot forward, or pausing and replaying whenever I felt my body react.

After a while, I wanted Evan to moan my name and so he did. It worked and I came, my body shuddering in both shock and pleasure.

After the sensation had receded, the cool, clear light of clarity returned, harshly illuminating the fact that I'd just successfully masturbated to a photo Evan's dead ex-girlfriend had taken.

eleven

"We have to ask 'why?'" the TED Talk speaker explained. He'd been trying to convince us of this point for five minutes already.

My phone vibrated in my hand. It was a message from Soph:

Why is Paul never in the office after 2 pm on a Friday?

I replied:

Why does Paul pay us 10k under industry average?

She replied:

:(

"'Why?' is a question of discovery. It's the most powerful question you can ask," the speaker continued. "When we don't ask 'why?' we lose an opportunity to learn."

To me, asking "why?" often felt like it removed meaning

rather than adding any. Looking too deeply for an answer to "why?" could invite complete dissociation.

"I challenge you to ask 'why?' more often and to see where the discovery takes you."

The loud round of applause that followed crackled and buzzed as it forced its way out of the cheap Bluetooth speaker. We all winced and Paul leaped forward to mute the video.

"So, what do we think, team?" he asked as he closed the laptop.

"I really liked it," Dave from customer experience confessed. "I think we should all make an effort to ask 'why?' more often."

I stifled the urge to ask him why.

"I completely agree," Paul replied. "It's August, everybody. The beginning of a new month. Let's make this the month of asking 'why?' "

Back at my desk, Monday extended before me in a series of tasks. The first was analyzing some session replays. This task involved me choosing a focus group user and following their journey around the app, while taking notes. If the user didn't navigate the app in the way we wanted I needed to figure out how to better guide them. I sat and watched my screen as a red line, like a piece of thread, was drawn around the interface of the app. There was something so personal about watching someone use an app, it was like observing them as they navigated an unfamiliar supermarket; seeing all the intimate decisions they made in the hopes of satisfying some need. This particular user tapped and tapped back, tapped again and tapped back again, seemingly unable to find the item they were looking for. I took notes.

I imagined someone selecting my ghost account for a session replay. They would most likely be baffled by this user who seemed to spend most of their time toggling obsessively between practically inactive accounts; never leaving a trace and never posting photos, only silently observing. Or maybe that was normal, maybe a session replay of anyone would reveal that we were all obsessively checking up on each other, wasting our time and sabotaging our own mental health. I checked my phone but it looked back at me blank-faced.

The high after my date with Evan had faded quickly in the silence that followed, and now creeping doubts and insecurities had emerged from the shadowy gaps in my memory. I knew I could reach out and message Evan, I could tell him I had a good time and ask him if he'd like to meet up again, but I'd missed the twenty-four-hour window of post-date positivity and now I felt paralyzed. This paralysis was mostly due to the fact that the passing of time had warped the way I remembered our date. Over the hours of silence my memories had morphed, displaying my behaviors in a new, unflattering light. I now remembered myself as having been arrogant and obnoxious. I dragged out everything I could remember saying to Evan and interrogated it. I grew concerned about the way comments and opinions I had shared may have been received by him. I recalled ranting to him about the way social media allowed unqualified people to disguise their opinions as facts and publicly declare them to large, impressionable audiences. I'd gone on to extrapolate that the desire to merge our opinions with our personality and share them online was a symptom of the divisive nature of the world we currently lived in, which then drove us to defend these opinions in increasingly aggressive ways without any acceptance of nuance. I remembered Evan frowning in concentration as I worked hard to make this convoluted and tenuous connection between ideas. Hadn't I even interrupted him? So, I was rude and insufferable after all.

There was one particularly painful memory, in which I took an opportunity to perform a stricken impersonation of Tom Hanks shouting "Wilson!" as he watched his beloved volleyball friend drift away, only to realize from Evan's blank expression that he had clearly never watched *Cast Away*.

I continued to legitimize these concerns about the evening by transforming my memories to confirm them, then I used the doctored memories to convince myself of a reality in which Evan was most likely hoping that I would save him the trouble of rejecting me by never messaging him again. As consolation, I looked to divert myself from my thoughts by conducting a hunt for interesting developments in the lives of people I knew. Like a prison warden, I wandered my phone's home screen, opening apps in a particular order and shining a torch into every dark corner that might be concealing something I could distract myself with. Inevitably I found myself looking at my ex's account. And there I found a new development: He'd been tagged in a photo with a woman. She wore all black and, as Beverly had mentioned, she had short pink hair. They were sitting side by side on a bench at the pub my ex and I had frequented. I tapped through to her account, which revealed a bio containing a mess of emojis and a chaotic grid of photos of herself, her cat, and her friends. So this was my ex's new girlfriend. I frowned.

She looked sweet and younger than my ex, and rather than harboring any ill feelings for her, I felt only concern and sympathy. I knew she would not emerge unscathed.

I sent a screenshot of the photo to Beverly.

It's official.

Gross, she responded, more out of solidarity than genuine opinion. Then she called me. I rejected the call and grabbed

my coat from the back of my chair as I typed a message back
to her:

Sorry, just getting out of the office.

I left the building, calling her back as I crossed the road to
a small park.

"Are you okay?" she asked as soon as she picked up.

"Yeah, I'm fine. I'm just wondering why I wasted four of
the 'best years of my life' dating someone who was clearly
wrong for me."

"You didn't waste them. I'm loath to remind you of this,
because I am the last person to sing his praises, but you did
have fun together, in the beginning. You were happy then."

I saw my ex and me laughing; his crooked teeth and face-
splitting smile. I remembered the complete thrill I felt when he
approached me after a gig on the night we met. I recalled the
way he'd get so excited when he found a new song he liked
that he'd dance around the house, changing the lyrics to include my name and performing them for me, and I would
laugh until it physically hurt. He was actually a great per-
former, he could genuinely dance and sing, but no one in the
world got to see that except me.

"I'm only reminding you of that because I don't want you
to say you've wasted years of your life. I have some great
memories from those years and I know you do too, it's probably just hard to remember them at the moment. I hate to
think those memories will be forever tainted by the fact that
you both fell out of love with each other, and things turned
sour. And anyway, your twenties are not the best years of
your life. Practically everyone in their thirties will say their
thirties are the best, and if you ask someone in their forties,
they will say their forties have been the best decade. So I

guess everyone just thinks they're in the prime decade of their life."

"That's a nice way to think about it."

"Although, I guess eventually it does have to stop getting better and start to decline instead." She paused briefly in thought. "When do you think it starts to decline?"

"I'd really rather not think about that. You were just starting to make me feel better."

"Sorry—you're right. How did your date on the weekend go?"

"It went well, or at least I thought it did. Now I'm not so sure. He hasn't messaged me since."

"It's been two days. I don't think you should be concerned yet."

"Is it so unreasonable to hope that he had such a great time that he would want to message me immediately?"

"People just don't really behave like that, do they? They play it cool."

"But why?" I asked her, imagining the TED Talk speaker beaming proudly at me.

"I don't know. Power? Why haven't you messaged him?"

"I have a paralyzing fear of rejection."

"Well, if you don't message him and he doesn't message you then it just wasn't meant to be. 'Rejection is protection.'"

"Rejection is *what*?"

"Protection. It means that when someone rejects you, it's actually just the universe protecting you from something that wasn't meant for you."

I frowned in confusion and began picking at one of my cuticles. "You sound like you've been speaking to my dad. Can we talk about your life instead? How's rock climbing and Spanish going?"

"Really well. Actually, we got a pasta machine last week, we've been making ravioli, but Matt is finding it hard with his crutches." She laughed. "It's so funny, he—"

"Wait—Matt's on crutches?"

"Yeah, he had foot surgery. Didn't I tell you?"

"No, you never told me."

"Oh, it's boring anyway. It was very minor, he's fine," she said distractedly. I could hear the muffled sound of someone speaking to her in the background. "I'm getting called off break, I'll call you soon, okay?"

"Yeah, sure."

"Okay, I miss you."

"I miss you too."

She hung up and I dropped my phone into my lap, sighing and looking around the park. I settled my gaze on two pigeons that were fighting, or maybe playing, in a dirty puddle of rainwater. After a few months of living away, I realized that Beverly and I were drifting apart. I spoke to her frequently, but it wasn't possible to adequately fill her in on my life over the phone. When we spoke I forgot things and didn't bother with the mundane details for fear of boring her. I could see now that she had been holding back details from me too. But our lives are an accumulation of mostly mundane details, and those details eventually form a whole and interesting image, like the way pixels form a photo. How do you continue to see the image of someone clearly, if you don't have all the necessary details? I frowned, wondering what destination this trajectory had us moving toward. A cold breeze picked up, making me shiver, and I stood to return to the office.

//

At the end of the day, I shut down my computer and caught the tram home, listening to music as I watched the green expanse of Princes Park pass by. Instead of obsessively checking my phone for a message from Evan, I was now pretending to be indifferent to the silence between us; applying myself to the kind of superstitious activity which only appeals to someone who is powerlessly waiting to be contacted. The universe works in mysterious ways, but there is one way in which it never fails to be obvious: It will give you what you want when you no longer desperately want it. I reasoned that if I was completely content with not hearing from Evan, he would message me.

The tram drew to a stop and the doors clattered open. A woman boarded with her small child, just as the rain had begun to lightly tap on the windows. She sighed with audible relief as she sat down, and the child, a little boy, climbed onto his mother's lap, before directing his vacant, drooly gaze at me. I smiled at him and he stared back at me impassively. My phone vibrated. It was a message from Evan:

Are you free this weekend? x

twelve

"You're an only child, aren't you?" Soph asked, appearing by my desk.

I turned and eyed her suspiciously.

"I can tell you what your 'sexual energy' is based on whether you have siblings," she explained without looking up from her phone. "I've got two older brothers, which means"—her eyes scanned—"apparently I 'like it rough.'"

"Well, this sounds thoroughly researched and reliable," I said.

"You're an only child, right?"

I nodded reluctantly and she resumed scrolling.

"It says you're 'self-obsessed.'"

"That's such a boring stereotype," I said dismissively, turning back to my computer.

"Or, hang on . . ." she paused to read ahead. "It says you're 'self-sacrificing' in bed. 'Too eager to please.'"

I gave her a flat look.

"Don't look at me, I don't make the rules." She shrugged, her focus already back to extracting more useless information. "*Ooh,* interesting, it says people who have two older sisters are the best in bed."

With that she turned to walk away. "*Daaave,*" she called out. "Do you have any siblings?"

I turned my attention back to the spreadsheet in front of me but failed to hold it there. The screen blurred and all the numbers and words, which were vitally important only moments ago, were now hollowed of meaning.

Instead I recalled an image of my mother: Her seat pulled absurdly close to the steering wheel, which she gripped with both hands. Her teased fringe gently bobbing in the breeze that was coming through the driver's window. She had a cigarette crushed between two fingers on her left hand and her face was a crease of concentration. My mother always drove her car, an old white Camry, like it was a wild beast that might at any moment wrest back its power. I remember observing her profile from the passenger seat; her strong jawline, which was also mine, providing a border to her face like the edge of a cliff; her nose, also mine, just a little too bold for her features.

On this particular occasion we were on our way to the doctor's so I could get a script for the pill. I'd got my first period the day before. At thirteen, I was ambivalent about contraception, but easily bribed by the promise of a post-appointment McFlurry from McDonald's.

I was born when my mother was a month shy of her eighteenth birthday. She'd always made an effort to refer to me as a "surprise" and to avoid demonstrating anything that resembled regret, but she had on occasion unconsciously used the word "accident," and whenever this happened I'd imagine that my sudden existence had marked her life like a car crash might. Although she seemed to have mostly made peace with my unexpected arrival, she was permanently scarred by the way it was thrust upon her and, as a result, she remained terrified of the potential one careless action had to instantly alter the trajectory of a life. When I was younger, her fear manifested in control. Whenever she could, she forced a distance between me and her idea of whatever danger lurked ahead of me. I remember even the doctor was hesitant about my need for contraception at thirteen, she'd looked back at us with one eyebrow raised and her hands hovering over her keyboard. My mother convinced her by saying my cramps were keeping me from going to school, and I nodded along complicitly, propelled by images of soft-serve and M&M'S.

As a result of everything I learned from my mother about pregnancy, I spent my teenage years viewing pregnant women with pity. I thought they'd all made a terrible, tragic mistake.

My mother was still refusing to return my calls or texts. Months ago, in our last conversation, I'd told her that I'd found a new job and would be staying in Melbourne indefinitely. Originally I'd lied to her and pretended I was required to go for a work trip. It seemed easier to act like the universe had orchestrated a series of events that would lead to a permanent move, rather than admit that I simply wanted to leave my old life behind. I knew that my mother would not enjoy being lumped into the category of my "old life" and I had felt that I would preserve her feelings by keeping my reasoning vague and therefore limiting the probability my words had of offending her. But I had not anticipated that she would behave so strangely in response. She was hurt, I assumed, and she was communicating that by ignoring me, punishing me for being my father's daughter: an abandoner of places and people.

I was not concerned for her welfare. I knew that some terrible accident had not befallen her because she was still regularly active online. Recently underneath a post about the extension they were building on her local supermarket she wrote: *Finally! Desperately needs more parking. Utterly ridiculous on the weekends!*

On a post about someone's missing cat—a ginger named Mr. Pants—she wrote: *Have shared! I hope he comes home safe and sound xx,* though her well wishes were trivial and useless among the surging tide of others wishing well, and were made even more useless given that Mr. Pants had gone missing in a town just outside Denver, Colorado—thousands and thousands of miles away. She adorned the comment with a sad face which was weeping a single tear. So yes, she was alive and well, and in possession of a functional phone, an internet connection, and apparently an unbridled empathy for complete strangers.

I believed that my mother hoped I wouldn't thrive in the absence of her attention and that I would eventually discard my dignity and beg to return to the familial warmth. But the truth was her imposed silence only made me feel a sad sense of pity for her, like she was accidentally giving me a glimpse of her hand, revealing her bluff and exposing her limits. I'd always felt that my own power lay in my ability to weather these storms and to remain unaffected, like a mother calmly walking away from a toddler throwing a tantrum on the supermarket floor. After I'd told her I'd be staying in Melbourne, I had called her a handful of times to no avail and then given up, resigning myself to the game and knowing that she would soon tire of herself.

My mother was an often-ignored child herself. She had on occasion shared stories with me about her mother and father pretending she didn't exist as punishment for her misbehavior. Her parents were tough; they grew up poor in their respective neighboring villages in southern Italy and were married as teenagers. Some turn of luck allowed them to migrate to Australia in the 1970s, and after that they never experienced the same hardship again. Everything I know about my grandparents I have stolen piece by piece. My mother rarely spoke of them, so I have only a vague idea: poverty, luck, Australia. But still, I could imagine they would have had no patience for the petulance they'd inadvertently afforded their daughter by giving birth to her years after they'd successfully elevated themselves to modest comfort. When my mother acted out and was being punished through silence, her brothers and sisters were told that they were also not allowed to speak to her. The family would even go so far as to eat dinner without setting a place at the table for her. At first, she told me, she found this exercise novel, like a game or a challenge, and then quickly she found it frustrating. Eventually, it would end with her in tears, screaming and throwing herself around on the floor, until her father bent her over his knee, conceding that she was once again real, and hit her with his belt until she was quiet.

Her father died when I was ten and her mother died when I was eighteen; there are no photos of my grandparents holding me. My only connection to that side of my family is my mother. She doesn't speak to any of her siblings. Whenever I have ventured to ask her why, she has vaguely referred to some disagreement decades ago. Judging from the fact that my uncles and aunties have never reached out to my mother, I can assume that, in my mother's family, grudges are not just held, they are clung to. I suppose at some point my mother did something bad enough to become permanently invisible and, judging by the timeline, I was fairly certain it had a lot to do with me.

There is a photo I've kept of my mother and father holding me as a newborn. I've held on to it as one of the few documents of my early existence, but it is usually with reluctance that I look at it. It isn't the joyous image of two exhausted but ecstatic young parents, it's the image of two children holding a child, and I've always found it terrifying.

CHAPTER

thirteen

Evan believed it was completely unacceptable that I had lived in Melbourne for nearly three months now and could still count the restaurants and bars I'd been to on one hand. He was determined to set it right and so he sent me a list of six places and wrote:

We will go to every single one. We
will fix this.

It was a playful, yet sophisticated gambit, and I was impressed by the way he had essentially managed to ask me out on six more dates while pinning his motivation to some plausible common goal: the rectifying of a currently squandered potential, which almost allowed him to maintain an image of mystery about his feelings for me. Of course, I didn't entirely buy that the goal of seeing me was solely to broaden my limited Melbourne culinary experience. But I played along while harboring a small but confident joy, polishing and caring for it like it was a precious stone, that the real reasoning behind this ploy was that Evan simply wanted to see me again and again.

The first place on the list was a small Japanese bar and we arranged to meet there on Saturday for our second date.

We drank sake and shared small plates of sashimi, enjoying the increasing comfort we felt in each other's company. Our conversations built upon themselves now that most of the characters and settings of our lives had been introduced— except Emily, whom Evan still hadn't mentioned. After our last conversation about breakups had abruptly reached a dead end, I'd carefully planned topics that would allow us to avoid any sudden roadblocks. Naturally, I was still deeply curious about her but I felt strongly that I couldn't bring the topic up. That was a part of his life that he would need to share with me. I was also wary of ruining my own plan for the evening by forcing him to speak about such a dark and traumatic experience. My plan was to invite Evan back to my apartment; a decision I'd made mere minutes into the date, or more truthfully, one I'd made when I spent the day tidying my apartment in preparation; a self-fulfilling prophecy.

I could sense Evan was feeling something similar. His gaze over the course of the evening had softened and, as he held eye contact, he seemed to communicate his desire to do more than sit across a table and talk. He often rubbed his hand over his jaw and neck absentmindedly as he spoke and I found myself envious of his hands. I wanted it to be my hands that were touching him and I wanted his hands to be touching me. All of these feelings, lingering so close to the surface, created an exciting sense of tension as we talked and ate, a comfortable precursory feeling that encouraged me. It seemed that Evan had conferred control to me and I enjoyed the feeling of authority as if it were a form of foreplay.

As I wound my way back from the bathroom to our table I saw that Evan was looking at his phone. Although he didn't really use social media, he used his phone a lot. He documented his running, catalogued his meditations, reviewed his sleep quality, monitored his cryptocurrency, consulted his budgets, listened to podcasts, and read the news. His life was incredibly organized and optimized. In this way he couldn't have been more different from my ex, who often forgot to pay his car registration or driver's license renewal, and who hadn't completed a tax return in years. With my ex I lived on edge, constantly terrified of the prospect of some forgotten expense crashing like a meteor into our finances, decimating holiday plans and savings progress in its wake. To avoid this, I took on the responsibility of reminding him about bills and tax returns and attempted to teach him how to budget, which gave my presence in his life an unpleasant parental aura of which he grew resentful; the entire dynamic effectively doubling the burden of living for myself. It seemed that with Evan I could relax. I was certain that, in this way at least, he had his life completely under control.

When I reached the table I could see he had his running app open.

"Good run this morning?" I asked as I sat down.

"Yeah, actually. Really good." He put his phone down, giving me another glimpse of Cefalù before the screen went black. I felt a flutter of excitement, a Pavlovian response due to the habit I'd recently formed of masturbating while imagining myself there with him. As I was struck momentarily with those visions, a woman approached our table, placing her hand on Evan's shoulder. He turned in her direction.

"Nadia!" he said, the surprise disrupting his usual calm.

"Hey, you," she replied and withdrew her hand from his

shoulder in the same casually confident way that she'd placed it. I sensed they were perhaps old friends. I was yet to meet any of Evan's friends and, although I was open to the idea of it, I had hoped I would have time to prepare. I watched as Evan half stood to accept her hug. She wore her long brown hair fastened to the back of her head with a claw clip and gold hoop earrings swung from her ears.

"This is Ana," Evan said, now regaining his footing on the familiar terrain of the conversation. "Ana, Nadia."

We greeted each other, Nadia's eyes moving quickly around my face. The look she gave me had the unmistakable feeling of someone performing calculations in their mind. She was trying to figure out where the person in front of her fit into the equation. She turned back to Evan.

"How are you?" she asked.

"Yeah, good. Good. What about you?"

The exchange was losing momentum quickly, and although Evan was doing a good job of concealing his discomfort, it was still visible in his strained smile and his sudden reliance on cyclical politeness. Despite not knowing anything about her, I had the odd sense that Nadia seemed more at ease with the awkwardness.

"Good. I'm just having some drinks with a couple of friends." She pointed vaguely across the room and Evan's eyes immediately followed her direction as if seeking something.

"It's no one you know," she added, and a silence began to stretch. "I should probably get back. It was nice to see you though."

"Yeah, you too," Evan replied quickly and conclusively, as if reanimated by his role in bringing the conversation to an end.

"Nice to meet you, Ana," she said, giving a small wave.

Evan watched her walk away for a moment before turning back to me to explain. "Nadia was my ex's best friend."

"Oh, okay," I said, attempting to supress any unusual reaction.

With those few words Evan had made Nadia infinitely more interesting and I searched for her across the room, watching as she slid into a booth among her laughing friends. An opportunity I was not expecting had suddenly presented itself and I could have used it as an organic transition to ask a question about Emily, but at that moment so many entered my mind that it became difficult to isolate the right one. Nor could I guarantee that the question I chose wouldn't lead to me accidentally revealing some of my inexplicably intimate knowledge of her, or cause the tension we'd built throughout the evening to dissipate in an instant. The conversation was stunted for a moment.

"Want to get out of here and go for a walk?" Evan suggested.

"Or maybe you could come back to mine for a drink?" I countered.

He smiled at me with obvious excitement and said, "Yeah, all right."

I caught a glimpse of his teeth.

CHAPTER

fourteen

At fifteen, I thought of my virginity as an embarrassing stamp of amateurism and I wanted to be rid of it. Beverly took a more romanticized view of hers and claimed that she wanted to wait until she had a boyfriend. I was more concerned with certification. In the "How Embarrassing!" section of the magazines Beverly and I frequently read, there were often horror stories of bodily malfunctions or parental interruptions that occurred during "first time" experiences. I'd read one particularly troubling story, a harrowing account of a girl whose hymen was attached to an artery, so that when she lost her virginity she immediately started hemorrhaging and the boy had to wake his parents so they could drive her to the emergency room. I reasoned that if something embarrassing, or potentially life-threatening, was likely to happen to me in the process of having sex for the first time; I'd rather it happened in front of a boy who I would probably never see again.

There was a boy I spoke to on MSN who went to a neighboring school and lived in the wealthier suburb next to mine. I'd never met him before but he was one of those boys whose online presence crossed school boundaries and postcodes, and he seemed to appear in the contact list of any given female between the ages of fourteen and seventeen. There were rumors about him, that he was "experienced" and "hot." He was a year older than me, which seemed to add conviction to his case. And so, he became my target.

These were the golden days when the internet still had defined boundaries; when it was a portal we kept in a certain room and visited on our own terms. In order to speak to MSN Boy, I needed to log in and wait at the computer for the status next to his username to change to *Online*. When it did, I willed him to message me. When that didn't work I conceded and sent him a message. It was an excruciatingly slow conversation, during which his replies were mostly *not much u?* or *thats kool.* Not exactly a fevered exchange between two pining lovers. Still, I eventually secured an invite to his house that weekend. I didn't tell him I had a grand plan of off-loading my virginity on him, even though in this new online world words were of little consequence and people said all kinds of things they never would in real life. The twelve-year-old boy who lived next door to me had a MSN status that read: *Pussy Master.*

I suppose I didn't want to tell MSN Boy about my virginity because, even to me, my behavior registered as odd, or unusual. From the movies I'd watched and magazines I read, it seemed teenage girls were not meant to be so forward and precocious in chasing down their "first time." We were expected to fight for our virginity in some way, or at least we needed to be bargained with, convinced or coerced. But I wanted to toss my virginity away and move on.

Saturday arrived and, even though I'd orchestrated the entire event, my stomach churned as I rode my bike to his house.

My nervousness was understandable given that by this point in time I'd only kissed a boy. I was never one to do things by halves.

When he answered the door, a small white dog came darting down the hall and bounded manically up my legs. The unexpected attack, coupled with my existing nerves, made me freeze in shock.

"Get down, Daisy!" he shouted, grabbing the dog by the collar as it continued to skitter its paws across the tiled floor and stare up at me with its crusty brown eyes. "Come in," he said to me.

MSN Boy was skinny with a sideswept fringe that reached his eyelids. He held his chin permanently lifted so that he could see and frequently shook the hair off his face, like a nervous tic, only for it to fall immediately back into place. He led me down a hall and through a lounge room that had the most astounding view of the ocean. I gaped at it as we passed.

"My parents are at my sister's netball game," he explained as we moved through the quiet house.

His bedroom had a double bed up against a wall and a TV, DVD player, and PlayStation against another. It was a hot day and he'd pulled the blinds down over the window, which created a halo of bright white light around the edges. I remember the walls of his room were plastered with posters of naked girls. One woman used her forearms to cover her nipples. Another laughed with a garden hose in her hand, her white T-shirt drenched. A few of the posters had more than one girl in the shot, hugging each other in lacy underwear and contorting their spines. They looked impossibly experienced.

I was small for my age, bony and flat-chested. Underneath my denim shorts, my underwear was decorated with dancing cartoon ice creams. Now, with an audience of these pouting, writhing, oily-looking women, I had my first doubts about what I'd planned to do. But I was resolute. I reminded myself that this boy was my sacrifice. I would never see or speak to him again.

MSN Boy plugged an MP3 player into his sound system and began browsing through his music while I stood awkwardly and observed his posters as if they were art on a gallery wall. He ended up choosing Linkin Park and so I lost my virginity to the sound of Chester Bennington growling.

The experience was mercifully short. There were a few false starts and some questionable technique. All in all, it was a quick and hurried exchange; a little clumsy, but nothing horrifically embarrassing happened. He somehow managed to keep his satin boxers on the whole time. I didn't expect to enjoy it. In fact, pleasure never even entered my mind. I expected my first time to be something I endured and ideally survived. Maybe because of this, I wasn't disappointed.

"Are you all right?" MSN Boy asked, as I pulled my denim shorts back on immediately after.

"Yep," I replied, relieved. "It didn't even really hurt."

"Cool," he replied, apparently not even a little confused by my response. "Are you going now?"

"Yep!" I said, tying my shoelaces.

I basically ran out of the house, collecting my bike from the front lawn where I'd dumped it on arrival and fleeing the scene. In later years, once I had more to compare it to, I would come to recognize the experience as disappointing. I would eventually find it sad that my younger self felt she needed to rush out and seek the company of a stranger, simply because the pressure of her virginity was too much to bear. But at the time I felt like I had freed myself of the shackles of virginity. I'd looked fear in the face and stolen its power.

I rode my bike home, standing up on my pedals and coasting down the hill toward my house. A warm breeze blew through my hair and I felt light with relief. I was certain the experience had matured me and I had a new sense of confidence, like the next time a boy made a joke about sex at school I could confidently laugh and no one would jump in to say, "Ana, why are you laughing? You're frigid."

Apparently I had lost something and yet I felt victorious.

Beverly stayed over that night and I told her everything. She giggled and gasped at my retelling, while I aggressively hissed at her to be quiet so my mother didn't hear me and call the police or something equally as dramatic. I enjoyed telling Beverly the story and she had seemed to enjoy hearing it, but afterward, for a week or so, it felt like she was behaving differently around me; like there was something about me she no longer understood.

//

Evan and I arrived at my apartment and I held the door open for him, before following him inside. We were both trying very hard to remain nonchalant and cool. I opened a bottle of wine and poured us each a glass while Evan wandered around my living room looking at my books, just like The Chef had. Again, I felt exposed. Living alone meant that my home was an extension of me and the data at Evan's disposal was extensive. If he opened my pantry cupboard, he would see so many supplements that he might conclude I had every known chronic inflammatory disease, and not that I was just simply a sucker for the slickly marketed promise of optimized bodily functions. He'd find my coffee and would probably be disappointed to learn that I bought cheap, brandless coffee beans, having never developed the palate to tell the difference. If he opened my bathroom cabinet he would find an array of cosmetic products, all with specific purposes for specific areas of my body and face. Proof that the way I looked, no matter how casually I presented myself, was not without extensive and costly effort. If he looked too closely at my bath towel, he might spot the stain where I'd bled during my last period. The stain had set permanently because I'd been too lazy to immediately wash it.

I walked across the room, switching the lights off and the lamp on to soften the details a little. Then I joined Evan on the couch.

"Your place is cozy," he said, looking around the sparsely decorated room.

"It's okay, you can just say small."

"I stand by cozy. I mean, it's practically empty but it does have a nice feel to it."

"Thanks," I said, placing my glass down on the coffee table as the silence began to extend itself dangerously close to awkwardness.

"I'll put some music on," I blurted, reaching for my speaker.

"Oh—actually I hate music," Evan said.

I turned back to stare at him.

"That was a joke, obviously." He laughed. "*Jesus*— I think I just saw a whole new side of you. The look you gave me then was pure judgment. What if I genuinely hated music? What would you do?"

"I'd still sleep with you," I admitted.

"Is that what's happening here?" he asked.

I smiled and said nothing, staring back at him and imagining that I was challenging him with my eyes. Then I nodded and he immediately launched himself across the couch. I laughed just as his lips met mine.

The urgency in our movements built quickly now that there was a clear destination. After a moment, he broke off to begin untying my boots and I wondered if he might be about to reveal a foot fetish. I would indulge that, I thought as I watched him, I would let him lick honey off my toes if that's what he wanted. But once he had my boots and socks off, he ran his hands up my legs and eventually, mercifully, all the way up under my skirt. I lifted his shirt and he kicked his sneakers off. Then he pulled away from me, standing to unbutton his pants.

"Sorry—I'll just take these off," he said, removing his socks.

"It's okay," I replied breathlessly, pulling off my sweater and unzipping my skirt.

I sensed that he had stopped moving and I looked up to see he was watching me; an undisguised hunger on his face; a sock held limply in his hand.

I laughed a little self-consciously at the sight of him staring and his face broke into a smile. He dropped the sock and we closed the space between us; our bodies and lips colliding.

We moved to the bed, where Evan then shifted his way down my body until his head was between my legs. His open desire to witness my pleasure was intimidating at first. The temptation to perform emerged so I could ease the pressure of the spotlight with a staged and jazz-handed rendition of an orgasm. But there was something about Evan that felt exciting yet safe, something so unlike my last experience that at no point was my mind interrupted by unwanted memories of The Chef's crushing weight, or his thick, imperious hands. I let Evan stay down between my legs until I found myself unconsciously moving my hips and pressing myself against his mouth. With one hand gripping his arm, I whispered, "I want you inside me." He made a low groaning sound and crawled up the bed toward me. He leaned over me and with a hand on either side of his hips I guided and pulled him slowly into me. When he began to move, a shiver of pleasure ran through my body. His movements became a little rougher then, but it was the roughness of enthusiasm and desire. Not the roughness of dominance and power; a notable difference. His focus was on me and his movements were responses to the sounds I made. It didn't seem like he was making any assumptions based on anyone else's preferences and I was relieved. It felt as if some spaces could still be private; they could be ours.

I signaled a change of position and Evan rolled over to let me climb on top of him. Any lingering pressure to perform melted away and, without intellectualizing it, I moved in whatever way felt good. When Evan moaned—an involuntary, primal sound—a rush went through my body. I came, giving in and crying out. Then I collapsed forward, my face pressed against the headboard and Evan's shoulder. I realized then that two single tears had leaked out of my eyes and rolled silently down my cheeks. Startled, I quickly rubbed them away so he wouldn't see.

//

Later, while Evan was in the bathroom, his phone lit up, vibrating dully into the mattress next to me as he received a series of messages from Nadia. She was the type to send each sentence separately, which meant the messages dropped down the screen one by one:

It was so good to see you tonight!

Sorry if I acted strangely

*It was a bit of a shock to see you
with someone else*

*I still think about Em and
everything that happened all the
time*

I miss her so much

*If you are open to it I'd love to
catch up*

I knew it was only natural for Nadia to be hurt seeing that Evan had moved on from her best friend. I imagined that seeing him with someone else would further confirm that Emily was never coming back and that even her memory was beginning to fade. Emily's death would have been a tragic experience that Nadia and Evan shared, and seeing him with me would imply that, for him at least, the pain of their loss was receding.

Evan's screen returned to black and I waited, aware that his reaction to Emily being brought up in those messages was going to be insightful.

He came back to bed, picking his phone up and sliding under the covers. The screen lit up again and he read the notifications but appeared to be unmoved by them. He left them unanswered, putting the phone back down. Then he turned to me and, as his eyes searched my face, a smile spread across his lips. He shifted closer and kissed me on the forehead. In that moment, it felt like I'd won something. I just wasn't sure what.

fifteen

My half-eaten sushi roll had leaked soy sauce onto my desk. I saw the coffee-colored trail was creeping toward the keyboard and grabbed my napkin, mopping it up before taking another bite. It was still cold from the fridge, flavorless and slightly stale. The longest workdays are those when even lunch does not offer a brief respite. I craned my head to look out the window behind me and chewed mechanically. It had been my decision to face my back to the window, a sacrifice that afforded me privacy and a grace period to prepare for any visitor to my desk. This was not my first desk job. I knew the frantic, guilty dance of toggling tabs when someone was suddenly looking over your shoulder.

The sky outside the window was dark gray and the plaintive sound of rain mollified the office. The effect was reminiscent of childhood, a regression to the idea that the rain signaled nobody would be doing anything exciting today, and that by sitting at a desk and working through a series of tasks, I wasn't missing out on anything. I put the sushi roll back down and returned my eyes to my screen.

Even though I'd now worked at Gro for a couple of months, no one I reported to had any idea how long anything should take me to complete. Early on I saw the opportunity this granted me and I began to manage expectations by giving myself wide margins to complete simple projects. Nobody had ever questioned it; they wouldn't know what to ask. As a result I tended to deliver all of my work ahead of schedule and still have spare time. This is why I was never found at my desk after 6 P.M., and why I had the time to visit Emily's account in the middle of the day.

Since finding her on social media, I had returned to her grid over and over, seemingly in search of something. Even though I knew the content would never change, I still made small discoveries every time I looked at it and the thrill of finding something new had become addictive. I learned that, prior to her relationship with Evan, Emily had gone to culinary school for a year before dropping out to teach yoga. I saw that she'd studied to become a yoga teacher in India, and had confused her family and friends by not immediately returning home after gaining her certification.

Will you ever come home? a friend had written under a photo she'd posted, in which a copy of the Bhagavad Gita lay open next to a small, amber-colored tumbler of chai.

Maybe xx, she'd responded.

Since Evan and I had slept together, his venue list agenda had taken a back seat. Instead, he began staying at my apartment a couple of nights a week. Together we would cook dinner, impatiently passing the excruciating moments in which we were both clothed as quickly as possible. Despite this, and despite the fact that Evan and I spoke every day, we still hadn't had a conversation about Emily. He hadn't even mentioned her by accident. The situation encouraged me to return to Emily's accounts so I could continue sifting through the rubble for clues as to what happened. Recently I'd recognized Nadia in some of Emily's older photos and visited her account, which was all beige tones, matcha lattes, activewear, and smiling selfies. I found Nadia boring, but Emily was different. There was more to Emily's account than a one-dimensional social media stereotype. There were facets of her interests that didn't fit together neatly on her grid, the way they did for people like Nadia who curated their lives into self-conscious blandness. Emily's account had unfiltered, exposed edges that made it less aesthetic, but more interesting. I liked this about her.

All the same, her account wasn't giving me the answer to the one question that had plagued me recently. What had happened to her? I stared at my screen, sushi roll all but forgotten, and took a step across an imaginary line; the line that separates those who can let it go from those who can't. I googled her.

I started with her name, but it gave too many results. I added *Melbourne* but it didn't take me anywhere. Finally, grimly, I tried adding *death*.

Cyclist killed in hit-and-run sparks new outrage over road conditions

There she was. I pored over the article and collected details. Emily was only mentioned once by name. The fact that she had been twenty-seven was shared, along with some cliché́d journalistic comment about how she was a treasured member of the community, bubbly personality, dearly missed, et cetera. Evan wasn't mentioned. There was no reason for him to be, but my eyes searched for his name nevertheless.

Overall the article was more concerned with the road and the safety of future cyclists than it was with Emily. But now I knew what had happened: Emily died riding her bike, hit by a driver who fled the scene. There were pieces I could now put together, she must have cycled to and from the yoga studio until she was killed one night on her way home.

Up until that moment I'd viewed Emily from a distance. I'd detached myself from the tragedy of her death by reducing it to a morbid curiosity. Worse still, I'd viewed what happened to her as a lens through which I'd hoped to learn more about Evan and, selfishly, I'd planned to use whatever I learned to better understand Evan's feelings for me. But discovering that Emily had died alone, somewhere on the side of the road, abandoned even by the person who took her life, broke my heart. I imagined Evan receiving the phone call. I imagined his shock, the speechless horror. I saw him collapsing to his knees and heaving great explosive gasps of distress from the floor. Before I was even aware of it, tears blurred my view of the screen. Surprised and embarrassed, I snatched the napkin out from under the sushi roll and used it to dry my face, transferring soy sauce directly into my eye. It burned instantly and painfully.

"*Shit,*" I swore under my breath.

Wiping my eyes with my hands and pulling my headphones off, I stood up and walked quickly to the bathroom.

I could never truly understand the depth of pain Emily's death must have caused Evan. But my feelings for him had let me access a small piece of it, and its potency had shocked me. More than ever, I couldn't understand how he could keep this grief concealed so neatly. In the same way that I maneuvered around my knowledge of Emily, careful not to reveal it, I imagined that he must maneuver around his grief. Maybe he was afraid that if he opened that door, he would not be able to control what came out. He was probably worried that the sudden display of emotion would scare me, which was understandable, but I couldn't see how we could continue to speak daily, while still leaving significant parts of us cordoned off from each other. I wanted to be there for him more fully.

After washing my eye and cleaning up my mascara, I went to the kitchen to make myself a cup of tea. I waited for the kettle to boil and stared at the motivational calendar. August's quote, which I'd previously ignored, now leaped out at me with sudden relevancy:

Visualization is the first step toward realization.

sixteen

"I've never dated someone who's attracted to women before," George admitted, leaning back and unconsciously rubbing his hand over his shaved head. "I've always had this fantasy of a threesome, but now? I don't know, what if she's more attracted to women than men? My deepest fear is that she ends up being more attracted to the other woman than me."

"That's ridiculous." Lauren laughed, without taking her eyes from the cigarette she was rolling.

"That's your deepest fear?" Evan asked, inciting a flat look from George and a conspiring smirk from Lauren.

Lauren and George were Evan's closest friends. He'd invited me to meet them while he and I were playing pool at a musty old pub, where the beaming faces of football players from the eighties and nineties smiled down on us from the faded posters on the walls.

"I'm starting to think this place made it to your list just so you could show off your pool skills," I'd complained as he cleaned the table for the second time.

"Well, it wouldn't be very feminist of me to let you win, would it? You don't strike me as the type who would like that."

My eyebrows involuntarily raised as I realized he was correct.

"No, you're right," I conceded. "Continue."

He smiled at me and then, while his eyes were focused back on his cue, he said, "My friends are having drinks at a bar nearby, would you want to join them? Just for a drink or two?"

"Yeah, that'd be fun," I replied casually as he finally sank the eight ball.

The idea of meeting Lauren and George had sounded exciting, but as we'd walked to the bar I fell silent. Sensing my apprehension, Evan reassured me that he'd told them all about me and they couldn't wait to meet me. He was right, they'd been very welcoming. They'd even launched straight into the incredibly personal details of their own romantic lives as if I was a close friend already. George, I learned, was newly dating a bisexual woman named Hannah.

"You know there's a chance that you'll be more attracted to this theoretical 'other woman' than you're attracted to Hannah too, right?" Lauren was saying in response to George's fear of being rejected during a threesome. "If anything, Hannah's bisexuality makes it a level playing field. It also means that she would *actually* be into what's going on, rather than just participating in some patriarchy-pleasing performative act." She selected a filter out of the small plastic bag on the table in front of her, ignoring George's huff of disapproval, and continued.

"And can I add that being bisexual doesn't mean you're automatically interested in threesomes. You've assumed that a threesome is now an option for you. And anyway, to be honest, this all sounds more like an issue of your self-confidence, rather than her sexual preferences."

"Well, it's been an absolute pleasure talking to you, Lauren, as always," George concluded, picking up his beer.

"I'm just saying." She shrugged and searched for her lighter in her tote bag. "You made an assumption."

"Well, so did you!" he shot back. "You assumed that any straight woman who participates in a threesome is just trying to please the patriarchy."

Lauren lit her cigarette, inhaled, and blew the smoke out the side of her mouth. "Well, if they aren't sexually attracted to women isn't that exactly what they're doing?" She turned to me in search of support. "Ana, surely you get what I'm trying to say."

I'd been content to spend most of the evening watching the two of them rally back and forth, but now Lauren had pulled me onto the court.

"I don't know," I floundered, immediately wishing I could go back to spectating. I didn't entirely agree with the generalizations and assumptions made by either of them and I knew there might be a danger in choosing sides, given I had only just met them both. I glanced at Evan, who looked back at me in a sympathetic but unhelpful way.

"Well, as a heterosexual man, would you ever have a threesome with another man?" I asked George, hoping to pose Lauren's point in a context closer to his own understanding.

"No way!" he scoffed, shaking his head.

"Give me Hannah's number," Lauren interjected, taking back control of the conversation. "I'm going to tell her to run for her life."

"Is this one vegan?" Evan asked.

Lauren threw her head back and let out a singular "ha!" of laughter before turning to me to explain. "George brought a woman who was vegan on a date here once, and then he ordered a bowl of mac and cheese and proceeded to eat it in front of her while she just looked at him in disgust." She laughed, while George shook his head. "He was so oblivious to how offensive he was being."

"Honestly, she looked like she was going to be sick," Evan added.

"It wasn't that bad," George said, attempting to defend himself.

"Are you kidding?" Evan exclaimed. "There was so much blue cheese involved."

"Well, I didn't know that her being vegan meant that *I* had to change my dietary preferences."

"It didn't!" Evan laughed. "It just meant that if you were trying to seduce her, you probably shouldn't smell like blue cheese."

"Anyway," Lauren resumed, "she made an excuse to leave and George followed her out to say goodbye and then he still tried to kiss her."

She smirked at George affectionately; the shade of his already perpetually flushed cheeks seemed to have darkened.

"Hannah's not vegan," he concluded.

We called it a night after the third round. George was going to hang out with Hannah, and Lauren was meeting up with someone she'd matched with. After we said goodbye, I turned to walk in the direction of my apartment but Evan stopped me.

"Want to stay at mine?" he asked.

"Okay," I answered, feigning casualness to conceal my

surprise. It was the first time Evan had ever invited me to his apartment. The sudden arrival of this invitation, at this particular moment, seemed to mark reassuring progress in our relationship.

It was a blustery, cold night. Cars sloshed past us and we squinted into the wind as we walked up Lygon Street. Warm light glowed from the small bars that appeared in between the stretches of dark or vacant shopfronts. Eventually we arrived at an apartment building. It was modern, both eco-conscious and self-conscious in design, and covered in wild green vines that scaled the black metal balconies and exposed brick walls, like a symbolic gesture to nature, or maybe an apology for the intrusion. It looked new and expensive.

Although his apartment was small with only one bedroom, it had high ceilings and polished concrete floors. He gave me a short tour and I realized that, prior to this moment, I had no idea of what Evan's place might be like. When I was not with him and I imagined what he was doing, I saw him against a vague, dark gray backdrop, like a storm cloud or the inside of my own mind.

"Wow, this is nice," I said. "Is it expensive?"

"Actually, it was pretty cheap when we first moved in and, surprisingly, the landlord hasn't increased the rent since then."

We. The thought that Emily had lived here felt oppressive and immediately I saw traces of her everywhere. The fiddle-leaf fig next to the TV was probably hers. The woven throw blanket slung over the couch arm would definitely have been hers. There were objects in the apartment that I knew immediately to be Evan's: the elaborate, gleaming coffee machine on the kitchen counter; the pouch of protein powder that sat next to the blender; the green bike, which leaned against a wall; the record player; the scale in the bathroom that could tell you exactly what percentage of you was water. But I knew if I looked too closely, inside cupboards and drawers, I was sure to find more evidence of Emily. You don't live somewhere without leaving traces.

"Lauren and George really like you. They both sent me a message saying they think you're great," Evan said as I took a seat on the couch next to him.

I smiled, pleased. "I like them too."

He returned my smile, leaning in and kissing me.

I shifted myself on top of him, continuing to kiss him while attempting to block out intrusive thoughts of Emily. Did they often have sex on the couch? What did she sound like when she moaned?

Eventually, when Evan was inside me, what I felt became more urgent than what I was thinking, and I began to experience only the singular dimension of physical feeling; the peace of temporarily being a body without a mind.

//

Later, while I sat in the bathroom, I visited Lauren's account. It was very active, featuring mostly film photos of her friends or herself, interspersed with images of tables covered in wineglasses and small plates of aesthetically pleasing Mediterranean food: anchovies on thin slices of bread and burrata garnished with zest. I scrolled a little further back, stopping when I saw a photo of Evan and Emily. It was a photo taken at a bar; Emily, wearing a black turtleneck sweater, was grinning up at Evan, and Evan, in a denim jacket, gazed lovingly back at her. They had the residual signs of recent laughter playing on their features. Below the photo was a rose emoji and the words: *Love you Em.* The time stamp showed that Lauren had posted it a couple of days after Emily's death. The discovery made me feel strange, as if my curiosity had opened like a trapdoor beneath me, revealing the disgusting depths of my obtrusive need to know more.

I moved on, finding George's account, which in comparison was relatively vacant: a handful of memes, some reposted photos of him and his friends taken by Lauren, and a few images from a recent snowboarding expedition in Japan. As I scrolled back I stumbled across a video in which I could see part of Evan's face in the thumbnail. George had posted the clip nearly four years ago, it depicted a party in someone's backyard. I watched as the video panned past Evan, taking in the impressive size of the crowd. It must have been summer judging by the presence of filthy bare feet and a limp-looking inflatable pool filled with murky water. When the video moved all the way to the left side of the backyard it revealed Emily.

I had never seen a video of her before. She was just as beautiful in motion as she was in photos. The additional perspective didn't reveal any angles that were less flattering. Instead, it seemed to show that she would have been beautiful at any time, on any day, from any angle. I'd always felt that kind of beauty was unfair. My sharp features had a tendency to look very different depending on how forgiving the light was. I watched the video again. Emily wore an oversized linen shirt with a black bikini underneath and, as always, her fringe was parted in the middle, perfectly framing her face. When she noticed George was filming, she grinned and waved at the camera. Even though I felt sick, I watched the video five more times.

seventeen

The next morning, I woke up in Evan's bed to the sound of coffee beans being ground. I reached up to pull the blinds open, revealing a bland, overcast sky, and then maneuvered myself back underneath the warm covers. Evan's room was relatively austere; the surface of his bedside table occupied by a lamp, a bottle of magnesium tablets, and a Malcolm Gladwell book. There was a wardrobe built into the wall and a chest of drawers. The walls were bare, but I could see a single blemish where a picture hook had once been nailed next to the door. I reached for the book and read the blurb on the back. It appeared to be about the way we think and how we make decisions, and why some people seemed to make good decisions while others didn't. *Never again will you think about thinking the same way,* it read. I put the book back down. I wasn't interested in thinking about how I think. I could do without that additional layer of self-analysis.

Evan, still sleep ruffled, appeared back in the room with a tea towel slung over one shoulder.

"Morning," he said, handing me a mug of coffee. "I'm making breakfast. It'll be about fifteen minutes."

I thanked him, watching as he left the room with a smile fixed upon my face. Once he was gone, I dropped the smile and took a closer look at the mug I was holding. It was peach-colored, a little wonky in shape with a thick handle. I recognized it immediately. Emily had once posted a photo of it with the caption: *Coffee in bed with my new favorite mug.*

Recently, I'd felt the burden of Emily's unacknowledged presence more acutely. My aim of shielding Evan from having to discuss her with me had at first felt like a noble cause, but I was beginning to wonder whether I was being complicit in his denial.

Until this moment, I had only come across Emily through the scattered internet trail of photos and thoughts she'd left behind. I had yet to brush up against any physical evidence of her, anything that wasn't digital and thus spectral. Here in my hand was a solid, tangible example of her legacy in Evan's life. An actual relic. I imagined her holding the mug, both hands cupped around it. Technically I had only myself to blame for the fact that I knew this had been her mug. Had I not obsessively looked at her account I would probably be having a markedly better morning. I might have even objectively appreciated the mug for its aesthetically pleasing design. But that was impossible now. Was it fair of me to find Evan's decision to give me this specific mug strange? I put it down on the bedside table and climbed out of bed.

"I'm just going to have a shower," I called out from the bedroom doorway, driven by the urge to escape the mug's looming presence.

"No worries," he called back.

In the shower there was a bottle of anti-dandruff shampoo and a fluorescent blue shower gel. I stared at the two bottles, anchored by their aggressively masculine branding and their Evan-ness. They began to color the apartment with him again. I wondered if I would still feel this way, vaguely haunted and insecure, if Evan and I had discussed Emily. By discussing her, Evan would add grit and dimension to my idea of her; he would paint a picture of an actual flawed human being. He would bring her out of the shadows so that I could potentially see a clearer image of her, rather than the intimidating idea that I'd—admittedly—mostly created myself. He could also fill in the plot holes of their story. No relationship is perfect; all lovers have disagreements and if they don't openly argue, they probably live in a prison of passive aggression. My mind had divided itself, half of it chastising the other for having such selfish needs. I found myself agreeing with both sides. It would be selfish to bring Emily up only to ease my own insecurities. But, on the other hand, we'd been dating for a couple of months now and I'd shared so much of the events of my life with him, why hadn't he told me about this? Was it due to some failure on my part? I felt ashamed, like our entire relationship so far had been one long dinner party during which I'd drunkenly overshared.

I walked into the kitchen just as Evan was plating up.

"Smells good," I said, inhaling the aroma of garlic.

He smiled, handing me a plate, and I took it to the couch.

"I really like your place," I said, sitting down and tucking my feet underneath me. "Although, I do think it needs more mold and lino."

Evan laughed, placing his own plate on the coffee table and sitting next to me.

"How do you find living alone?" I asked tactfully.

"For the most part I like it, but it can be disorientating at times," he answered.

"I know what you mean, when I first moved into my apartment I went two whole days without speaking," I said, choosing not to add that—on the other side of the spectrum— there'd been a few times when I'd found myself soliloquizing without even realizing I was doing it.

"Yeah, that still happens sometimes. Time can do strange things when you're alone a lot," he said candidly, and I leaned in as if to catch every word. "I have to get outside a lot, go for a run, or have people over. Lauren and George are good, I'll invite them over if I feel like I'm losing it a bit."

"Have you lived here for a while?" I asked.

"Three years next month."

"Have you always lived here alone? Or did your ex live here too?"

I tried to say it as casually as I could but it came out strangely, both blunt and sharp. I glanced at Evan's face from the corner of my eye and saw a muscle in his jaw working. I was being intrusive, peeping through the keyhole to the past, and none of this was any of my business. He placed his fork down, picked up his coffee, and cleared his throat.

"Yeah, she lived here for a couple of years," he answered.

It was dismissive, but it was enough to tell me that I had been right. The fiddle-leaf fig was hers. The handmade beige ceramic plates we were eating off were most certainly hers. I realized that by aiding in this avoidance of the topic, I'd most likely prevented any opportunity for discussion of her to occur naturally. I decided to give him a chance, to bravely extend a clear invitation to him.

"I know about what happened to her," I admitted. "After

you sent me that friend request I saw it all. I'm so sorry. I can't even comprehend how hard that would have been."

Evan said nothing.

"You really don't like to talk about her, do you?"

"Of course I don't." He put his mug down as if I had ruined his appetite. "Why would I like talking about her?"

He ran a hand through his hair. I'd learned that this was a signal that he was uncomfortable. I felt guilty; I was the reason for his current discomfort. My resolve to ask him about her directly crumbled.

"I'm sorry," I blurted. "I shouldn't—"

"It's fine, Ana. I just think it would be weird for me to talk to you about her."

We sat in silence, and as a child who had been mostly disciplined through passive aggression I had the immediate and distinct feeling that I was being punished. Evan drank the last of his coffee. Then he stood up to take his plate to the sink, before walking to the bedroom without saying a word. After a moment I followed his lead. I found him in his gym gear, tying up his sneakers. His eyes flicked up at me as I entered the room.

"I'm going for a run," he said.

Not only was I dismissed from the conversation but I was dismissed from his apartment as well.

"Okay," I replied and began to collect my things. The energy in the room felt tense. I didn't want to leave his apartment like this. I wanted to reinstate a feeling of affection between us. I still wanted to explain myself.

"Evan, I'm sorry I brought her up. It's really none of my business. I should have let you—"

"Ana, please," he pleaded as if I was torturing him. "I just don't want to talk about it."

I fell silent and once Evan was ready, we left his apartment. He gave me a distracted kiss at the front of his building and then he was gone. I stood with a frown on my face as I watched him sprint down the street away from me.

//

A memory plagued me as I walked home: My ex and I were arguing, as we were prone to do after we both realized we didn't love each other anymore but remained paralyzed by fear at the prospect of tearing our shared life in two. In our desperation to be heard and understood the disagreement had escalated to shouting. We stood on either side of the living room glaring at each other.

"You don't know when to stop," my ex declared, his eyes wide and incredulous; his face a mask of complete contempt. "Can you just give me a fucking break for once?"

He stormed off down the hallway to the bedroom and I stood there livid and trembling with rage. This was his favorite move: toss a grenade at me and walk away. It ensured the last word was always his. Not this time, I thought. I followed him to the bedroom.

"You don't just get to walk away every—"

He looked up at me from where he sat on our bed and I saw his eyes were wet. I instinctively recoiled at the sight of him. I'd never seen him cry.

"Please," he said, turning away from me, "just leave me alone."

So I did. I turned around and walked away.

eighteen

Evan didn't message me at all for the rest of the day. The motives for his unusual silence were transparent: Like a dog being trained, I was supposed to learn that he would withhold the affection I had come to depend on if I crossed this particular line again—The Emily Line.

Even though I often understood the mechanics behind the way I was being treated by the men I dated; even though I could clearly see the intention behind the games I was being subjected to, I couldn't make any of it hurt less. I could intellectualize it all but I could not control how I felt; a paradox that often resulted in me not only being punished by someone else, but then punishing myself for not being able to emotionally rise above it all. In some ways, I'd come to think of it as a necessary evil; a required suffering along the journey of becoming intimately close with someone. It was an uncomfortable teething period where two people learned how to have their needs met, or their boundaries respected, before they were able to be vulnerable enough to actually verbalize them. It was always messy. Despite my understanding of all of this, the sudden severing of a connection had always created a liminal space; a sort of waiting room charged with the slowly fading hope of reconciliation. I would reluctantly linger in that space, keeping watch over my shoulder, ever optimistic that a door would open and I could return from where I had been banished. Silence is rejection in slow motion. It's an injury sustained from a blow that was never dealt. There is, in theory, nothing to recover from.

Silence as a form of punishment was not new to me—it was, after all, my mother's love language—but Evan wasn't even the first or second man who had used this tactic on me. In fact, it was through silence that I had been delivered my very first heartbreak.

//

The Drummer was in a Perth band I discovered on Myspace. I was sixteen and, having lost my virginity the previous summer, felt myself in possession of a maturity that far surpassed that of the boys I went to school with. At that age I also wholeheartedly believed that there was nothing more important in the world than music, especially that which spoke to the deep anguish of my soul. I played the band's songs on repeat for weeks and one night I privately messaged their Myspace page to ask if they were going to do an all-ages gig anytime soon. I never got a reply, instead The Drummer sent me a friend request from his personal account.

The Drummer was always at the back of their band photos. He was thin with long dark curly hair that he wore tucked behind his ears. He was always dressed in tight black jeans and T-shirts sporting the violent logos of other bands he liked. My Myspace page purposefully gave the image of someone older than sixteen. I decorated my page with selfies in which I wore thick eyeliner and proudly demonstrated that I listened to music that was beyond my years. Online I was made out of only pixels, liberated from the humiliating pantomime of adolescence I felt forced to perform. Online I could exhibit the person I was on the inside; free of the label of "schoolgirl" and all of its connotations of braces, acne, and uniforms, all of which seemed to render my self-proclaimed precociousness less convincing. My online persona felt like the real me, while the real-life me felt like a persona.

After I accepted The Drummer's friend request, he commented on two of my photos:

:)

Hot

Then he sent me a message:

Ur really pretty

I stared at the message in disbelief. I couldn't believe that he had instigated a private chat with me, let alone that a twenty-year-old thought I was pretty. A thread of unbroken dialogue continued between us through the beginning of my final year at school. I worked up the courage to admit my age to him and was relieved when he seemed completely undeterred. He messaged me every single day, unashamedly double or triple messaging when I didn't respond for hours while I was in lessons and away from a computer. A lot of what we shared in those early conversations was about music. I obediently downloaded every single song he mentioned and played them on repeat. I was guaranteed to like any music he liked, purely through my determination to connect with him. I even looked up the lyrics of songs he mentioned and carefully read each word, searching for clues and encouraging myself to believe that any lyrics about love and lust were a secret message for me. I became addicted to the idea that he was concealing a powerful undercurrent of desire for me. I wanted to believe that his feelings were so strong that he was afraid of revealing them entirely; I imagined he could only hint at them through the words of others.

One day he asked me to send him a photo, specifically one no one else had seen. It was a Saturday and I was home alone. I put on eyeliner, teased my hair and changed into a band shirt. Then I conducted a photo shoot in front of my bathroom mirror with my digital camera. I sent him the best photo I took. His response was:

Sexy! wat bra r u wearing?

His compliments and encouragement ignited the exhibitionist within me. I began to take more provocative photos, posing like the women I'd seen in a copy of *Zoo* magazine Beverly had once stolen and shown me. At his request, I started sending him photos of me in my bra and underwear. I learned quickly that this temporarily guaranteed his undivided attention; he would remain logged in and his responses would be almost instant. It felt strange and intoxicating to know that I possessed a kind of power over this man, that I could command him to sit at his computer and speak to me. That a photo of me could make him feel, for a brief moment, that nothing was more important than the conversation we were having. Or, at least, that's how I imagined he felt.

Weeks passed and we continued to speak every day. He would ask me about school and I would ask him about the band or how his shift at the bottle shop was going. He continued to send me music. One day he sent me an image of him and the other band members practicing. In the photo they were smiling and waving at the camera. It made me feel special, like my place was more on their side than in the crowd with all their other fans.

Then, one evening, he asked for a photo of me naked. I tried to take some in the privacy of my bedroom, but I was embarrassed by them. While he pushed for nude photos, I pushed to hang out together. I wanted to go to the movies. He told me he wanted to meet me in real life, but he was too busy with the band, and so we continued this game in which no one was winning.

He grew colder and less talkative. I was being punished for not complying with his demand, though at the time I didn't understand the mechanics of what was going on. In fact, it was only later, as an adult, that I fully grasped the predatory nature of the dynamic. After messaging me every single day for over a month, he suddenly stopped responding for two or three days at a time. I would obsessively log in and check for contact. At school, I started hanging around in the computer lab at lunchtime, using a proxy site to access Myspace. I was confused.

I logged in after dinner one night and saw he'd messaged me, but my elation was short-lived:

I dont think we can talk anymore :(

unless u send me pics

I wanted to go back to talking every day again. I wasn't ready to give that up. Sending a naked photo suddenly felt like a simple solution. I took one in the bathroom mirror and sent it to him and he responded:

Wow. You're amazing :) :) :)

My heart leaped and I smiled at the message, thinking that wasn't so bad. But after a couple of days, he requested another photo and when I didn't send one he immediately ceased responding.

After days of silence I would relent and send a photo and we would go back to talking, until he requested another.

Eventually, he must have tired of our arrangement because he stopped messaging me altogether. I was completely blindsided. I struggled to process the sudden severance. I didn't know how to deal with the feeling that there was nothing to process, despite the fact that my emotions declared a different reality. I hung around in his inbox, having completely overstayed my welcome, and sent him occasional messages to see if I could elicit a response. I was in denial that he could be rid of me so easily, when the idea of us simply never talking again caused me so much anguish. I began to make up theories that would explain his silence, so that I could separate him from the blame. If he was blameless, I could preserve the delusion I'd sustained myself on: that something was preventing him from speaking to me, not that he simply didn't want to. He could have been locked out of his account. Or maybe he was incredibly busy with band stuff. But the more I clung to these delusions, reciting them like mantras, the thinner and more worn through they became. Soon I would find myself facing the unavoidable truth: If he wanted to speak to me, he simply would.

Beverly knew all about the situation, though she didn't have much advice. She was interested solely in the boys who existed in "real life." She lived in a completely different realm from me. Her versions of heartbreak were definable and widely relatable in the movies and TV shows we watched; boys wrote notes that said, *I don't want to be your boyfriend anymore,* or teary breakups unfolded by the bike racks after school. When Beverly's first high school boyfriend, Jake, broke up with her right before the school holidays I spent a week consoling her. In solidarity, I even participated in her completely deranged idea of a "spell casting" exercise that would make Jake fall back in love with her. I sat with her while she drew elaborate symbols on a piece of paper she'd sprayed with Lynx Africa and I never once cast judgment.

But when I first tried to explain how hurt I was by The Drummer's silence, hoping that the same gentle counseling would be returned, Beverly shrugged and said:

"But you guys never even went to the movies. You never even kissed him."

Four weeks after our last contact, The Drummer changed his display photo on Myspace to him and another woman. Her profile now also proudly resided in the number one place of his top friends list. She was much older than me, at least nineteen, and her photos were all professional studio shots of her wearing high heels, red lipstick, and corsets. She had tattoos that covered her arms and two smiling cartoon swallows underneath her collarbones. The rejection became inescapable.

//

Sunday arrived. I made coffee and spent hours reading a novel on the couch. A storm hit in the afternoon, the sky darkening prematurely, and for a minute or so hail beat against my window like pebbles thrown by an overly enthusiastic suitor. By nighttime I was hurting a little that I still hadn't heard from Evan, but I was resigned. I told myself that he was trying to communicate his boundaries but was unable to do it with words, so instead he used passive-aggressive behaviors. I tried to view the situation with compassion. I came up with ways that might help him better communicate in the future. I made a kale salad for dinner and had a long bath with a mug of tea. I put a face mask on and listened to a podcast about gut bacteria. After the bath, I played ambient music in my bedroom and took my body through a yoga class I'd found on YouTube. I followed all of this up with a ten-minute guided meditation, where I focused on different body parts and commanded each of them to relax, but when I finally emerged from my self-care spiral, I felt just as bad as I had hours before.

In bed, I visited Emily's account. I now only had to type *E* in the search bar for it to correctly recommend both Evan's and Emily's profiles. Evan's reaction to my mention of Emily made me return to her account with a stronger edge of desperation. I now knew without a shadow of a doubt that he would not help me to understand any of this. I scrolled until an image caught my attention. It was Emily behind the counter at the yoga studio she had worked at. She was leaning on her elbows with her hands cupping her face. The caption read:

Midweek Flow 6 pm @bendstudio

I tapped through to the studio's account. It was filled with professional photos, clearly taken during classes; the faces of the students looked strained and flushed with effort, their eyes staring directly ahead at the exposed brick walls or down at the birch floors. I scrolled a year back, curious to see if Emily was mentioned. She was. I found a post with a picture of her and the other teachers standing in a line with their arms around each other's shoulders. There were six of them, all smiling and wearing matching activewear. The caption read:

*It is with the heaviest of hearts that we deliver this
news to our Bend community. Yesterday we lost our
much-loved teacher Emily. Our little family is
shocked and reeling, we are unable to believe her
loving, bubbly face will not be seen around the studio
anymore. We will miss you so much, Em. Rest in
peace, angel.*

*Out of respect for our grieving teachers and
community, we have shut our doors and will reopen
on the 7th of November. No classes will be held until
then.*

The post had hundreds of comments, a stream of heart
emojis and repetitive messages saying how much they would
miss Emily. I found that I was not moved by this heartfelt
post in the same way I had been by the news article about her
death. The article's tone was cold, almost indifferent, toward
the tragic end of Emily's life and that indifference had made
me feel sorry for her. This post showed me that she was surrounded by love, probably more than the average person, and
definitely more than me, given I couldn't get a text back from
the man I was sleeping with, or even my own mother.

I scrolled back to the top of the studio's account and visited the link to their website. They had a free first class offer.
It occurred to me that I could sign up and go. There was nothing truly preventing me from doing this, other than a vague
sense that it was a strange thing to do. It felt like an appropriate rebellion against the silence Evan was inflicting on me.

I checked the schedule. The first class with vacancies was
Midweek Flow on Wednesday at 6 P.M.

nineteen

I do actually like yoga. It was my father who introduced me to it when I'd visited him in Bali for the first time; a trip that eventuated out of some backfired plan of my mother's, in which she tried to blame my dad's departure for my sudden downcast mood. The change in my behavior was actually due to The Drummer's decision to sever contact, but I couldn't tell her that. I imagined myself confiding in her and then her attempting to ban me from the internet.

After my parents separated, my mother burned with palpable rage and envy at my father's ability to drop everything and leave the country, and so my noticeable melancholy, though mostly unrelated, gave her an opportunity to hold my father accountable—something she was not often able to do. My mother's anger toward my father blinded her and she didn't seem to grasp the effect turning my sudden unhappiness into a consequence of his actions might have on me. In frustration, she might say, "The only reason your father calls you once a fortnight is because I remind him to."

In this way, my feelings were often struck by the shrapnel

of my mother's resentment. There was also the fact that her words were almost always at odds with my father's, who went to great lengths to reassure me that he missed me and wanted to talk to me. They were both the voices of authority in my life and, as confusing as it was, it was my responsibility to remain bipartisan by checking my sources, developing critical thinking skills, and always applying my thorough understanding of bias.

My father was immune to all forms of emotional manipulation, especially my mother's, and despite being far less qualified, he believed himself to be more enlightened than doctors, teachers, and school therapists. When my mother told him I was displaying signs of depression, he decided I would spend the next school holidays with him in Bali. He sent me a text:

Chin up bug see you in two weeks :)

My father, a belligerently optimistic man, assumed that if he took me to yoga every day, I would find myself simply unable to be sad anymore. Turns out he was partly right.

And so, in the midyear holidays of my final year at school I arrived at Denpasar airport. At first I didn't recognize my father as he emerged out of a group of Balinese taxi drivers with his arms spread wide. He was so tanned and thin from endless hours of surfing. His singlet flapped around with nothing to cling to. I realized later that he looked so different because he was genuinely happy and I'd never seen him genuinely happy.

"There's my bug," he said, smothering me in a sweaty hug. He took my backpack and began to lead me through the car park to his scooter. The air around us was thick and muggy, perfumed with incense and the smell of damp concrete and mold. I was uncomfortably warm in my combat boots and black skinny jeans. My eyeliner and mascara had smudged in the humidity and were stinging my eyes. Nothing about this environment was conducive to my very specific aesthetic. I knew then that half of what I'd brought in my backpack would remain untouched: my hair straightener, my liquid eyeliner, my fishnet stockings. On the first day of the holiday my dad had to take me to the market to buy shorts, singlets, and a pair of sandals.

At the airport, I followed my dad through crowds of disheveled tourists, who were still adjusting to the ambush of sight, smell, and sound, and the taxi drivers who were competing with one another for business by shouting and waving their hands.

I kept my eyes on my dad's salt-and-pepper hair, which he'd grown out and tied back in a bun with an elastic band. We stopped when we reached a silver scooter.

"Put this on," he said, passing me a helmet. "And put this back on."

He handed me my backpack and put his own helmet on. I noticed that he wasn't wearing any shoes.

"Don't worry, bug." He laughed, sensing my hesitancy, but not realizing that it wasn't scooter related, rather I was grappling with an instinctive, though misdirected, stranger danger response. He was overusing his pet name for me in an effort to reinstate some intimacy or to remind me of our shared history, but it wasn't working quickly enough. It had been nearly a year since I'd last seen him. I suddenly wished my mum was there. I wanted to look over at her and have her nod in approval.

My father kept his promise of taking me to yoga every day. He would wake me at 8 A.M. and we'd walk the winding alleyways, past the barking dog, the clucking chickens, and the old Balinese woman who would always be emptying a bucket of dirty water out on the path. My father would call out to her, "Selamat pagi!" which meant "good morning" in Bahasa Indonesia, and the old woman would wave her hand dismissively as she turned her back. The soft light of the morning sun seemed to make everything glow and without fail, at some point every morning, my dad would turn to me and say, "Isn't this just beautiful?"

He was like a small child in constant awe of the world around him. He had truly been reborn.

The yoga classes my dad attended in Uluwatu were held on a patch of grass by a pool, in the garden of a hotel. The air was thick and if it rained, which would always be heavy and sudden, we would shelter in the hotel's conference room. The class would go on, our bodies adjusting themselves around chairs and table legs. To my embarrassment my father would do yoga in a pair of tiny Speedo shorts, his hairy body dripping with sweat and vibrating with effort. In every class he would attempt at least three handstands, his face growing increasingly more red and veiny. He was surprisingly flexible and though I was mostly impressed, I found the image of him almost doing the splits in his Speedo shorts deeply disturbing.

The yoga teacher, Elke, was German. She was strong and muscular and always dressed in tie-dyed singlets. Occasionally, she brought her harmonium along and would invite us to accompany her in singing long, repetitive kirtan songs at the beginning and end of class. I found the singing humiliating. I played along, opening and closing my mouth silently like a fish. My father, however, sang with his eyes closed, smiling blissfully. I would sometimes peek at him during these lengthy, tedious performances and every time I saw that he knew all the lyrics I was startled.

I struggled with other newfound multitudes my father contained, like his declared love for "all beings in the universe"—except, of course, my mother—or his belief that everyone should do what "lights their soul on fire," which for him apparently didn't include living in the same country as me or spending more than a fortnight a year in my company.

During this trip I witnessed my dad begin on a path that, months later, had him reintroduce Elke as his partner and "twin-flame," and embrace the yogic concept of "ahimsa," which encourages the idea of doing no harm to yourself or others. He became a vegetarian shortly after that, shedding the last few distinctions that made him recognizably my father.

In response to my mother's concerns about my melancholy, my dad tried to give me a pep talk a couple of times, mashing together concepts from different self-help books he'd read, or attempting to sell me on the simple idea that I could just choose happiness.

On the walk back from yoga one morning toward the end of the trip, he must have sensed an opportunity in the calm quiet and began to search for some piece of advice to offer me. On reflection, as an adult, I can understand that a complex struggle took place between his desire to be compassionate to me and his desire to be seen as wise. He wanted to be both a father and a guru, but there was an awkward leap toward vulnerability required in being a father, and in the end, he took a step back from me, choosing the universal over the specific, and without asking me what had happened, or why I might be feeling sad, he told me:

"You know, whatever is making you unhappy, none of it will matter in a few years' time. By the time you're nineteen, you won't even remember the names of most of the people you went to school with. If someone has hurt your feelings, just remember that."

Obviously he didn't realize the potentially nihilistic thoughts such a complex idea, unaccompanied by the prerequisite of hindsight, might ignite in the mind of a teenager. Thankfully I disregarded his advice immediately, unable to comprehend that my pain meant nothing. Later I would understand that he was in some ways right, of course, but I would also know that for all his grand wisdom he was not the one to go to for advice. I was better off seeking the solace of anonymous relationship advice threads online, where strangers would share their experiences or console one another, and after reading their stories I would no longer feel alone.

Though it was not in response to any of my father's wisdom, I did have an enlightening experience during those two weeks in Bali. It happened when we bumped into a friend of my father's at the warung where we were having lunch. I sat there pushing the last of my nasi goreng around my plate and pretending to read an Eckhart Tolle book my father had given me while they talked about the surf. When they hugged goodbye, I heard my dad say, "Love ya, brother," as he clapped his friend on the back. I realized then, as I watched him embrace this stranger, that he had yet to ever tell me he loved me. I looked back down at my book to disguise my hurt and continued reading:

Feeling sorry for yourself and telling others your story will keep you stuck in suffering.

CHAPTER
twenty

I took off my shoes and stepped into the studio where Emily had once worked. I looked around, taking in the concrete floor partially covered with a rattan mat and the shelves of overpriced yoga paraphernalia; the smell of lemongrass essential oil diffused into the air. I imagined Emily here; she would be walking around with perfect posture, her blond hair tied up. She would be wearing tights and a slouchy crewneck jumper and would probably be holding one of the pastel-colored stainless-steel water bottles the studio sold. I imagined her smiling and floating among the arriving students, greeting each one. I imagined her greeting me.

"I'm Emily, I'll be your teacher today," she'd say to me, showing her dimpled smile.

Instead, I was greeted by a lithe, middle-aged woman with dark hair.

"Hi, you must be new here," she said enthusiastically from behind the reception desk.

"I am. I was hoping to try the intro offer?"

"Of course." She pulled out a clipboard and gave me a

pen. "I'll just have you write your name here. I'm Kirsty, by the way, I'll be teaching the class."

I had bolstered my confidence to come here, to a decidedly Emily-owned space, by telling myself that I simply wanted to do a class. But I also hoped that by being somewhere she had been so frequently, I might glean a little more information about her. What I hadn't expected was that I would turn from the reception counter and immediately see Nadia, sitting on the concrete bench where I was also supposed to wait until the class started. She was scrolling on her phone, oblivious to me standing only steps away. I spun in the opposite direction and went straight to the bathroom, locking myself in a cubicle. My heart pounded and I stared at the back of the door, taking deep breaths. This act of hiding comforted me, a soothing mechanism first formed during a strange period of my childhood when a boy in my year one class suddenly began insisting on holding my hand all through recess and lunch. I was so disturbed by this sudden imposition that I began to hide in the bathroom until the bell rang. After a week of hiding, an absolute eternity at that age, I eventually rejoined my peers on the playground. By then the boy had changed tactics. Instead of reaching for my hand, he hid in the bushes next to the swings and began throwing rocks at me. I felt only relief.

In the toilet cubicle, my heartbeat slowed and I began to consider how ridiculous I was being. I reminded myself that Nadia didn't know I'd come here on purpose. In fact, Nadia hardly knew me at all. I'd only met her once, she probably wouldn't even recognize me. Anyway, there was no point in wasting a perfectly good intro offer. I checked the time, it was two minutes to six.

When I entered the studio, the room was practically full. I'd managed to time my arrival to the exact moment when everyone was distracted and busy, laying out their mats and warming up. Feeling invisible, I scurried to the back corner, far away from Nadia, who had taken a spot in the front row and was serenely arranged in pigeon pose.

During the entire sixty minutes of vinyasa, no concrete facts about Emily presented themselves. Instead my imagination once again filled in the gaps. I decided, while in downward-facing dog, that Emily would have been a great teacher. I assumed she would have been less abrasive than Kirsty, who seemed to teach yoga like it was just another tool used to punish the body into a smaller shape. Kirsty talked a lot about "challenging yourself." She said "push" and "you're doing great" so often I thought someone in the room might be in labor. From everything I knew of who Emily was, I decided reluctantly, while in child's pose, that she had been a compassionate person. I had some clues to go by, like the way she'd once posted a plea on her feed for people to donate and help the refugees fleeing war-torn Syria. Even though sharing a donation link is a drop in the metaphorical ocean of actionable steps, it spoke to an inherent empathy that was confirmed throughout the digital paper trail she left behind. Her account also had over two thousand followers, but she wasn't any sort of influencer. It seemed that Emily was just somebody many people liked.

Kirsty drew the class to a close with savasana. As commanded, we all lay on our backs, a chorus of grateful sighs echoing around the room. I stayed there, feigning death, even after namaste was said and the room returned to life and chatter, hoping that Nadia would leave and not see me. But when I opened my eyes, she was passing right by my mat toward the exit. We made eye contact briefly as she walked confidently past me, while I appeared to be playing dead. She glanced away, seemingly without recognition, and I closed my eyes in relief.

I pulled my shoes on at the door then checked my phone and saw that Evan had broken his silence. As always the message seemed to come through at the exact moment in which I'd briefly forgotten that I was waiting for it:

How was your day?

I assumed this signaled that I was now forgiven and the punishment was over, but I didn't feel freed.

I stepped out onto the street and saw that the sun had almost entirely set during the class; I'd forgotten I'd need to walk home in the dark. Ahead of me I saw a woman walking her dog, so I set off at a pace that kept me within screaming distance of her. As I walked I deliberated on how to respond to Evan. He hadn't spoken to me for nearly five days, the longest lapse in communication since we'd met. That wouldn't seem like a big deal if a precedent had been set that lapses like this would occur frequently, but it hadn't. Since the beginning of our relationship, Evan had been attentive, responding within minutes, rather than hours, and never shying away from starting a new conversation when one had inevitably tailed off. I knew what was expected of me now. I was supposed to compartmentalize this period of disconnect. I was supposed to suffer through it, but never openly speak of the hurt I felt. I was supposed to experience amnesia, and cleanse myself of any negative memories. Already, I was beginning to view the last few days in a different light. Before the memory of the hurt disappeared entirely, I took a moment to imagine how it might feel if I forced an acknowledgment. If I suddenly refused to do my part in suspending the disbelief and ruined the whole performance by sending back:

Hey, glad to see that you've
stopped ignoring me. In the future,

it would be far more productive
and mature if you just told me what
you were thinking, instead of hiding
from me until you'd successfully
buried your emotions again.

I tried to imagine how Evan might react to a message like that. Would he apologize, or never message me again, maybe even call me crazy? I reasoned that it wouldn't be exactly fair to say that to him. He had every right to assert his own boundaries, if that was what he was genuinely doing, and I was also guilty of suppressing my emotions and of manipulating others. I too had secrets. I opened the message again and saw that Evan was typing another. I watched the three dots dance and then disappear.

Nadia said she saw you at Bend?

//

As I walked home I responded to Evan, keeping my answer vague:

Yeah, I went to try the intro offer.

He replied:

Can I see you this weekend?

I was relieved that he wanted to see me, but at the same time the conversation had changed course too quickly. I wanted him to tell me that Emily had worked at Bend, which would have given me the opportunity to feign subtle surprise, or if necessary, to claim some bizarre coincidence. By not asking any further questions Evan was allowing an implication, that I had gone on purpose to the studio where Emily had worked, to hang in the air, and I couldn't dismiss it without looking suspiciously proactive.

I knew that my love for yoga was a piece of information that wouldn't fit conveniently into Evan's existing idea of me. It would link Emily and me, like the center of a Venn diagram, and clearly Evan didn't want us to be connected in any way. Because Emily's love for yoga had been more vocal and vocational, I told myself that she had a stronger claim over it, and because of this—as well as the delicate situation with Evan— I should never speak of yoga again. It registered as odd, even to me, that I felt yoga, which had a lineage hundreds of years old, could be deemed Emily's. The alternative path was to reject this feeling, to instead aggressively claim yoga and mark it as my own until Evan no longer associated it with Emily, but I was afraid of reminding Evan of Emily too often, given that I now knew his tendency for sudden withdrawal. To be safe, I decided I would need to keep my interest in yoga to myself moving forward, but I immediately resented the decision. It was as if I was being forced to give away a prized possession. I wondered what else I would be required to hand over to her.

When I got back to my apartment I immediately ran a bath. I was making Evan wait for my response, as he had done to me, although I knew my own silence was only symbolic. It was not the same as his, I didn't have the stamina to extend my petty punishment beyond a couple of hours.

I visited my ex's account, a decision completely at odds with the entire concept of having a relaxing bath, but one I felt had been made for me given that I could summon no resistance to the act, physical or mental. My willpower had long ago been weakened against the dopamine release of online search and reward. When I arrived at his account, I saw his new girlfriend had tagged him in another photo. This time the two of them were standing in front of a beige brick apartment building with a SOLD sign next to them. The caption read: *So proud of you!!!* and was adorned with the emoji of two champagne glasses clinking.

He'd bought an apartment. For a moment I stared at the image, my mouth agape and my heart hammering. I might have felt some mature and deep objective happiness for him, like two ex-lovers in a film meeting by chance and sharing a knowing smile from across the bar with tears glistening in their eyes, if—*if*—I hadn't spent the last two years of our relationship desperately dragging him into the future as he sulked and kicked at the dirt behind us. I'd wanted to buy an apartment with him and his refusal to participate in the commerce-and-currency-driven nature of the world we lived in meant he'd floundered around as a casual audio technician, turning down shifts and spending every single cent he earned as if to spite me. This had left me pointlessly accumulating savings toward a deposit, despite not being able to afford a mortgage on my salary alone. And now here he was, somehow a property owner all by himself. To add to the sting, he was smiling in the way he had at the beginning of our relationship; toothy and genuine. He was happy and I was hurt anew at the realization that his restless dejection, the trait I'd come to believe was intrinsic to him, was actually just a symptom brought on by our relationship; by me. I closed the app and opened the message from Evan, my resolve to fight fire with fire disintegrating in my desperation to feel better. I texted him back a demure:

I thought you'd never ask

CHAPTER
twenty-one

The first weeks of October flew by while I tried and failed to dress appropriately for the weather, finding myself either sweltering under too many layers or suddenly thrust, exposed, into arctic wind. Everyone on the tram in the mornings was appropriately dressed and I began to grow suspicious that they all knew something I didn't, seeing as the weather forecasts were almost always wrong.

The sun revealed and concealed itself as if it were a game. On one Sunday morning I hung my sheets out on the line in the hopes of capitalizing on its sudden arrival, only for it to immediately slip behind a dark gray cloud, leaving my soggy sheets stranded, whipped and flung around by the wind and rain for days afterward.

I struggled to stay on top of my laundry in general now that Evan and I had begun to split our time between our two apartments, each of us packing a bag and moving back and forth like children of divorce. Our messages had long ago changed from long-winded, carefully edited paragraphs, through which we got to know each other, to memes and simple, practical updates like:

Be there in 10 or *Red or white?*

What would you do? we continued to ask each other in honor of the time he'd told me he hated music and I'd told him I'd still sleep with him.

It was the perfect inside joke. What atrocities of character, opinion, or taste could we pretend wouldn't affect our attraction to each other; what barriers of incompatibility would we commit to scaling?

What if I told you I don't believe in the wage gap. What would you do? Evan might ask.

I'd ask if you want to stay at mine or yours this weekend, I might respond.

It had unlimited iterations and could always be made relevant, and it had room for surprising creative freedom; all the while it reminded us that we were unreservedly into each other.

The calm sailing of our relationship was in part owed to my diligent steering, which tracked a course away from the topic of Emily. Though on occasion, as we watched a sad movie on my couch, or were forced to endure a sad song at the supermarket, I watched Evan's face subtly transform; his eyebrows knitting together and his jaw muscles showing themselves. I stole glances at him as these facial reflexes came and went ephemerally, like ripples in a pond. I took them to be glimpses of his suppressed pain and I felt helpless in their audience.

Lauren and I began meeting for coffee and wandering around various parks and gardens. She shared with me the tribulations of her dating life, which made my relationship with Evan feel like a warm jumper, shielding me from the harsh cold outside. At times, when our conversations reached the topic of Evan, I wondered if I should ask Lauren about Emily, but I never did. Evan was one of her closest friends and she'd only known me for a couple of weeks, so it would be presumptuous to assume she would keep my inquiries in confidence. Mostly I found myself just appreciating our new friendship and the way our senses of humor overlapped each other's almost perfectly. She would often send me memes and on one occasion I cackled so loudly I caused a fellow shopper in the produce aisle to clutch their trolley in surprise.

Toward the end of October, George finally introduced us to Hannah by bringing her along to drinks one night, his face flushed with heat and anxiety as he watched us all greet her. Hannah was tall, almost the same height as him, and pretty in a vague sort of way. That is to say, she was basically flawless, but because her appearance was so frictionless, my eyes seemed to slip over her with nothing to grip to. She had short blond hair and wore a pair of designer clogs from a brand that must have an aggressive digital strategy, seeing as their ads had been optimistically following me all over the internet via pop-ups, banners, and sponsored posts.

Hannah had a fine arts degree and worked in a private gallery selling art to wealthy people. She was suited to the task for her knowledge of art, but also for the connections her father, a senior equity partner at a top-tier law firm, brought into the gallery. These were affluent businessmen looking to decorate the wall space behind their receptionist's head with tax-deductible art. I wondered how Lauren felt about that, given that she had held a few exhibitions for her photography, and was not shy about her opinion that artists who sold their work for what she termed as unreasonably inflated prices were perpetuating the elitist idea that art was made only for the rich, and that this idea was largely contributing to the ruin of the industry. But as Hannah spoke about the gallery and how the current exhibition was going, Lauren nodded along, seeming mildly impressed.

Still, when George and Hannah went to get another round of drinks, Lauren fumbled through her tote bag and said, "Well, she seems nice," with a slight lack of conviction.

"Be nice, Lauren," Evan responded.

"What?" Lauren retorted, the sound muffled by her attempts to keep a filter in between her lips, as she pulled tobacco out of its pouch. Evan looked at her imploringly and she took the filter out of her mouth. "I am."

When George and Hannah returned, the conversation continued and I took a moment to sit back and observe, watching as Hannah risked a joke which paid off; Evan laughing and Lauren smiling; George grinning along, his face still flushed, only maybe now with a little bit of pride too. I thought about the next couple of months; the weather, though currently unstable, would settle into long days of sunshine, which would end with warm, still evenings lit up by pink and lavender skies. We would spend Friday nights at the pub, laughing and decompressing after a week of work. We'd have picnics in the park and sprawl under the shade of the elm trees. Maybe we'd even take a few trips to the coast. For the first time in a long time, I viewed the future not with indifference or apprehension—as a destination I was uncontrollably careening toward—but instead with genuine excitement. My decisions had helped to create this vision of the future and I felt now that I had the power to continue to craft it; I could make it everything I wanted it to be.

CHAPTER
twenty-two

My alarm went off at 6 A.M., a harsh and unrelenting buzzer like a fire alarm. It took a little while for me to remember that I was going to Evan's straight from work that night and so, in an optimistic burst of late-night motivation the previous evening, I'd decided to go for a run early. I pulled myself up and stared blankly around my room. There was no chance I was going to be able to fall back asleep now. Manipulative past Ana knew this too; I spotted the running clothes she had set out on the end of the bed. I dressed, made coffee, and then ventured out into the cold.

My feet hit the pavement and the bass of Kate Bush's "Running up That Hill" thumped into my ears. I had ironically added it as the first song to my running playlist many years ago, but I now habitually played it at the beginning of every run. It eased me into the right frame of mind, as though a muscle memory in my body was activated through sound. The air around me was cool, but as I eased into the rhythmic motion, my body began to warm and my mind began to clear. I emerged from a smaller road and took a left turn. There were no lights on in any of the houses I passed, which gave their façades an uninviting presence, like they were glaring at me with distrust. Even the streetlights seemed to beam down on me accusingly, as if my motives for being out in the dark could only be suspicious.

Running in the morning was unusual for me. I normally preferred an early evening run so I could release pent-up energy after a long deskbound day; running in the morning felt a little like I was stealing energy from my future self, rather than taking care of a surplus. But I'd always aspired to be the type of person who runs before the world wakes up and gains an additional runner's high from the sense of accomplishment.

I glanced behind me and noticed a man jogging in the same direction. Besides the two of us, there was another man waiting at the bus stop across the road. He was holding his phone sideways with his earphones in, entranced by the images jumping across his screen. As someone who belongs to the smaller-statured part of the population, I've always known that I can't rely on the "fight" part of my fight-or-flight response; a theory that felt confirmed by the fate of the woman murdered on the bike path.

I ran for a moment before stealing another casual glimpse back. The man had gained on me slightly. Instead of continuing, I decided to alter my route and turn down another street. I was aware that he might also feel uncomfortable running behind me. It was nothing personal. He could now alleviate any awkwardness by continuing down the street he was on.

But when I glanced back shortly after, I saw he had taken the same turn as me and was behind me once again.

It was annoying that he'd chosen the same street as me

and I was frustrated that I now needed to stop my music so I could be more alert. But, at the same time, I was embarrassed by the jury of my fear, which was declaring malicious intent without supporting evidence.

I paused my playlist and I could hear his feet hitting the pavement, sometimes in time with mine, sometimes not. I picked up my pace. The man's footsteps also increased in speed, as though in response to my own, and a physical change took place in my body; something primitive in me had perceived a threat, and my heart began to beat faster even as my mind tried to deny it.

I assessed my surroundings, looking for ways to take back control. I had unknowingly turned down a laneway lined with garage doors, and now there was no one else around. I was running at a pace just outside of sustainable; I could feel my pulse in my neck; my lungs burned and my throat was tight. I put my hand into my jacket pocket and pulled out my apartment key. I clenched it between my knuckles, a mostly useless, though instinctive, response. I can scream, I thought, and if I need to I can bite and kick.

The man coughed, like he was clearing his throat, and the sound echoed down the quiet street, sounding far closer than his footsteps had. I turned my head and saw the vague shape of him only steps away. Fear poured down my spine like cold water.

I calculated my next move: If I ran to the end of this street, I could turn left and head for Sydney Road, where I hoped there would be more people around. With a plan in place, I dropped any pretense and ran as hard as I could. Still he was gaining on me. When I sensed that he'd reached me I flinched and let out a small scream. He ran straight past me. I stopped running, my chest heaving painfully as I watched him continue down the street without looking back. There was no change in his pace. His running shoes hit the pavement rhythmically, his earphone cord swung back and forth. I bent over, put my hands on my knees, and threw up coffee onto the pavement.

twenty-three

That night I watched Evan as he moved around the kitchen. He was cooking us dinner and I was contemplating whether I should tell him about my run that morning.

I'd thought about it all day at work. I'd planned to tell Soph but she'd taken the day off, so instead I stared at my screen with eyes glazed over, replaying the scene in my mind and analyzing it. My body seemed sure that something had happened, my hands trembling whenever I paused typing and hovered them over my keyboard. Yet my mind was less sure. My memory was fluid; it morphed and changed as I grasped for the details and certainties.

For a start, I wasn't sure I had actually been followed. Maybe I was the one who had detoured onto that man's route. Maybe he was just returning home and was required to take the same turn that I had. But what if he had planned to seize me there in that laneway? What if he had placed a hand over my mouth and muffled my screams? I thought about The Chef and the size and weight of him against me; the way he'd overpowered me without even meaning to. I thought again about the woman who was murdered walking home, her body crudely discarded in the bushes for someone to find. What if, when I flinched and screamed, I had successfully scared the man and caused him to abandon his plan? The fact that he didn't even turn around and look back at me seemed to say something, but I wasn't sure what. Maybe his music had been so loud that he never even heard my small scream. It's possible that he didn't even notice me there at all. What exactly was there to tell Evan? I played out scenarios in my head; in some Evan grew protective, in others he accused me of being melodramatic. I tried to figure out how I wanted him to respond, settling on the desire for him to be sympathetic and acknowledge that it was unfair for me to feel this way if a man runs behind me down a street.

I watched Evan as he placed two fillets of salmon into a pan, leaning back as hot oil was spat at him. He then washed his hands and dried them on the tea towel that was once again slung over his shoulder.

I thought about when, a couple of years ago, my drink had been spiked when I was at a bar with my ex and his friends. I'd gone from sober to being unable to stand within minutes. My ex looked after me, taking me home and putting me to bed. In the morning when I woke up, with what felt like an ice pick lodged in my skull, he told me I needed to be more careful where I left my drink.

I suspected that if I told Evan what had happened on my run he would be concerned for me, and his concern would lead him to want to fix the situation, and the solution was simple: carry pepper spray, buy a big dog, learn jujitsu, don't run while it's dark. Be more careful.

I decided not to tell him.

twenty-four

Dave from customer experience was sitting across from me in the staff kitchen the next day, shoveling broccoli and chicken from a plastic container into his mouth. I watched for a moment in fascination as a clump of over-steamed broccoli made the onerous journey from heaped fork to his mouth, only to fall back out of his open mouth and onto the table, where it remained unnoticed by him, as he read an article on his phone.

I looked down at my own phone apprehensively. A couple of days ago my mum had tagged me in a meme on Facebook; a glittery, clip-art graphic of a wineglass captioned with some joke about the hilarity of latent alcoholism. The image was irrelevant, because the tagging only served the purpose of informing me that she'd decided she was no longer ignoring me: *I suppose I forgive you.* This was my mother's daring half step toward reconciliation. It was a relief in some ways to know that we were no longer in the midst of an active conflict, and in another way it represented the reemergence of other issues. Mostly because it signaled that she felt she had done her part and would be expecting me to cover the vast remaining distance. She would be assuming that I would call her soon, but after resigning myself to being ignored for so long, and having grown accustomed to the peculiar comfort it had come to offer me through its unchanging stability, I felt anxious about entering back into the unknown.

"Do one thing every day that scares you," Dave said.

"Huh?"

"*Do one thing every day that scares you,*" he repeated, this time pointing to the motivational calendar on the fridge door, which had been turned to a new page.

"Oh," I replied. "Right."

"I can't believe it's November already."

"I know." We shared a moment of silence for the unrelenting forward march of time, during which Dave scraped the last of his lunch out of the corners of the container, before returning his attention to his phone. I needed some fresh air. I grabbed my things and left the kitchen. Once out of the building, I crossed the road to the park and found an empty bench. I sat down and picked nervously at my cuticles, envious of a small group of smokers clustered over on the other side of the park. I wanted some sort of reliable, purchasable stress relief that would scar my lungs instead of leaving my cuticle beds red and raw-looking. I sighed and squinted in the bright daylight, watching as a group of pigeons fought over the soggy remnants of an abandoned sandwich.

I knew I shouldn't feel so apprehensive about speaking to my mother. I knew many people were happy to speak to their parents. Some people, like Beverly, spoke to their mothers multiple times a week. I thought about the two photos Emily had posted of her mother. In the first, her mother was standing in front of a shiny, stainless-steel stove. Her dark gray hair was loosely and elegantly scooped away from her face; she wore a cream boatneck sweater. On top of the stove in front of her was a blue cast-iron pot and she was stirring its maroon contents while smiling at the camera. The caption read: *Maman Henderson's famous Boeuf Bourguignon.* A couple of things were apparent to me from this photo: the first being that Emily came from a wealthy family, which was obvious from the marble countertops and the fact that the stove had seven gas burners. On top of that, Emily's mother exuded an understated and glamorous aura, and she appeared to be cooking while wearing cream-colored cashmere. The second discovery was that Emily's family was cultured. Her mother was French and très chic and I imagined her cooing to infant Emily softly in French and cooking her elaborate and fancy meals. My mother was never into food. In this way, her Italian heritage barely left a mark on her. Other Italian children at my school had homemade continental rolls their parents had lovingly packed them for lunch. I imagined their mothers wore red-and-white gingham aprons and their nonnas had twinkling eyes and pockets filled with treats.

My mother occasionally makes pasta with tomato sauce, the condiment version. I'm certain my nonna has turned in her grave each time my mother served this concoction until she was spinning, gaining speed and drilling her way toward the center of the earth.

The other photo Emily had posted of her mother was taken at a cozy-looking restaurant. Emily and her mother sat next to each other at a large mahogany table, embracing and smiling radiantly; their identical hazel eyes lining up alongside each other's. The caption read:

So much love for this woman,
thank you for everything you do for
me maman. I love you x

Her mother had replied in the comments:

I love you mon chou xxx

Like my dad, my mother has never told me that she loves
me. This was something that had caused me pain for a short
period of my life, after I was old enough to observe other
mother-daughter relationships and find my own lacking in the
same evident warmth. But I learned with age and experience
that love is not spoken only through language, and I'd come
to understand that my mother's love for me was communi-
cated in her fear for my well-being, in her desperation to pre-
vent anything bad from happening to me. Even so I had once,
years ago, worked up the courage to tell her that I loved her
over the phone. I did this after deciding that, as mature adults,
we should be able to easily overcome the rigidity of our so-
lidified child and parent roles. On this particular occasion I'd
waited, with a hammering heart, until the conversation was
naturally drawing to a close before I said the words.
"Bye, Mum. I love you."
She responded in a stricken and confused voice, "Yes,
okay." And hung up on me.
In the park, as I stared at a particularly diseased-looking
pigeon, which had wrestled away a piece of crust too big to
carry, I realized I'd temporarily forgotten that Emily had trag-
ically died. When I remembered once more I was mildly disgusted with myself. Emily's mother had lost her daughter, she
could never call her *mon chou* or tell her that she loved her
ever again. I chastised myself for my selfish comparisons and

for being envious of Emily's life and discontented with my own, when I was here, alive and well, and she was gone. There were women in war-torn countries who were forcefully separated from their children, I scolded myself. They would probably give the clothing off their backs if it meant they could speak to their children on the phone. The audacity of my complaints sickened me. I should call my mum, I thought, I should just do it. I knew the call would begin with her making a comment along the lines of, "Good to know you're still alive," or "I haven't heard from you in a while," as if it had not been possible for her to pick up the phone and call me. Still, I should just let it go and call her.

It would be just after 9 A.M. in Perth and I imagined my mother leaning against the counter in the kitchen, having her morning Nescafé and a bowl of canned peaches, followed by a cigarette. She would be wearing her fluffy purple robe, her hair already teased and petrified. The metallic mauve lipstick she always wore, even first thing in the morning, would be lining her tightly drawn lips. Just by conjuring this image I could almost smell the mustiness of the house, which originated from the old shaggy brown carpet that lined nearly every room. That carpet was almost certainly responsible for my childhood allergies, but still, it is the smell I most associate with growing up and even recalling it caused something to tug at my heart.

I imagined that soon she would be preparing for her first client. My mum ran a beauty salon out of my old bedroom. When I was growing up she had a salon, and for years she made reliable money doing nails, waxing, and facials. But her business began to dwindle when she refused to embrace laser hair removal. By the time I was eighteen, most of her clients had left her behind for the new laser salon in the shopping center near our house. After that my mum moved her salon into our house. She serviced only the die-hard clients who stuck with her; masochists who persevered with Brazilians and leg waxing.

I'd only ever let my mum wax me once. She did my eyebrows for a school dance, giving me what she called "The Sophia Loren." She tore away at my usually thick brows until they were thin lines that arched menacingly in a way that was far too harsh against my soft adolescent face. Then she tinted them, ignoring the instructions on the box and leaving the solution on until they were pitch-black.

Now every year for my birthday, Beverly sends me a photo of us at the dance in which my eyebrows were the unfortunate focal point; they appeared to have been drawn on with permanent marker, giving what would otherwise have been the adorable image of two teenagers making peace signs at the camera a disturbing and villainous undertone.

Pirouetting through my cyclical thoughts had wasted the rest of my lunch break. I sighed and stood, feeling the guilty relief of my successfully executed procrastination. Then I returned to my desk, woke up my screen, and recommenced staring at it with a frown on my face.

CHAPTER
twenty-five

The anniversary of Emily's death arrived like an exam I had not adequately prepared for. I woke to the sound of Evan's alarm and his fumbling hands attempting to turn it off. I reached for him under the covers but just missed him as he left the bed. All morning, I stole glances at him, wondering if I should say something. I watched him as he frowned while making a smoothie, as he scrolled on his phone with his brow furrowed. I wondered if he was receiving messages of condolences, but when I caught a glimpse of his screen, I saw he was reading a *Guardian* article about the climate crisis. We then discussed the article and for a moment my concerns about him and my silly little life were eclipsed by the stark image of a future far more threatening. Eventually we kissed goodbye at the door and separated to go to work.

As I walked to my tram stop, my thoughts returned to Emily. I wanted to feel a sense of relief that this occasion seemed to have no effect on Evan at all. I suppose I liked what that implied about his feelings for her, but logic demanded that I accept he was putting on an act. I knew there was no way he simply didn't care at all. Forced to abandon the illusion of relief, I was hurt that he couldn't show me the side of him that was still grieving. Even after all this time he still felt the need to hide it from me. Of course, Evan didn't know that I knew what the day represented; he continued to live in a world where I remained mostly ignorant of Emily. I wondered if he truly believed that I'd have done nothing to source more information about her for myself, or if he'd imagined that I was content with the little he had shared. It's not like her social media accounts were hard to find, and yet I was required to continue pretending that I knew nothing about her. Admitting that I had thoroughly investigated her seemed to be a confession that said: "Yes, I guess I do care about you a lot, possibly more than you care about me, because I know what your ex-girlfriend's coffee order was and you can't even remember my ex-boyfriend's name."

My need for information about Emily seemed to reveal that I'd been playing a character all along: nonchalant Ana, who was so self-assured she never felt compelled to compare herself to an ex-girlfriend.

I'd read enough self-help books to be aware that humans have an inbuilt fear response which causes us to catastrophize and torture ourselves with imagined worst-case scenarios. I knew that our brains formed this defense mechanism because once upon a more primitive time, it served us well to assume that what we feared was bigger and faster than us. That assumption allowed us to be constantly prepared and ready for threats. But people like me, who enjoyed a privileged life, didn't have much use for this old, inherited software. All it did was send excessive cortisol flowing through my body at the flick of a hypothetical switch. It encouraged me to do things like google my symptoms when I was sick and con-

clude I had cancer, or an ovarian cyst, or deep vein thrombo-
sis. In times of peace it incessantly asked: "What can you be
afraid of?"

My need to know everything about Emily was in part an
attempt to override this old programming, to uncover a piece
of information that would prove I ultimately had nothing to
fear.

At intervals throughout the day I continued to think about
her. I wondered what she would be doing if she was still here
and I wondered how the world would be different. I tortured
myself thinking of an alternate reality where she was the one
who woke up next to Evan. Where did I exist in that reality?
My life was so entwined with Evan's now that I kept a collection of my possessions at his apartment permanently. I bought
groceries and stored them in his fridge as if it were my own.

Emily's death was an event that affected the trajectory of
my life for the better and despite the neurotic tendency of my
brain to overanalyze, I was for the most part happy. These
facts combined to reveal an uncomfortable truth: I didn't like
the idea of a reality in which Emily hadn't died. I wondered
whether if Evan and I continued to date, he would eventually
reach a place where he felt these same conflicting feelings.
Would he begin to struggle with the troubling idea that losing
Emily was a necessary trial on his journey to find me? Or
would he forever see her death as an event that recast his life
into a new shape, neither better nor worse, but simply different? Would we ever be able to openly discuss such complicated thoughts and feelings?

Throughout the day I checked Emily's tagged photos every
couple of hours. I had exhausted the information divulged by
the photos she'd previously posted, but I harbored an admittedly strange hope that, on the anniversary of her death, one

of her friends might share a post that would teach me something new. I grew increasingly more surprised to find that there was nothing. Nadia, despite being perhaps overly active on any other day, remained silent. Evan, unsurprisingly, didn't break his silence either. Eventually, Bend posted a photo of Emily teaching; her hair was tied back and her eyes were focused upward at her hands, which were reaching toward the ceiling. A full class reflected in the mirror behind her. The caption read:

> *Tonight's 6 pm Vinyasa with Kirsty*
> *is held in Emily's honor. Come*
> *down and practice in memory of*
> *this wonderful teacher and dearly*
> *missed friend. We miss you every*
> *day Em x*

Unsurprisingly the post had collected a high number of likes and comments. The room would be full tonight.

After work, I made myself dinner along with a mug of tea and sat on the couch half watching a documentary about fungi, while mindlessly scrolling on my phone. I messaged Evan and shared a meme I'd found funny; some satirical rendering of an image originally created to glorify "hustle culture" and to perpetuate the idolization of a problematic tech billionaire. It was a simplistic guise for my real motivation of wanting to check in on him. He replied in his normal tone, *haha*, but his responses faded off quicker than usual. I let it be.

At about eight-thirty Emily's brother, Adrien, tagged her account in a photo of them both, one that I had already seen because Emily had originally posted it years ago. They stood side by side, squishing their faces together and grinning into the camera, each of them holding a glass of pale wine. Emily was wearing the white-rimmed cat-eye sunglasses I'd seen in previous photos.

Adrien was undoubtedly Emily's twin brother; they shared the same thin blond hair and eye color. He was pretty, like Emily, with the same open and kind face. His smile creased his cheeks in the exact same way as hers. The caption underneath the image was heartbreakingly simple:

I miss you

I saw that Lauren had commented:

Thinking of you today x

I'd visited Adrien's account previously and I knew already that he was a hairdresser at a salon in Brunswick: *Senior stylist @shockwavessalon No bookings via DM (unless ur Timothée Chalamet).*

He mostly posted photos of himself, or photos of his clients' hair, which was usually colored in bright artificial hues or pastel tones.

Despite the fact that Emily could no longer be close with her brother, I was envious of her for having had a sibling at all. I'd always wanted one. In the years after having me, my parents realized that having one child wasn't really for them, let alone having another, but I'd always held the selfish desire for a sibling to level the playing field, make things two against two. I imagined having an older sister who would be fiercely protective of me but also tender; we would have shared clothes and slept in each other's rooms; we would have had a secret language for when we didn't want outsiders to know what we were saying. I based much of my longing for a sibling on what I had observed of Beverly's life. Her sister, Reyna, was three years older, and despite the fact that Reyna mostly ignored us, we idolized her as if she were a celebrity. On occasion we'd even sneak into her room when she was out and smell her perfumes or touch her clothes, or we'd wait up to catch a glimpse of her when she arrived home from a party, like two little paparazzi. We watched Reyna as she performed the responsibility of the eldest child and clawed freedoms one by one from Beverly's parents. I saw her as a brave explorer, summiting all the adolescent mountains that lay before her, so that when the time came the path was already marked for Beverly. When I imagined having an older sister, I imagined her like Reyna, taking the brunt of my mum and dad's experiments in parenthood so that I received a more polished second draft. Maybe that's the sort of selfish idea that can only be conceived by a child without siblings.

Beverly also had a younger brother, Jerome. The first time I went to Beverly's house, Jerome was sprawled on the couch watching cartoons and Beverly walked straight up to him and punched him in the leg. He cried out and swung back, missing her as she laughed and leaped out of his reach. We left the room just as a launched pillow narrowly missed my head.

Despite the fighting, I saw many moments of casual affection between the siblings. I could recall watching a movie on their couch one night and seeing Reyna stroke Beverly's hair while Jerome rested his head in her lap. I quickly lost interest in the film and instead watched the siblings from the corner of my eye with a strange feeling of longing I was much too immature to fully understand. Often when I left their house to return to mine, it felt as if I was leaving a party early. I knew the fun would continue after I had gone and that my absence would be only faintly registered. During the Christmas holidays between years nine and ten, Beverly, Reyna, and Jerome were sent to the Philippines to visit their grandparents for a fortnight. I remember feeling physically sick with envy at all the fun they would have together, while I rode my bike aimlessly around the neighborhood, alone and forgotten. Back then loneliness felt as dramatic as that: A lone vulture circled in the empty sky; a ball of tumbleweed rolled by.

As an only child I frequently felt as if I oscillated between the uncomfortable feeling of being the center of the universe and the feeling that I didn't exist at all.

I looked at the image of Adrien and Emily hugging again. The photo was not meant for my eyes, it was meant for friends and family, those who would be thrust back into the thick of mourning by this anniversary. Once again I felt like that teenager: the outsider; the malcontent observer; the lone bike rider.

twenty-six

Soph was showing me a photo of a dick. A poorly taken, badly lit, slightly blurry, terribly angled photo of a dick. "Wow, Soph. It's a bit early." I pushed her phone away.

She laughed and tilted her head to better look at the photo. "This is a football player, I'll have you know."

I swiveled my chair to face her and gave her what I imagined was a confused but amused smile. I knew Soph well enough to know that there was a story and she was waiting to be invited to share it. To give her some credit, her anecdotes, though they often contained more information than I cared to hear, were reliably entertaining.

"He came back to my place on the weekend; he's *obsessed*." She beamed. "He hasn't stopped messaging me."

She flipped her phone around and showed me the photo again. This time I looked at it, tilting my head. She was grinning from behind the screen, practically begging to tell the story.

"Okay, tell me." I sighed.

She pulled a chair from an empty nearby desk, just as Paul

entered the office with a group of five other middle-aged suit-wearing men. We paused our conversation and watched as they walked solemnly to Paul's office, the only closed-off room in the open-plan space. The office door shut behind them, and I could see them all standing around with nowhere to sit in the minimalist room. Paul sat at his desk, his legs crossed and his expensive loafers twitching nervously.

"What's going on there?" I asked Soph.

"That's the board. Something serious, I guess," she said.

Dave mouthed, *What's going on?* to Soph from behind his computer. In response she shrugged, and then mimed using a keyboard and mouthed back, *I'll message you.* Everyone went to Soph for information.

"Anyway," she said, turning back to me, "I'm the one with the real news here."

On Saturday night Soph had met the football player in a bar. He bought her a drink and they started flirting, which then led to her taking him back to her apartment. To her surprise he'd messaged her the next day asking if he could see her again. Soph wasn't a football supporter and so, after googling him to find out which team he played for, she learned he was married. She showed me his account, which consisted of images of him in action, kicking a ball or tackling another player, shirtless photos of him at the gym, and a sparse scattering of his stunning wife and perfect children. Then she showed me his wife's account, which contained one photo after another of herself or their children. The wife was an influencer. She promoted everything from dubious teeth-whitening strips to plant-based protein powder and "nontoxic" fabric softener.

"Doesn't she suck?" Soph laughed. "God, look at her."

She held up her phone to show me a particularly vacant-looking photo the woman had posted of herself; the skin of her face and arms was blurred and overedited and her teeth were bizarrely white. It was common now to see app-produced faces like this online: mattified, monotoned, and devoid of texture; doll-like and dead behind the eyes. I felt the same eerie feeling that I always felt when I looked at the image of someone like this. Someone who had taken one step too far while editing and slipped straight off the cliff into uncanny valley.

But even so, I failed to muster any negative feelings toward this woman. I imagined her alone on the weekends looking after a newborn and a toddler, while her husband was out sleeping with women like Soph. I imagined her holding her phone out with her graceful, sinewy Pilates arms, switching the camera to forward facing as she smiled. I imagined her sitting down, while her toddler played on the carpet in front of her, and setting to work using an app to erase every flaw from the photo that she liked the best. Then she would post the photo, and immediately the likes, the compliments, the disguised and undisguised envy would come flooding in and she would feel good.

"I feel so powerful," Soph continued. "I mean, I could take these photos to the media. Can you imagine?"

She showed me a row of his explicit photos in her camera roll.

"They'd probably pay for these."

I had the sudden sense that I should intervene.

"You wouldn't do that though, right?" I asked. "They'd end up all over the internet. The wife would see them on the *Daily Mail* or something."

"Well, I'm sure his wife already knows," she responded. "I mean, isn't that what you sign up for?"

"Wait, are you seriously considering this?" I asked.

"No, of course not." She laughed. "Unless he ghosts me."
I looked at her imploringly.

"I'm joking. Don't worry, I'm just going to keep them forever with all the other nudes I've been sent."

"You keep all the nudes you've ever been sent?"

"Yeah, in my Nudes Receivable album."

I stared at her, imagining the album as a writhing orgy of flexed muscles and bad lighting.

"It's not weird. Lots of people do it." She was now slightly distracted by her phone. "I happen to know for a fact that two of my exes still masturbate over my nudes and one of them has just got engaged."

She changed the subject jarringly: "Want to get sushi for lunch later?"

When Soph eventually pushed off my desk and rolled back to her own, I turned to my screen and put my headphones on. But instead of the latest analytics report, I found myself dwelling on the idea of Soph's Nudes Receivable album. I tried to place the idea in the context of my own life, but the thought that my ex still had naked photos of me was an unbelievable and self-indulgent idea.

Evan often asked me to send him photos and he'd been honest early in our relationship about how much he liked to receive those kinds of images. I knew he had a collection of explicit images of me, just as I had a smaller collection of ones he'd sent in return. The photos were important to him and I enjoyed sending them. Many, many years had passed since my experience with The Drummer and I'd long ago learned to delineate between sexy naked photo sending and emotionally manipulative bribery.

There was something about the idea that Evan could get himself off to just a hollow image of me that gave the real-life version of me an inflated sense of sexual power. It turned me on that Evan wanted a photo of me, even when he had the whole internet at his disposal. If there were two categories of people—those who kept nudes and those who didn't—I knew that Evan would most likely belong to the first category. That idea set my mind on a troubling path. If Evan showed such an interest in photos from me then I could only assume he'd asked Emily to do the same. What does one do with the naked photos of a dead girlfriend? I couldn't begin to comprehend how complicated the idea of still being sexually attracted to a girlfriend who passed away would be. I tried to find some piece of my life that was relevant, something I could call upon to help me understand, but I'd never suffered such a loss; I'd never even come close. Looking at those photos of Emily would be difficult. Deleting them, harder still. If your ex remained a living, breathing reminder of why things didn't work out, then deleting the images would be easier. But in Evan's case, once those photos of Emily were deleted he could never, under any circumstances, get them back. I'm sure that would make the act of discarding them far more difficult. After all, they weren't just photos, they were memories too.

//

Later that evening, Evan and I were walking home from the supermarket. The air was still and the sun had almost set behind the clouds, turning the sky both red and gray, like smoldering ashes.

"Do you keep the nudes I send you?" I asked.

"Yeah," he replied, before pausing to consider. "I hope that's okay. I probably should have asked."

"It's fine," I continued. "It's just that Soph told me today that she keeps all the nudes guys send her, even the ones her exes have sent her. I think the idea of keeping nudes from a past relationship is strange."

"That is a little strange," he agreed. "Threatening, even."

"Yeah, I've always deleted them after a relationship ended."

"*Shit,*" he hissed, and stopped walking. Alarmed, I turned to look at him, wondering if I'd said something wrong. "I forgot the soy sauce."

At his apartment, Evan took a shower and then started cooking. When I stepped into the bathroom after him I saw he'd left his phone by the sink. He had a habit of leaving his phone lying around, sometimes in unusual places. I would frequently have to call it while he tiptoed around trying to hear the vibrations.

Throughout my life I had worked very hard to convince myself that I was not the type of person to look through someone else's phone, but now more than ever the temptation weighed down upon me. I shut the door, closed the lid of the toilet, and sat on it. I shouldn't look, I thought as I reached for the phone. I should just let it go, I thought, as I performed from memory the path his finger took across the screen. The phone made a successful clicking sound and unlocked. I opened his camera roll and noticed my hands were shaking slightly, an almost comedic response. Apparently my body thought I was dismantling a bomb.

At first, I saw photos I recognized: screenshots of memes, my own naked body posing provocatively, my own face smiling. I ran my finger down the screen and watched the small squares disappear downward in dizzying waves. When I saw blond hair my finger froze.

I began to scroll slowly through the photos: Emily smiling

across from Evan at a café; memes; screenshots of restaurants, articles, and clothing. I wanted to slow right down and analyze every photo. I hadn't until this moment thought about the fact that someone's camera roll was a veritable gold mine of information, infinitely more than any polished and published feed, but I didn't have time to absorb it all.

I scrolled on. I saw Evan trying on a jumper that he evidently never purchased, more screenshots of sport headlines and related memes, a book that must have caught his interest, someone's dog, Emily at a park, a screenshot of his myGov log-in details, small artfully arranged pieces of food on a plate, a naked body. Emily.

I froze.

It was a selfie she'd taken in front of a mirror, though I didn't recognize the mirror. Her hair and face were out of the shot. The first thing I noticed was that my body was very similar to hers. I didn't know what to think about that. If we were more differently built, I could potentially convince myself that any variances were reasons why Evan desired me, specifically me. But the likeness between us showed me that anything Evan desired in me, he had clearly desired in Emily. I suppose I ultimately hoped I wouldn't find any photos. Or, at least if I did, Emily would be in some way noticeably flawed so that when I measured myself against her, I could at least conclude myself a winner in some category. This was a ridiculous longing of my ego; an ego that had been trained my whole life to view one woman's beauty as a competitive edge against another's. It was my unchecked internalized misogyny rearing its ugly head and I felt ashamed and angry that some neural pathway which belonged to me continued to be hijacked by thoughts that weren't truly my own, but rather some lingering conditioning.

I had already spent too long in the bathroom. I locked Evan's phone and placed it back the way I had found it, not anticipating the immediate repulsion I would feel toward myself after going through his camera roll. It was similar to how I felt after I masturbated to images of him that Emily had taken: a dull postclimax disgust.

twenty-seven

"It's important to look back on the relationships that surrounded us growing up," the podcast guest explained, as my tram crawled through the morning traffic. "Close your eyes, take a couple of deep breaths, and start from as far back as you can remember. Were the relationships that surrounded you healthy? What did you learn about love by watching these dynamics?"

I paused the podcast, leaning my head against the tram seat, closing my eyes, and casting my mind back.

My mother had boyfriends after my father. I remember little about the first besides his watery, red eyes and his constant sniffing. He had allergies, which were no doubt exacerbated by the old, dusty carpet in our house. He hung around for a couple of months and then disappeared along with the coffee machine he'd bought my mum as a gift.

After him, there was a butcher with a high-pitched laugh. Phil, I think. Phil found my mother hilarious and he would tell her all the time as he wiped tears from his eyes: "You are unbelievable, Ros, you just crack me up." Or sometimes he would turn to me: "Your mum is unbelievable, Ana."

He stuck around for the longest. I have memories of him joining Mum and me for Christmas lunch at the pub, a tradition of ours. I remember he found something so funny that he spat a mouthful of beer all over his half-finished plate. I think at some point Mum got sick of his laughter; she probably realized that nobody was really that funny and became suspicious that he was laughing at her. At least she had a freezer full of steak at the end of it all. Well, the steak that remained after she threw most of it at him as she screamed for him to get out of her house.

The ends of my mother's relationships were often dramatic and sudden, and rarely conducted behind closed doors. One man, a schoolteacher, demanded to say goodbye to me when my mother ended their brief relationship, and so my mother stood in my bedroom doorway, arms folded over her chest, as the man sat down on my bed next to me and explained that my mother had decided they weren't a good fit. I remember the way he told me, his eyes pleading with me and filling with tears, as if he was begging me to fix what was happening. I felt no allegiance to him, so I simply nodded and said, "Okay, bye."

After the turbulence of a breakup had settled, my mum would knock on my bedroom door and say, "Want to go get a movie?"

Then we'd drive to Blockbuster and select a stack of DVDs and whatever snacks I wanted. Sometimes she'd tell me to invite Beverly and the three of us would sit on the couch in a complete sugar stupor, transfixed by Julia Roberts as she fled her own wedding, or dated Hugh Grant, or taught a rude shop assistant a valuable lesson. These were good memories for me; my mother's sudden and often startlingly loud laugh, the smell of microwave popcorn, her high heels discarded on the floor and her red-pedicured feet resting on the coffee table.

It was easy to see what drew men to my mother. She was beautiful, even with her predilection for outdated hairstyles and makeup. She was also comparatively unencumbered, having only one ex-husband, who lived in a different country, and one teenage daughter. Men were attracted to this lack of baggage. I think they saw the potential of relief in my mother, the same relief you might feel when a bellboy approaches you in a hotel lobby and offers to take your suitcase.

One man, a newly divorced mechanic with three children in primary school, promptly dumped his kids on Mum after their second date. He would drop them at our house in the morning and collect them in the evening. The first time this happened, it was because my mother had offered. The next few times were because my mother had offered the first time. This all transpired during the school holidays while I was in my final year at school. I remember waking up and walking out of my bedroom every morning to see their small, bewildered faces staring up at me from the couch; they were just as confused as I was. That breakup was conducted via a phone call, because if she invited him over it was likely she would open the door to find only his children standing there. I remember her screaming "I'm not your fucking babysitter, Clive!" before slamming the phone down.

When I was eighteen, she dated Barry and ever since then Beverly and I have referred to any man who behaves poorly as a "Barry" in his honor. Barry told my mother he was a pilot to explain why he couldn't see her all the time; a lie that came undone when she bumped into him at Target with his wife and daughter. He was supposed to be in Singapore. Turns out he was an accountant. On reflection, the most confusing part was the presents he bought her: trinkets with the look of having genuinely come from an airport in Phuket or Tokyo. I imagine he'd been ordering them off eBay.

"What did you learn about love by watching these dynamics?" the podcast guest had asked. I considered the question. It was an uncomfortable idea to think that the scenes I'd witnessed between my mother and the men she dated were my formative experiences of love. What had I learned? That dating was hard for my mother? That it was hard for everyone? That the act of being vulnerable with another person was always going to leave you exposed to pain and suffering, and that the more vulnerable you were, the deeper the potential for pain? Or, that you could never *really* know someone and instead you had to choose, day after day, to trust that they weren't going to hurt you?

I opened my eyes, briefly observing the downcast faces of the other passengers. Then I looked back at my screen and began browsing for a different podcast to listen to.

twenty-eight

On the morning of my birthday I left my apartment early, treating myself to a coffee and an almond croissant on my way to work. As I sat on the swaying tram, attempting ineffectually to brush the crumbs and powdered sugar off my pants, I received a message from Evan:

> *I have a surprise to give you*
> *tonight.*

Hot, I replied.

Without a human resources department, there was no one at Gro to keep track of birthdays, and so, to my relief, I was able to coast through the morning without attracting any attention.

My dad called me while I was taking a lunch break.

"Happy birthday!" he shouted, his voice booming directly into my ear via my headphones.

"Thanks, Dad." I grimaced, adjusting the volume down. I could see Elke's shoulder to the right of my father. "Hi, Elke."

"Happy birthday, Ana!" she said, waving her disembodied hand.

"Elke's got you an amazing present," my dad said.

"Oh—thanks, Elke," I said, concealing the dread I was feeling.

Last year, my present was a one-on-one astrology session with Elke. It was my twenty-eighth birthday and so she decided it was pertinent that I understood the celestial phase I was soon to be entering: my Saturn Return. Elke had warned me then that in a year's time my life would most likely look very different. In this phase, which apparently lasted for up to three years, life had a habit of changing rapidly and drastically, she told me. I'd laughed it off, but on sobering reflection I was, one year on, living in a different state, dating a different person, and working in a different job. Vaguely accurate or not, I wasn't keen to hear what the stars were conspiring to now.

"You really don't have to give me anything," I said, hoping she might agree and change the subject.

"She's done up your astrocartography chart," my dad explained, ignoring me.

"My what?"

"It's how your stars relate to different places in the world and what that means." Elke stepped more fully into the frame to answer. Her dark hair was slicked back and she looked dewy and damp, like she'd just showered. She always looked like that; her flawless, deep olive complexion and the humidity worked prosperously together.

"She's going to go through it all with you," my dad continued. "It's incredible stuff. She did my chart and it just—" He made a sound that symbolized his head exploding.

"I'll email your chart to you, so you have the whole map," Elke said, "but for now I'll just go over which lines intersect with Melbourne. There's no point in me telling you all about your Venus line if it cuts through Albania." She laughed.

I laughed too, though I had no idea what she meant.

"So," she began, moving herself into the center of the screen and referencing a sheet of paper she had. It was then that I realized that my present was going to happen right now.

"*Hmm*—okay, so your Pluto line cuts through Melbourne," she told me. There was a presentiment lurking beneath the surface of her words. Her brow furrowed almost indiscernibly.

"Is that a bad thing?" I asked.

"Well, it means transformation."

"Is that a bad thing?" I repeated.

"Nothing is ever really a bad thing," my dad chimed in unhelpfully.

"Exactly, nothing is bad," Elke continued. "It just means that you will learn things at an accelerated pace. You might find yourself thinking of the past and seeking closure." She was now reading directly from her phone. "Or, feeling the need to break negative cycles for good. Your ego will be broken a little, but then you'll be reborn. In a necessary way, like a realignment with your true self."

I imagined a chiropractor performing a spinal adjustment.

"That sounds painful."

"Yes, it can be." She nodded. "But it will be worth it."

"Thanks, Elke. That's very eye-opening," I said, hoping to draw the conversation to a close.

"I'll email the rest through. Let me know if you want to go over it all."

Perhaps sensing my deflation, she added, "Pluto lines are very powerful. It really is a gift to be near yours." She consulted her phone again. "Oh, but just be careful around cars. Proximity to a Pluto line increases the chances of road accidents."

I immediately thought of Emily.

"Hey, we have some news," Dad said, before looking shyly over at Elke. "Do you want to tell her?" he asked, whispering loudly.

"No, you tell her," she said, rubbing his arm.

I braced for the announcement that at twenty-nine years of age I was about to become an older sister. I immediately imagined their child: shoeless, wild, and uninoculated. Their child would grow up in a world where they'd be sound-bathed more than they were actually bathed. They'd think "namaste" meant "thank you" and would believe that depression was caused by misaligned chakras. They'd assume everyone they met was made out of light and love, except for my mother, who they'd probably be trained to assassinate on sight.

When I'd wished for a sibling as a child, I hadn't even considered that the wish might eventuate on a timeline like this.

"We're officially certified intimacy coaches!" my dad shouted, interrupting my visions.

"Oh—congratulations," I said.

There was a pause as they both beamed at me.

"So, what does that mean?" I asked.

"Well, we help other couples learn how to be truly intimate with each other," Elke explained.

"Like therapy?"

"No, it's more about helping them to open their heart space," my dad explained. "We work mostly with energetics."

I realized that more information was likely going to confuse me further.

"That sounds great. Do you have any clients yet?" I asked.

"Yeah, actually we have twelve in Bali and nine overseas," Elke said.

"Oh, wow," I said, genuinely surprised.

"We only put out our offering three weeks ago, but the clients just keep finding us. People need guidance more than ever," my dad said. "It's such rewarding work, you know, just helping people get out of their own way. Hey, speaking of which, has your mum called you for your birthday?"

"Nope," I said. "I think she's waiting for me to call her."

He looked concerned. "Well, are you going to?"

"Yeah, yeah, I will."

Elke touched my dad's arm and disappeared from the screen, as she did every time my mother was brought up in conversation.

"How long has it been since you last spoke to her?" he asked.

"I don't know, about five months."

He sighed. "I know it's hard to be the bigger person all the time, but you've got to reach out to her."

"I did, I called her twice and she didn't pick up. She's ignoring me." My voice sounded more petulant than I would have liked.

"I know, but just give her another call. Ros isn't as self-aware as you or me. You're going to have to go to her."

"So how much do I owe you for the session?"

"Ana—" he began, exasperated.

"I'll call her. I promise."

After we ended the call, two notifications from Beverly lit

up my idle screen. She'd sent the forbidden photo from our middle school dance, along with a message that read:

Happy birthday to you and your
eyebrows xxx

//

When I got to Evan's apartment that night, he answered the door coyly; only opening it enough to reveal half of his face.

"What?" I laughed.

"Come on in . . ." he replied mysteriously before disappearing from sight.

I laughed again and pushed the door open to see him standing proudly by the coffee table amid a collection of small, oddly shaped presents and a handmade sign that read: HAPPY BIRTHDAY ANA.

"Oh my god." I dropped my bag. "What is this?"

We sat and I unwrapped the presents one by one, each revealing an item that frequented my life: a specific sriracha I liked; my favorite tea; the brand of spirulina I blended into my smoothies; a candle to replace the one I'd almost finished; a bottle of wine he'd once bought that I'd mentioned I'd liked. There were fifteen presents in total, most of them common grocery items I often selected for myself, and yet every time I unwrapped one my heart soared and I grinned stupidly. It was a present that seemed to say "I know you" and "I love you" at the same time. It couldn't have been more perfect.

For my last birthday, back in Perth, I'd booked a table at my favorite restaurant and invited a handful of friends. My ex and I were still together at that point, but he didn't show up.

When the awkwardness of waiting for him extended beyond what I could cope with, I feigned receiving a call and left the table. When I returned, I explained that he wouldn't be coming due to a migraine and left it at that. Beverly knew better, I remember her glancing at me with pity and concern.

Later that night, my ex came home. I woke to the sound of his boots thudding down the hall and into the bedroom. He stripped his clothes off and climbed under the covers.

"Ana," he said, drunkenly attempting to whisper. "I'm sorry I missed your birthday dinner." He wrapped his arms around me, smelling of sweat, weed, and alcohol.

"Please don't," I responded.

He moved his whole body under the covers and across my legs.

"What are you doing?" I asked.

"I'm giving you your birthday present."

He fumbled with my underwear and attempted to tug it off.

"No, don't. I'm serious." I wriggled away from him. "Don't."

He put his head between my legs. I could feel his warm breath on my thighs.

"I said don't!" I shouted, jerking my knee defensively and feeling it connect with some part of him.

"*Fuck*," he hissed, pulling the sheets back and resurfacing with one hand covering his face.

"Jesus Christ, Ana. You kneed me in the nose." He pulled his hand away and I could see that there was a single drop of blood on it.

I said nothing and rolled away from him. He stormed out of the room and didn't return.

The next morning, I walked through the living room on

my way to the bathroom and saw him sleeping on the couch, a couple of bloody tissues on the floor next to him, a threadbare towel he'd retrieved from the bathroom and used as a blanket. He rolled over on the couch to face me, the towel pulled up to his chin.

"Ana," he announced, the words sounding rehearsed. "I think we should break up."

We didn't break up, instead we continued to torture each other for months—still, that moment held a significance in my memory. It was the beginning of the end.

Evan was opening the bottle of wine in the kitchen. From the couch, I watched him, his brow furrowed endearingly as he extracted the cork. The vision gave way to the sudden conviction that I was in love with him. There was no other way to describe the welling of emotion I felt as I watched him perform this mundane task. I would not have felt the same way were I watching anyone else open a bottle of wine. I loved him, specifically, and it was very possible that he might also be in love with me.

We hadn't yet said those words to each other, but I had the sudden desire to tell him; I wanted to hear him say it back. But then, as usual, I thought of Emily. I thought of the casual *I love you* messages that were left scattered all over their accounts, which seemed to imply that those words were said often. If I told him I loved him, he might think of Emily. He might then react strangely and shut down, packing all my presents into a bag and sending me home. I didn't want to risk ruining this perfect moment. I tucked the words away, saving them to use another time.

Evan poured the wine into two glasses and carried them over to the coffee table. I stood up, threw my arms around him, and said, "Thank you for my presents, I love them."

twenty-nine

"I mean, to ghost me for three weeks and then send me this? That's *heartless*." Soph showed me a text the footballer had sent her the night before, where with strangely formal legal language, he'd withdrawn consent for her to keep any of the explicit photos he'd previously sent her.

"And trust me, I know he didn't write this. He can't even spell 'definitely,' he writes 'defiantly.' So some lawyer or publicist or something has probably helped him craft this whole message."

"That really sucks, Soph." I sighed sympathetically.

She groaned, rolling her eyes to the ceiling and gathering her thoughts.

"I was waiting to hear from him, hoping that he'd want to see me again and instead I get this." She gestured at her phone. "It's such bad timing too, I've got all this to deal with."

She was now referring to the spontaneous end-of-year performance reviews taking place today. In the email, Paul had tried to disguise the seriousness of these interviews by telling everyone that he wanted to have a *friendly chat* indi-

vidually about our *role in the company* to *close out the year,*
but the fact that he felt he needed to use the word "friendly"
created a ripple of panic. A couple of days later, he'd informed
us that the board would be present in these interviews and
since then a small, but persistent, frown had attached itself to
everyone's face. "Agility" was one of Gro's company values,
but everyone knew that historically speaking Gro's "agility"
mostly manifested in the form of sudden restructures, where
roles would disappear and their responsibilities would be dis-
tributed without any extra remuneration. It went without
saying that this chat was an opportunity to convince Paul and
the board that we were worthy of keeping our jobs. The atmosphere was somber. I spent the morning getting ahead on
my workload and messaging Beverly:

> *My dad and Elke are now "certified*
> *intimacy coaches"*

What does that even mean???

> *It's like counseling other couples on*
> *how to be happy, I think.*

Like . . . sexually?

> *Probably*

Omg I bet they have so many
orgies. I've always known your dad
is a freak!

> *DON'T*

"Ana, are you ready to come through?" Paul asked from
the door of his office. His voice was very serious, as if to con-
vey to everyone that there were no favorites. I nodded and

collected my laptop. Paul's office had been set up in an intimidating scene; spare chairs had been sourced and arranged in a semicircle, and the board members, including Paul, occupied the chairs on one side of the room, leaving the seat closest to the door free. When I sat down, they all looked at me, each of them sporting the same serious expression. I wondered if they'd all agreed beforehand that they should avoid smiling in order to make this situation even more daunting.

I've always used a certain tactic during situations like this: I imagine the most intimidating person in the room masturbating. In this case, I chose the man to my far left, who was emanating an aura of being in charge. I imagined him straining and groaning; his red face deepening a shade with the effort; his wispy gray hair flapping about as his hand vigorously pumped away, a complete slave to his own uncontrollable urges. You're just like me, I thought, you're not that special. Masturbation: the great equalizer. I made sure I smiled at each of them individually.

"Right, Ana," Paul began. On closer inspection, he really didn't look good. His usually polished and unshakable confidence had not yet been broken, but it had at least been bent. He explained that he was going to ask me some questions about my role within the company. I nodded and he began with some technical questions. I explained the various tasks I performed daily; the overarching projects the tasks contributed to, and the goals and objectives of the projects themselves.

"And how do your own personal values overlap with the company's?" one of the board members, a nondescript man who was very pink, asked.

"Sorry?" I was confused by the question.

"The company values: innovation, honesty, agility, and integrity. How do they relate to your life outside of work?"

I wanted to say that honesty and integrity are kind of the same thing and that having them both in the company values seemed like a wasted opportunity. I also wanted to say that after I left the office at the end of the day the last thing—literally the last thing—I thought about was how the company values fit into my personal life.

"Well, I treat those around me with respect and I value honesty and integrity very highly."

"What do you feel is your purpose in life?" asked another board member. His neck was spilling over his collar.

"Ah . . ." I floundered. "In my work life? As in my career goals?"

"No—what is your purpose in *life*?"

"Oh. To be happy, I guess."

There was some sudden note-taking.

"Was that the wrong answer?"

"No, no, of course not." Paul smiled. "Where do you see yourself in ten years?"

"Just healthy and happy, I hope."

My answer sparked more note-taking.

"If the company was an animal, what animal would it be?" the first board member asked.

I was unable to disguise my confusion.

"An animal?"

"Yes, which animal? It can be any. There is no right or wrong answer."

"A giraffe."

The room was tense, one of the board members shifted uncomfortably. I'd chosen the wrong animal.

"A giraffe," he said. "Could you explain your answer?"

"Well . . ." I riffed, "they're fast and they can also see really far ahead of themselves. They're very agile."

Paul raised his eyebrows, apparently impressed, and shocked by the fact he was impressed. More notes were taken. Paul's body language then signaled that the meeting was wrapping up.

"Well, Ana, is there anything you want to ask us? Any questions?" he asked.

All of them looked at me expectantly and I shook my head.

//

"Did you hear the news?" Soph asked, leaning against the counter in the kitchen as the kettle rattled its way to a boil.

"No, what news?"

"Well, turns out Hayley found out Greg's salary and it's a fair bit higher than hers."

Hayley and Greg were app developers, though Greg had started a year after Hayley.

"What? Really?"

Soph nodded in response, her eyebrows lifted toward her hairline. "She saw his salary in a document that Paul accidentally sent them both. I think it was something to do with the performance reviews. It's bad. He's on fifteen thousand more than her."

"Whoa," I responded.

"Apparently Greg asked for a pay rise last year and got it, but Hayley never asked. So when she addressed the salary difference with Paul, he basically said it was her fault for not asking," Soph went on. "Naturally she's mad. She demanded a raise in her review to match Greg's, but Paul told her that they will need to do a proper performance review to assess it first, which obviously sucks for her. I mean, now she has to justify why she should earn the same as Greg. And we all know she works way harder than him."

We stood in silence for a moment, staring at the vibrating, sweating kettle.

"Have you ever received a pay rise?" I asked.

"No. Have you?"

I shook my head.

Dave walked into the kitchen, an empty mug in his hand, and went straight to the coffee machine.

"*Daaave* . . ." Soph said with a drawn-out inflection.

"Yes . . ." he responded, artlessly mimicking her.

"Have you ever received a pay rise while you've been working here?" she asked.

"Yeah," he replied. "Why?"

"Just wondering."

"Is this about the Hayley thing?" He leaned against the counter while the coffee machine dribbled out an espresso shot.

"Yes, it's ridiculous."

He turned back to the coffee machine. "Well, to be fair," he said, his voice casual, "it's really up to her to ask. Everyone knows you ask for a pay rise at the end of every performance review. They expect it."

Soph and I looked at each other, both of us processing the fact that Dave almost certainly earned more than us.

"But I didn't know that!" Soph cried. "Who told you that?"

"What?" Dave looked confused.

Soph turned to me. "Were you ever told that?"

I shook my head, recalling, with a sinking feeling, the moment in my performance review when Paul had said: "Well, Ana, is there anything you want to ask us? Any questions?"

//

For the rest of the afternoon, I attempted to busy myself, toggling between tabs. Soph and I messaged back and forth, discussing where to apply for jobs, and I spent some time halfheartedly browsing the careers page of a few user experience consultancies, which were often cultishly titled *Join Us!* and boasted *dog-friendly offices* or monthly *whisky tasting events,* none of which appealed to me. I searched until I found a consultancy that didn't boast anything and sent them a query email.

Later I watched as Hayley crossed from Paul's office to her desk. She pulled the sleeve of her jumper over her hand and used it to wipe her eyes as she collected her bag. Then she stormed out of the office, letting the glass doors clang shut behind her. I met Soph's eyes over our screens, both of our brows raised.

I looked around the office. The ping-pong table was covered with artwork and paper because it was mostly used as a conference table due to the fact we had a ping-pong table instead of a conference table. The beer and snack fridge hadn't been restocked in weeks. The office plants that covered surfaces and filled corners of the room were dusty and mostly dead or at least nearly finished dying. When I'd interviewed at Gro, Paul had declared his vision of a progressive, new model of working which was "disruptive and different." A counterweight to the rigid and stifling conventions of traditional corporate culture. But none of his grandiose speeches, or theories, or vague company policies and values had made the journey from words into something more meaningful, like actions or decent and fair salaries. I now saw his vision for what it truly was: a mirage; an inviting oasis of palm trees and water that shimmered away into nothingness the closer you looked. I started picking at my cuticles.

thirty

"Your dad's name is Mark, right?" I asked Evan. He nodded in response, keeping his eyes on the road. We were on our way to visit Evan's family for Christmas and I was doing some last-minute cramming to try to assuage my anxiety about meeting his parents for the first time.

Christmas had never really been a big event in my household. In the years when other men were not involved, the day usually started with my mum waking me up and sitting on the end of my bed while I unwrapped my present. Later, we'd go to the pub for Christmas lunch and while I pushed the dry slices of turkey around my plate my mother would get drunk on cheap prosecco and flirt with everyone. After that we would go home and she would lie on the couch, headache-ridden with a cold flannel over her face.

Evan told me Christmas was a small event for his family too, but no matter how I tried I couldn't reduce the meeting's importance, or my perception of all the opportunities I had to make a bad first impression. My experiences with meeting other people's families often left me feeling like an alien, thrust into a new type of human interaction and forced to have to learn how to blend in quickly. I was reminded of just how vast the space on the spectrum between normality and my family was. Even my ex, who I believed had more issues assimilating successfully into society than I did, had a great relationship with his parents and brother. They even had a wholesome annual Christmas camping tradition.

"So what does Mark do? Does he work?"

"He's retired, but he was general manager at a biomedical engineering company. He mostly plays golf now and recently he's really been into gardening."

"Okay, what about your mum?"

Evan paused to consider. "Honestly, I don't really know. She likes to cook. She has a book club, I think. She didn't work when I was growing up."

I was sure the image he was painting of his mother was missing a fair few strokes of detail but I moved on.

"What about your sister?"

"Olivia's eight months pregnant and there's Milly, who's four, I've mentioned her already, right? My niece?"

"Yes," I said, frantically flipping through my mental notes for a mention of Milly.

"Olivia is a stay-at-home mum at the moment, but she also paints and sells her work sometimes. Tim, her husband, is an accountant."

I looked down at my cuticles, urging myself to leave them alone.

We parked in front of an old two-story Victorian house; neat, ornate, and imposing. Evan opened the front gate and we walked through a small courtyard of manicured garden, which was filled with rosebushes heavy with white flowers and perfectly shaped hedges. Even the usually pedestrian agapanthus that lined one side of the courtyard were standing up straight and orderly as if at attention; Evan hadn't been joking about his father's gardening obsession. The door opened before we knocked, revealing Julie, Evan's mum. She embraced Evan warmly, asking how he was.

Julie was tall with short blond hair. She wore a matching beige blouse and pant set, which seemed to drape and hang from her body in a way that could only be described as expensively. She was neat, polished, and adorned with shiny gold jewelry.

Evan moved through into the hallway and her eyes turned to me.

"Ana, so nice to meet you," she said, though she didn't move to hug me. I felt a little relieved that I'd avoided that opportunity for awkwardness, but at the same time I wondered if things were already going badly. I followed the two of them past an elegant staircase, stepping lightly over the dark floorboards, which were so shiny it felt rude to walk on them. I already knew that Evan came from a wealthy family; there had been certain indications: He'd once asked for a "carafe" of water at a bar and, on another occasion, he mentioned his parents had spent September at their villa in the south of France. I also knew, theoretically, that this type of wealth existed, but I had never stepped foot in a house like this before. In the hallway, we passed a huge vase of lilies that sat on a narrow glass table in front of a mirror. My reflection, creased with nervous concern, looked back at me and I attempted to relax my face. Evan and his mother were making polite small talk about the weather and I took the opportunity to remain silent while I still could. We walked past an opening in the hallway that revealed a lounge room. Two marble fireplaces faced each other from opposite walls, and a

huge beige couch sat in between them; more vases, more flowers, more mirrors. The hallway expanded into an open-plan
kitchen and dining room. The back wall of the house was
mostly glass with large double French doors that led to the
backyard, where Evan's father could be seen pulling something out of a vegetable bed. Evan placed the bottle of wine
he'd brought on the vast kitchen counter.

"Your father's in the garden as per usual," Julie said as she
checked something on the stovetop.

I followed Evan into the garden, his father's voice sudden
and booming as he greeted us. I watched them embrace. Evan's
resemblance to him was clear in their eye color and skin tone,
but also subtly present in their shared mannerisms. They had
the same smile and they were the same height. I was struck
momentarily by the eeriness of how genes replicate themselves.

Evan introduced me and Mark held out his hand formally.
We smiled as he vigorously shook my limp hand.

"Ana, do you like zucchini?" he then asked in a voice that
was self-assured and clear. The type of voice that would have
once easily asserted itself in a room full of people and pep-
talked teams of entry-level employees, perhaps a little conde-
scendingly.

"I do," I admitted.

He leaned in conspiringly. "Remind me, and I'll give you
some before you leave. Julie's sick of the stuff."

He took us on a garden tour, where it quickly became apparent that he treated his garden the way he would have
treated an office of employees. Everything was ruly, the plants
were tied and restrained; all of it bent to his will. Most of the
vegetables were huge, far larger than a conventional size. I
imagined them forced to grow overtime in the evenings and
on weekends.

After we had returned to the corner of the garden where we began the tour, Evan and Mark chatted about Evan's job until Mark asked me what I did for a living.

"I work in user experience design for a start-up."

"Okay." He nodded as if waiting for me to continue, but the conversation was interrupted by the sound of voices coming from the house. Olivia, Milly, and Tim had arrived. They stood by the patio doors, Milly sulking and clinging to Olivia's leg, while Julie attempted to reason with her. We walked back toward the house to greet them, reaching Tim first.

"Mate," he said to Evan, shaking his hand before turning and introducing himself to me. He had a round, boyish face and a receding hairline. Both attributes seemed to contradict his age.

"Watching the cricket tomorrow?" he then asked.

"Yeah, maybe," Evan replied.

They began to discuss the test match, so I turned and watched Olivia and Julie as they tried to calm Milly, who was now teary and alarmingly red-faced. She was holding a pink plastic convertible car with a doll strapped into it. The doll was upside down, flapping helplessly about at the mercy of its owner. Julie took Milly by the hand and led her into the kitchen, freeing Olivia, who walked over to greet us. Olivia looked more like Julie than Evan did, slightly lighter in coloring, her features sharper but her jawline less so.

"Hey, you," she said, giving Evan a hug before hugging me. "You must be Ana."

Evan and Tim resumed their cricket discussion, and Olivia stood back, surveying the backyard with one hand on her lower back and the other around her pregnant stomach.

"God, I'm dying for a glass of wine," she said to me, as we watched Mark continue to potter around the garden.

"When are you due?" I asked.

"I've still got four weeks to go." She sighed. "Well, maybe less, Milly was early. Less would be good."

Mark was now unwinding a hose and clearly displaying no intention of finishing up to join the family.

"I should go and say hi," Olivia said, excusing herself and touching Evan on the back as she walked past him and out into the backyard.

Evan was still deep in cricket talk. Meanwhile Milly was entertaining herself on the floor under the dining table while Julie was busy in the kitchen. I contemplated what to do. I could stand next to Evan, offering nothing to the conversation until they were forced to talk about something else, or I could help Julie. I looked over at her as she attempted to lift a cast-iron pan out of the oven. Her face was flushed from heat and effort. I walked over, grabbing a tea towel from the island counter.

"Here, let me help," I said, bending over and supporting the pan.

Julie's eyes glanced at me briefly and she smiled. "Oh, you're a doll, Em. Thank you."

I flinched slightly at the sound of Emily's name as we shifted the heavy pan onto the counter. I glanced at Julie's face but she showed no recognition of what had just happened. She hadn't even realized that she'd called me Em. I watched her transfer chicken from the pan to a wooden board, and looked over at where Evan was standing. I could see only a small sliver of his face but still I could tell his jaw muscle was working. His posture had altered slightly and become almost indiscernibly tense. Had he heard?

"I'm going to get Mark in here to carve this," Julie said, washing her hands in the sink and smiling at me.

I took an empty wineglass from the counter and filled it to the top.

//

During lunch I was able to sit back and observe the conversation. No one in the family shied away from starting or adding to a discussion, which was a relief, until a question was directed at me.

"What do you do for work, Ana?" Tim asked. Caught off guard, I made a show of apologetically finishing my mouthful of bread.

"I work in user experience design."

"Oh, who for?" he asked.

"It's a start-up called Gro. They help to build share portfolios."

"Like a hedge fund?" Tim offered.

"Yeah. Basically."

"The term 'start-up' gets used a lot these days. Why don't these 'start-ups' just call themselves a company?" Mark asked.

"Well, they would probably have to start paying their employees proper salaries for a start," I answered. I took another mouthful of wine as Tim chuckled politely.

"It's a bit like the way everyone calls themselves entrepreneurs these days," Olivia added. "Instead of just saying they're a small business owner—"

"Or just an idiot who fell for a multilevel marketing scam," Tim interjected. "So many of Olivia's friends fell off the face of the earth for years, only to reappear selling supplements and meal replacement powders."

"I know a few people from school who have done the same thing," Evan joined in. "Suddenly their bio reads *CEO*."

"Well, that's just your generation in a nutshell," Mark said, leveling his next comment directly at Olivia, Tim, Evan, and me. "Everyone wants the title of CEO without having any concept of how hard you have to work to get there or how many years you have to be committed for. It's all about the label. Your generation just want instant recognition. They want the praise without having to work for it."

Olivia shook her head. "Well, actually," she said, "it's more that the multilevel marketing business model preys on women who have recently become mothers, and are dealing with the loss of their financial independence at a time when they're still coming to terms with losing their independence in every other area of their life. After I had Milly, I considered going back to work part-time but the childcare costs meant that I would basically break even. It made no sense."

Tim nodded in agreement.

"So you have these women at home alone all day and someone approaches them and offers them a way to make money from their couch? Of course they're going to buy into it. I don't think that—"

"That's not what I'm talking about," Mark cut through. "I'm talking about the way your generation expect that stepping into a senior management role is guaranteed just by showing up for work every day."

I shifted food around my plate, distinctly feeling like I was in between two different conversations.

"Why do women put all this pressure on themselves to go back to work anyway?" Julie asked. "Being able to stay home with your children and look after them is a gift."

"Some people don't want to be just a mother," Olivia said, picking up her water glass.

"I remember this one kid," Mark said, smirking and shaking his head, clearly determined to bring the conversation back to areas he knew more about. "He asked me for a pay rise six months after he had completed his probation period. Can you believe that? He wanted more money just for not being fired." He laughed.

After lunch, gifts were exchanged in the lounge room. We all politely received our gift cards from one another, before turning our attention to Milly, who, on the verge of being overwhelmed with happiness, sat in front of the fireplace with a pile of presents to tear through. Each of us was quickly employed to help extract toys from their impenetrable plastic fortresses. When a present was revealed, Milly squealed with delight but then quickly discarded it in favor of the mysterious allure of the next unopened package. I pulled out my phone. My mum still hadn't responded to the *Merry Christmas* message I'd sent her hours ago. It was almost midday in Perth, and I knew she'd be getting ready to head to the pub for Christmas lunch. Despite the simplicity of our Christmas traditions, I did enjoy them, maybe because I had nothing to compare them to, or maybe because I couldn't view them through anything other than the rosy tint of nostalgia. I even recalled that some of the sweet older women who also attended the same yearly lunch would occasionally bring me gifts: lavender talcum powder that I'd never use or cheap chocolates that tasted like slightly sweet chalk. I was surprised, maybe even a little impressed, that my mother was able to sustain her grievance even through a day as sentimental and family-orientated as this. I tucked my phone back away so I didn't look rude.

On the ornate mantel above the fireplace, I noticed a row of framed photos, one of which appeared to be a school photo of teenage Evan. I stood up from the couch to inspect it. Teenage Evan had braces and a shiny forehead with a few token blemishes. His face was open and his smile was confident. I moved on to a photo of Olivia as a teenager. She was wearing a hint of some rebellious eyeliner and she had pulled two thin pieces of hair forward out of her ponytail. The next photo was displayed in a large mirrored frame. In the middle stood Olivia in a white dress, Tim was next to her holding her hand, and the family fanned out on either side of them. It was obviously a photo from Olivia and Tim's wedding. I located Evan to the left of his dad and then next to Evan I saw Emily. The reminder of her beauty was a surprise attack I wasn't prepared for. She beamed into the camera with such confidence, such complete belonging. She was radiant. One of her arms was delicately wrapped around Julie in a symbol of casual affection.

I imagined her here in the room, topping up Julie's glass and laughing along with her; handing her the perfect gift, Julie gasping in surprise, "How did you know?" Evan smiling proudly at the two of them as they embraced. I suddenly wondered what I was doing here; physically here in this room, metaphorically here in this relationship. I was kidding myself to think I was well adjusted enough to be able to deal with these circumstances. It was uncharacteristically optimistic to think I could cope without projecting an unfair need for constant reassurance from Evan. I wondered whether I was truly the right person for this job, the job of being The One Who Came After, which required the responsibility of delicate handling and constant concealing. I stared at Emily's face and she smiled back at me through the glass like she knew the answer.

thirty-one

Hannah invited us to a New Year's Eve house party and we were all relieved that the burden of figuring out what to do was no longer on any of our shoulders, except Lauren, who was invited to two other events she'd rather attend, but was struggling with the idea of her closest friends being separated.

Fineeeeeeeeeee, she wrote in our group chat thread, *I'll come but I'm out of there straight after the countdown.*

The party was in Carlton North, in a share house occupied by three housemates; two of them, Josh and Veer, were close friends of Hannah's.

We made plans to meet at Evan's for drinks beforehand, to which Lauren arrived late, bringing with her a cloud of oud and sandalwood perfume.

"Whoa, Lauren," George said as she sat down on the couch. "As your close friend I think I should tell you that I can see through the top you're wearing."

"Fuck off, George," she said, putting her beer on the coffee table.

"Sorry." He laughed, as if genuinely surprised by her reaction. "I didn't know if you knew."

"Of course I know, you idiot." She didn't meet his eyes as she spoke and rummaged through her tote bag for a filter. "As if I, a woman, who has had to hide her nipples her entire life, isn't going to be aware when they might be visible."

The conversation should have stopped there, but George wasn't done.

"Well, having them on display is probably one way to guarantee attention."

His tone was cruel. Lauren's narrowed eyes flashed up at him.

"I'm not doing it for attention."

"Anyway," Evan said, attempting to change the subject. He cast a meaningful look at George, which was ignored.

"Oh, right," George scoffed. "That makes no sense."

There was an undertone to the conversation, as if a different conversation were simultaneously taking place, implied but not spoken, and also not going well. I took a sip of beer.

"Why don't we talk about what you're wearing, George?" Lauren said, her frustration blatant.

"Ah—okay." George frowned, looking down at his clothes in mock confusion.

"Well, your knees are on show. You must want attention."

I understood her point but wished she had polished it a little more.

George scoffed again. "You know that's not the same thing. My knees aren't sexual organs."

"Whoa, whoa, I'm not sure I agree with that," Evan joked.

"Breasts aren't sexual organs, they're reproductive organs," Lauren shot back.

"Now you're just being obtuse," George said, picking up his beer. "C'mon, Lauren, you know perfectly well that you have incredible tits, and clearly you want to show them off. I would too if I were you. It's okay to just admit it."

Lauren didn't respond. Color rose on her cheeks underneath the artificial shade she'd applied.

//

Just after ten we arrived outside an old house; the type that had been a share house for so long that its state of neglect was easily recognizable; peeling stucco, rotting weatherboards, an old bookshelf abandoned by someone on the front veranda, a garden that was both overgrown and dead. Hannah greeted us at the door; her eyes, which were decorated with black eyeliner in a way that made them appear cat-like, were unfocused, seeming to look both at and through whoever she was speaking to. She was clearly drunk and high. Loud music and red light leaked down the hall from the end of the house. We filed around the two bikes stacked against the wall and followed Hannah.

In the lounge room a group of dusty indoor plants congregated around a boarded-up fireplace and a row of empty liquor and wine bottles lined the mantel, seemingly to imply a conscious decorative decision. Stacks of vinyl and a record player were neatly organized on top of a collection of milk crates. Two women were swaying and spinning on a Persian rug in the middle of the room. A man was sitting on the couch either watching them or staring at the wall behind them, I couldn't tell. The party did not look promising. I looked back at Evan and could read the same thoughts on his face; behind him, Lauren looked around sulkily. It was the type of house I'd lived in throughout my early twenties, a revolving door of strangers and parties, but now that I was nearly thirty it no longer looked like fun. I no longer possessed the air of youthful optimism necessary to float above the sea of existential dread that would occasionally rise in a house like this; in the same way that my hangovers had recently become as much an assault on my mental state as my physical. Hannah led us through the kitchen, animatedly gesturing and talking to George. A woman leaned against the kitchen counter, scrolling on her phone, while a man shouted into her ear to be heard over the music. We continued on, past a dining table that looked as if it was reaching the end of a hard life, and out into the backyard.

To our collective relief, the energy outside was of a party in its prime; groups of people crowded on the cracked and uneven concrete slab, some sitting on milk crates, others standing or crouching to avoid the old Hills Hoist that leaned precariously in the center of the space; clouds of smoke were dissipating into the air above.

It was now possible to talk over the music and we found a spot to stand and drink, while Hannah moved off to fetch someone. George procured some unclaimed glasses on a table nearby and we poured our wine, while Lauren set to work rolling a cigarette. Moments later Hannah returned and began to introduce us all to the host of the party, Josh.

He dressed as if to exhibit a lack of care, except that everything he wore was clearly expensive and sourced from limited edition collaborations between hiking and streetwear brands, betraying a self-consciousness that broke the illusion. His pants were made of some kind of parachute material and were covered in odd-shaped pockets. I wondered what the purpose of all of them was, until he opened one halfway down his leg and pulled out a little bag of white powder, handing it to George, before opening a different pocket and pulling out a blunt and lighter. When Hannah introduced Lauren, Josh's eyes lingered on her, but she was too obliviously distracted by her phone to notice.

The night progressed relatively uneventfully. At one point, Lauren got into a heated debate with George over whether "all-boys" schools should exist.

"Misogynistic arsehole factories," she called them, instantly recruiting Evan and Josh, who had also attended one, to George's side.

"Lauren, what would you know? You never went to one," George argued. "You've never even set foot in one."

"Yeah, well, I've met enough guys who have!" she cried.

The conversation segued then to other generalizations about the poor behavior of men. That's when Hannah chimed in, her confidence perhaps bolstered by her inebriation.

"It's funny though," she interjected over Lauren, who had held the floor for too long anyway, "I think a lot of heterosexual women romanticize the idea of other women. Like, when it comes to dating, men are the worst and women are all unappreciated saints, but I have to say, the two worst relationships I've ever been in were with women. Dating someone who is both highly emotionally intelligent and incredibly manipulative is *terrifying*."

"Well, you don't have to worry about George being highly emotionally intelligent," Lauren said, her eyes cast down at the cigarette she was rolling. Hannah laughed, as if just to fulfill an expectation, while George watched Lauren with a frown on his face.

//

Just before the countdown started, I found myself in the bathroom giving a woman on the verge of passing out a glass of water. I watched her taking small child-like sips from the cup and tried to think of what to do next. I couldn't leave her there, alone and sitting in the bathtub, but I also didn't want to spend the countdown standing next to a sink where someone had recently vomited.

"Can you stand?" I asked her.

She was wearing some sort of furry black bucket hat, which at this point was nearly covering her eyes. She didn't respond. I checked the time on my phone: 11:54. I had a text from Evan: *Where are you??*

"Oh my god, Laila!"

A woman had appeared in the bathroom doorway behind me.

"Are you her friend?" I asked.

"Yeah," she said, wobbling as she kneeled down next to me. "I didn't know she was so fucked-up. She was fine and then she just disappeared."

"I gave her some water, I think she's okay. I wouldn't leave her alone though. You should probably take her home."

"Yeah, okay," she replied, before turning her attention to her friend. "Laila? Come on, get up, you're going to miss the countdown."

I left her tugging at her friend's limp arms and went to find Evan.

I located him as the countdown hit five. He handed me a drink and we shouted through the last seconds of the year. Evan and I kissed, and then George pulled me into a hug. I turned to find Lauren, but she was deeply preoccupied with

Josh, kissing and writhing against him. Instead, I found Hannah, who grabbed me and *woo*-ed directly into my ear. Then we all turned our attention to the fireworks exploding in the distance, somewhere else in the city.

It had been an eventful year. I'd found myself in a life completely unrecognizable from the one I was living a year ago. When I looked back, the reasons why I'd left Perth now seemed vague and hard to define. I'd rehearsed and repeated them in a way that seemed to detach me from their meaning. With the wisdom of hindsight, leaving Perth was less about those reasons and more about the indefinable feeling that something better was going to find me if I left in search of it. As Evan put his arm around me, I felt I had been right.

"I'm so glad I met you," he whispered against my hair, as if he knew exactly what I was thinking.

//

At the end of the night, as I stood with Evan on the sidewalk and waited for our car to arrive, I recognized the furry black hat of the woman I'd tried to help in the bathroom earlier. She was farther up the street with a man, who seemed to be attempting to keep her upright and kiss her at the same time. She pulled away from him and I watched as he stepped in closer to her, moving his face toward hers once again. Something flared inside me and I started walking toward them.

"Hey!" I shouted. "She's too drunk."

"It's fine, I'm looking after her," the man responded. He held the woman against a letter box, so that her body was upright, but her head hung in a way that made it obvious she couldn't stand by herself. Her eyes were closed.

"It looks more like you're trying to kiss her."

"I'm her boyfriend, chill out. I'm just trying to get her home."

"*Ana,*" Evan said, catching up with me.

"Where were you earlier? When she was passed out in the bathroom," I said.

"What?" The man glared at me and I turned my attention to the drunken woman instead.

"Hey, hey, do you know this guy?" I asked her.

"Are you serious? I'm her boyfriend."

"Do you know him?" I asked the woman again. The woman looked up at me and Evan and then shook her head.

"She thinks you meant me," Evan said.

"Can you show me a photo of you both on your phone?" I asked the man.

"No." He scoffed. "Are you actually implying that I'm attempting to assault my own girlfriend? Mind your own business."

"Well, can you at least tell me her name?" I persisted.

"Fuck off!" he spat, his frustration with me escalating.

"Whoa, mate." Evan stepped in. "She's just trying to make sure your girlfriend's okay."

The man directed his glare at Evan. "And I'm telling you to *fuck off.*"

Evan's phone started ringing, our car had arrived.

"Ana, c'mon," he said, pulling me back down the street.

I let him lead me away, climbing into the car with my heart pounding.

"You saw that, right? She needs help," I said.

"Yeah, maybe," he said, putting his seatbelt on. "He did say she's his girlfriend."

He sounded annoyed at me and I was confused.

"But even if she is, there's something really off about the whole thing."

"Well, what did you want to do?" he asked, frustration rising. "Did you even consider that guy might suddenly get aggressive with me, or worse, you?"

He sighed, lowering his voice. "I understand you were trying to help, but I'm not going to get in a fight with a guy like that over some drunk girl I don't even know."

"I just wanted to make sure she's okay."

I still wasn't convinced that the man was actually her boyfriend. I recalled her friend in the bathroom had said: "She was fine and then she just disappeared."

"He might have spiked her drink," I insisted.

I imagined articles appearing all over the internet tomorrow morning: **Woman's Body Found in Park**.

"What if she's in danger? How am I supposed to help?"

"I don't know," Evan concluded, his voice despondent.

CHAPTER
thirty-two

Evan and I were at a gallery opening in Collingwood for a friend of Lauren's. It was held in a converted warehouse space with a polished concrete floor and white walls. The artworks were simplistic line drawings, quiet and contemplative and ignored entirely in favor of conversation.

We found Lauren shortly after we arrived and she pointed out her friend, the artist, but I couldn't distinguish who she was indicating.

"She has curly dark hair. A mullet," Lauren explained, expanding the potential candidates, rather than narrowing them down. I left the two of them and went to the bar. When I returned, Evan was chatting to someone he knew, a friend of Lauren's, who had a peroxide pixie cut and an eyebrow piercing. I handed Evan a glass of wine and he introduced me before they continued talking about someone I didn't know. Not wanting to intrude on their conversation, I looked around the room and attempted to appear self-sufficient.

My eyes roamed quickly over the crowd of unrecognizable faces, until they abruptly landed on Nadia. She was wearing a black dress and her long hair trailed down her shoulders. I watched her as she laughed at something someone had said, clutching their arm as she did so. Then she nodded, turned, and began to make her way over to us. I quickly drew my attention to the conversation in front of me.

"Hey," Nadia said, hugging Evan. She was wearing dark red lipstick, although the color only outlined her lips; the rest of it was now lining the rim of her wineglass. She seemed drunk.

"Hey, I didn't know you were going to be here tonight." Evan sounded genuinely surprised.

"Yeah, Abby knows Melissa," she explained, gesturing randomly into the crowd. "They went to RMIT together."

"Oh, right," Evan replied. "You remember Ana?"

Lauren's friend, now ignored, took the opportunity to leave the conversation and I shifted to let them pass.

"Of course," Nadia exclaimed, pulling me into a hug. "Anyway, I should go find Abby, she's a bit drunk," she said, addressing us both with her slightly glazed eyes. "But I'll come back and say hey later."

"Ah—sure," Evan replied.

"That was weird," he said after Nadia had left. "I don't know why she's here. This really isn't her type of thing. She doesn't even like Abby."

I shrugged.

"Anyway," he said, looking down at his empty glass. "Should we get another drink?"

I was speaking to Lauren when a woman began to address the room via a wireless microphone. It took a little while for her to gain control over a couple of particularly drunken hecklers, but eventually the room was quiet enough for her to be heard clearly. She asked us all to move back against the wall to make room for the performers. I leaned over to Lauren and asked her what was going on.

"It's a performance art piece," she answered as we all shuffled backward.

In the space the crowd had left, a woman and a man were unrolling a large piece of paper across the ground. Once the paper was set down, they handed out small torches to some of the people in the front row, whispering instructions into their ears. Then they stood on the paper and faced the crowd. At the same time they removed their shirts, revealing that the man had the word "Capitalism" painted across his chest and the woman had "The Mother" painted across hers. The performance suddenly took on the appearance of a rushed high school art assignment.

The lights went out and the audience members with the torches turned them on, aiming them at the performers. I heard some laughing from the other side of the room, but it was drowned out as "I Wanna Be Your Dog" by the Stooges began blaring from the gallery's sound system. Capitalism placed his hands in a bucket of black paint and began to smear it over The Mother's body. I turned to Evan but he was no longer next to me.

Quickly, the performance took a more aggressive turn. Capitalism was now pretending to attack The Mother, shoving her and streaking her with more paint, in turn covering themselves and the ground in thick, oily lines. In an overly exaggerated movement The Mother, her face contorted with theatrical sorrow, began to slowly lie down on the canvas, and I had a sinking, ominous feeling about what was going to happen next. The male performance artist climbed on top of the woman and began simulating thrusting movements. I averted my gaze around the room and saw some heads nodding along, appreciating the symbol, while others were visibly uncomfortable. Capitalism was now pulling The Mother's hair, while she remained stoic, unmoving, and lifeless. When Capitalism put his hands around The Mother's throat, I found myself, very suddenly, at my limit. I turned and left for the bathroom.

In the cubicle I stared at the graffiti on the back of the door:

He said I'm ugly :(

Someone had responded underneath:

Tell him to fuck off

And underneath that:

And this is why I only date women now

A final comment was scrawled below:

Women can be cunts too

When I exited the cubicle, I saw Nadia standing at the basin, reapplying her lipstick. The girl next to her, who I assumed was Abby, was entirely engrossed in the act of composing a message.

"Hey," I said, smiling at them both and washing my hands.

Nadia made eye contact with me through the mirror and smiled back. "Did I see you at Bend a while ago?" she asked. "Did you like the class?"

"Yeah, it was good," I replied, matching her casual, conversational tone.

"It's such a nice studio," she went on, putting her lipstick in her bag. "I go there all the time. It makes me feel closer to Emily."

Hearing her say Emily's name out loud, without any hesitancy, startled me. It was a strange way to feel given Emily had been Nadia's best friend. Of course she could use her name whenever she liked. She hadn't asked a question so much as made a statement, and so I took the opportunity to say nothing as I dried my hands with a paper towel.

"You knew she taught there, right?" Nadia pressed.

I wondered if she actually hoped I would make that admission to her.

"I didn't, actually," I said, feigning mild surprise. "I was looking for a studio to go to and I heard they did a free trial class."

Nadia frowned. "Wow, what an awkward coincidence. What did Evan say about that?"

"Nothing." I could feel her watching me.

"Can I ask you something?" she said, her tone softening as if to indicate a confidence between us. "Does he talk to you about Emily much?"

Out of pride I contemplated lying and saying that he did, and then out of reason and a desire to help Evan I contemplated opening up to her and admitting that he didn't. In the pause I took, she continued, "The only reason I ask is because he talks to me about her a lot. I think he's still really struggling with it. You might want to speak to him, offer some support."

I remained silent, processing her words, which were an admission that she spoke to Evan about Emily frequently and that she knew he never spoke to me about her. I suppose I knew back when I first saw Nadia's messages light up Evan's phone screen all those months ago that he would talk to her about Emily. It made sense, and it should have been a relief to know that he was getting support from somewhere, but still, it hurt to hear that he was seeking out those conversations, just never with me.

"I was a little worried that he maybe wasn't dealing with any of it," I admitted. "I'm glad to hear he's talking to you about it."

A line appeared and disappeared between Nadia's brows.

"I'm so sorry for your loss," I added. "It must have been so hard."

"Thanks," she said, nodding and pursing her lips.

I had the sense that whatever vengeful desire she'd had to hurt me for replacing her best friend was losing its momentum. At that moment, a group of people entered the bathroom and the small space became cramped and loud. She and Abby left, the door swinging closed behind them.

Back in the gallery, the lights were on again, and the paint and paper was being packed away, but the energy in the room was struggling to recover. I saw Lauren desperately trying to help revive the atmosphere by handing out more wine. Evan was waiting for me by the door.

"Ready to go?" he asked.

On the walk back to Evan's apartment I linked my arm through his and snuck my hand into his jacket pocket. We discussed the performance art piece, Evan explaining that, while I was away, Capitalism had gotten paint in his eye and the performance had to be stopped.

"Capitalism failed in the end," he concluded.

The conversation I'd had with Nadia lurked in the back of my mind. I contemplated whether I should bring it up. When I closed Evan's apartment door behind me, I made a decision.

"So, I ran into Nadia in the bathroom," I said. "She brought up Emily."

Evan's eyes flashed up at me as he poured us both a glass of water. "What did she say?"

"She was just saying that you and her talk about Emily often and that—"

"Why are you so interested in Emily?" he asked, cutting me off. "First you went to Bend—"

"That was a complete coincidence," I lied.

"And now you're asking Nadia about her?"

"Nadia started the conversation, for the record."

His eyebrow twitched as if this piece of information was confusing.

"I just want to be there for you, that's all. I want you to talk about her with me—"

Evan scoffed. "You want me to talk about her?"

"Well, no, I only meant if you feel like it would help," I replied cautiously. "I just want you to know that I'm here if you want to talk about her."

"Fine," he said, holding his arms out wide in exasperation. "What do you want to know?"

"I didn't mean—"

"Should I tell you about how incredible she was?" He dropped his arms back down.

I stared at him, both shocked and confused by the turn the conversation had taken.

"And intelligent? Like genuinely so impressively smart. She was beautiful too, obviously—I mean, you've seen photos." He looked at me then, as if to assess whether this comment had hurt. It had, but mostly because I realized then that he was trying to hurt me. I kept my expression still.

"This isn't what I meant—"

"She was funny," he continued, ignoring me. "She had this dark, dry, witty sense of humor. I loved that about her. She could make pretty much anyone laugh."

I flinched and he saw it.

"Too much?" he asked cruelly. "You said you wanted me to talk about her."

"Evan—" I implored.

"I'll keep going then. She was the kindest person I've ever known. Even when she didn't need to be—especially when she didn't need to be. I've never met anyone as compassionate as her."

His words seemed to be hurting him too now. He sat down on the couch, putting his face in his hands, and drew a deep breath. He wiped his eyes and I realized he was crying. I froze. All this time I had wanted him to open up to me, but now that he was showing me vulnerability I was frightened by the emotion.

"*Jesus,* Ana." He sighed. "I was on top of this." He ran both hands through his hair. "Things were going so well."

I sat down next to him, tentatively placing my hand on his back and stroking it. "Evan, I'm so sorry."

He turned his head away from me, wiping his eyes with the back of his hand and sighing again.

"Maybe I'm not ready for this," he said, standing and moving away from my hand. "I think I just need to be alone."

thirty-three

I ordered a car and stood outside Evan's apartment building with my belongings. Then I cried, for the entire journey home, while the driver cast worried looks at me through the rearview mirror. The next morning I practically woke up crying and continued, at intervals, for the whole day. I sobbed while trying to read and while attempting to follow a guided meditation. I teared up while piling my laundry into my washing machine at the laundromat, and again while I carried it home. I took a short break from crying to masturbate and then recommenced my weeping almost immediately afterward.

All day I contemplated calling Evan and apologizing, telling him he was completely right and offering to do whatever was necessary to appease him. But it seemed that in order to appease him I needed to stay away like he had asked. All I could do was wait for a verdict.

A life with Evan, even with his ability to wield mercurial silence in a way that my mother could only dream of, was still better than a life without Evan. I was terrified things were over between us, all because I'd wanted too much. I con-demned myself for this endlessly, dragging out any vaguely related flaw or fault and forcing myself to examine every sin-gle one of them. I dwelled at length on everything Evan had said, and in the light of my perceived shortcomings, the long list of honorable traits he had given Emily seemed insur-mountable. She was intelligent and beautiful and funny and caring, a declaration that left little room for what she was not. Was I intelligent? I'd never had reason to think I was and certainly no one ever went out of their way to reassure me. Through both school and university I'd done enough to stay close to the mean, enjoying the comfort and anonymity of the middle of the bell curve. I imagined that if asked, all of my teachers would clear their throats or avert their eyes: "Well, if she'd only applied herself more . . ."

Was I beautiful? This was disputable and subjective, but I knew one thing for sure: I was no Emily. Was I funny? Maybe. Was I caring? To a normal degree.

I considered calling Beverly and explaining what had hap-pened so that she could console me, but I was embarrassed by how upset I was. I was even more embarrassed by my actions, all the lurking and stalking. For these reasons, I'd left Emily out of our conversations about Evan. I guess I'd hoped to re-solve it all alone. To bring Beverly into my current situation, I would need to start from the beginning and confide in her completely. For the story to make sense, she would need all the details and I was too ashamed to admit them.

Beverly was logical, everything in her life made sense. Every decision she had ever made was the right one. Her life had always been linear, she never backslid, never cycled. Even the messiness of her early twenties was controlled within cer-tain boundaries, as if she knew she was just playing a temporary part. She never got any tattoos. Never, not even at the height of her recklessness, did she do anything that would leave a permanent mark. Now, as an adult, her life was well organized: Sunday morning Pilates; fermented foods; whatever book Oprah's Book Club was reading. She had never once posted a photo and deleted it minutes later, and she was always up-to-date with her cervical screenings. For this reason, her advice style was pragmatic to the point of being reductive. She might say things like, "Just dump him," as if it were ever that simple. I imagined her saying, "Let it go, you freak."

Ultimately, in moving to Melbourne, I was the one who had chosen to leave the comfort of our friendship in favor of the potential of change, and because of that I felt the need to behave as though the decision was not in vain; that I hadn't left the reliability and support of her presence just to spend my time crying alone in a black-mold-infested apartment.

Once again, my phone became a source of great pain. Its black-screened, idle presence taunted me. Its apathy made me resent it. At one point I even turned it off and back on again, thinking a message may have got lost from Evan to me. I googled *How does messaging work?* hoping I might discover that it was a flawed system, like a poorly run post office, which could explain that a message from him was probably on its way, just delayed and slightly behind schedule. But when I restarted my phone for the second time and no message revealed itself I was forced to accept my delusional state. I wanted to throw my phone off a cliff and watch it sail helplessly through the air, farther and farther away from me, but I knew if I saw the screen light up as it fell, I would dive after it.

In the afternoon I saw Maria from my kitchen window.

She was attempting to hang some sheets on the line but was having difficulty. I put my mug down in the sink, wiped my eyes, and ventured out to help her.

She eyed me with suspicion until I was close enough to be recognized, at which point her expression relaxed into a smile.

"I thought you might like some help," I said.

She thanked me just as a gust of wind whipped at the sheet, causing it to billow upward. I managed to grab hold of a corner and bring it back down to the line. On closer inspection the white sheets were decorated with small blue embroidered flowers.

"You know, these sorts of patterns are very popular at the moment," I said, indicating the floral embroidery. I'd recently seen a popular linen brand offer a similar sheet set for nearly five hundred dollars.

"My mother and I made these together," she explained, touching the stitching proudly. I realized that meant the sheets were decades old and likely very sentimental to her. I continued to adjust the sheet to make it fall evenly over the line, only now more carefully.

"They're beautiful," I said.

The sheets barely showed their age. I could feel the way they had been made with the intention of living a long life, and it made me sad that we no longer prioritized this type of care and quality. That we had lost it to mass production and meaninglessness. I wouldn't even know how to care for something, like a sheet set, in order to make it survive such an extended life cycle. I pegged a pillowcase to the line, feeling Maria's eyes on me.

"You look sad today," she stated.

"I am," I admitted.

"Do you miss your family?" she asked. I found it so endearingly incorrect that I nodded and said I did.

"It's hard to be far away from them," she said. "When I married my husband and migrated to Australia, I didn't want to leave my family. I cried and cried. I was very lonely until we ran the bakery and had our children; until I could speak English well. You never fully feel whole when you're away from your family."

I nodded in theoretical agreement, though my mind was imagining how terrifying it would have been for Maria to move to Australia alone with her older husband. She'd told me she'd been eighteen when they married.

"My grandson Alexander moved to London but he's moving back home soon," she continued. "In a few months, my granddaughter Zoe will have a baby and he'll become an uncle. He wants to be closer to the family."

"That's nice of him," I replied, wondering if this was some thinly veiled attempt to encourage me to move back to Perth. "Does that mean you'll become a great-grandmother?"

Maria smiled, deep lines etching into her face. "Yes," she said.

"Congratulations," I said, hanging the last pillowcase.

She beamed proudly as she collected her empty clothes basket.

Back in my apartment, I thought about time, about how it just keeps piling experiences, one on top of another, until one day you find yourself saying you're about to become a great-grandmother.

//

On Sunday night, after a whole day of silence, I sent Evan a message:

> *I invite you over for dinner and tell you that I'm going to make my specialty. You arrive and I serve you this.*

I sent a cursed image that had somehow appeared before my eyes via the mystery of the algorithm: a grotesque use of baked beans and gummy bears.

What would you do?

It seemed like an odd message to pin my hopes on, especially after Evan had instigated a Very Serious Break. But I thought that maybe if I kept things light by summoning an inside joke, he'd shake his head, smile at his phone, and then respond. But he didn't.

My *What would you do?* echoed out into the abyss. The answer was: Nothing. He'd do nothing. Worse, he'd ignore me.

//

Monday morning arrived and I had no intention of going to work. The environment at the office had soured since the performance reviews. The panic and anger had turned employees against each other; gossip was rampant and bitching was constant. I'd sent an email to the office to let them know I would be working from home because "my dog" was "sick." Luckily nobody seemed interested in hearing about the dog I'd never before mentioned. I received back a stream of sympathetic GIFs and teary-eyed emojis; there was an overuse of the words *doggo* and *pupper*, as everyone attempted to maneuver around the mystery of my dog's name.

Soph sent me a message:

Dog? Lol. Job interview?

Much needed self-care day, I replied.

I spent most of Monday lying on my back on the floor, which I had done a lot as a child when I would play a game where I imagined that I was dying. In this game I would lie perfectly still and slow my breathing down, until I was floating serenely in the limbo between awake and asleep. I was a slightly morbid child, fascinated by death, but I didn't actually want to die. It was more of an unconscious relaxation technique or something a therapist might call "self-soothing." On occasion, it was an intellectual exercise in imagining the effect my death would have on others. I would wonder whether my mum or dad would find me first; whether they would cry and hug me. I would imagine the emotions that were never shown pushed to the surface and channeled through their grief. I imagined their love meeting me with a force I'd never known but had vicariously identified in sad films.

On Monday afternoon, I found a copy of Emily's memorial invitation online. Strangely they had chosen to use a photo of her as a cherubic blond toddler. It looked like one of those shopping center photo shoots of the early nineties, with a marbled blue backdrop. Emily's mother, probably wearing a jacket with shoulder pads, would have been shaking a toy from behind the camera to get that dimpled smile in the shot. Emily looked like the perfect child and she grew up to become a perfect adult. When I was young, I rarely smiled in photos, instead I stared somberly into the camera, apparently burdened by the weight of my existence already. My mother often laughed about how serious I was.

"You hardly ever cried," she'd told me countless times, "even if you fell over, you'd get straight back up and keep going. You took care of yourself."

This was always meant to be a joke, or at times a compliment, but it was repeated and repeated until it embedded itself into familial folklore, and from then onward it became an expectation. My father, after discovering spirituality, began to claim that I was an "old soul." This seemed like a convenient way to bypass the fact that I'd been incapable of sharing my emotions; I was not a wise and ancient reincarnated being, I was just an emotionally constipated child.

Underneath the photo of Emily was her full name, *Emily Lucille Henderson,* followed by the dates of her birth and death separated by a dash. I looked at this small and unsuspecting symbol, burdened with the task of summarizing her entire existence so neatly and so crudely, and a sense of hopelessness descended on me at the thought that, no matter what happened in my life, it would one day be summarized by a dash. I was feeling melancholic.

By the evening, I was having communication withdrawals in the most literal sense. The fatigue; the anxiety; the nausea. I even had hallucinations, phantom limb experiences where I swore I felt my phone vibrate. On Tuesday morning my phone actually did vibrate, but it was only a reminder from my meditation app: *Now would be a good time to meditate.*

On Wednesday afternoon, I found myself sitting on my bed for nearly half an hour with a towel wrapped around me, my damp hair dripping onto my shoulders. My phone browser was open to the online booking portal for Shockwaves salon and I was contemplating a simple question illuminated on the screen before me.

Truthfully, I needed a haircut, and I lived in Brunswick, so going to a salon in Brunswick was a completely logical and reasonable thing to do. Specifically booking an appointment with Emily's brother, Adrien, was where the logic and reason became harder to justify. I didn't want to do it to spite Evan. In fact, I had absolutely no intention of Evan ever finding out. I wanted to meet Adrien because I wanted to know more about Emily; this intelligent, beautiful, funny, and caring image of perfection. Evan's words had painted a picture more intimidating than the one I'd created. Rather than laying my curiosity to rest, he'd succeeded in making Emily even more fascinating and elusive. I needed to know more, and with Evan already refusing to speak to me, I had nothing to lose.

The question was: *Would you like to book this appointment?*

The answer: *Yes, yes, I would.*

thirty-four

I watched Adrien through the mirror in front of me as he moved across the salon's concrete floor. He was more petite than I anticipated: fine-boned with impeccable posture. He wore a white singlet with loose pinstripe trousers and black sneakers; silver earrings swung from his ears, concealing themselves in his peroxide blond mullet, before revealing themselves again as he moved.

He hadn't greeted me yet. A receptionist with fluorescent orange hair told me, as she velcroed a black plastic poncho around my neck, that Adrien was running behind and would be with me soon.

Seeing him in real life had more of an effect on me than I thought it would. He was really pretty, which implied that I'd probably underestimated how pretty Emily had been. I was already in a fragile state—it had now been six days since Evan had severed contact—and I felt nauseous. Despite my inner turmoil, I noted that the salon was more welcoming than it looked from the outside. Through the windows it had the intimidating look of a sparsely decorated art gallery. But inside, the space's sharp edges were softened by welcoming smiles and the intermittent sound of laughter shared between stylist and client. I noticed, as I sat down, that everyone was well dressed, and I was glad that I'd risen to the occasion and changed out of the coffee-stained singlet I'd worn every day for the last week.

As I sat there, forced to face myself, I took a closer look at my reflection. Getting dressed properly had made a difference to my appearance, but the bags under my eyes were a dark purple hue that made me look somewhat unhinged. My eyes were glassy and dull, and my lips dry and pale. I looked like someone who would benefit from standing in the sun for twenty minutes.

I watched through the mirror as Adrien positioned a hair dryer over a client's head. He said something to her, smiling, and then he was walking toward me. I glanced away while I waited for him to reach my chair.

"Hi, Ana," he said, pulling up a small stool and sitting next to me.

I hadn't thought to use a fake name. It was obviously my plan to keep my identity as Evan's girlfriend—if I could still call myself that—a secret; now I wondered whether it had been a mistake to use my real name.

"I'm Adrien. Sorry to keep you waiting. It's been crazy in here today," he said, holding eye contact with me through the mirror.

After looking at so many photos of Emily, I had disregarded the hazel color of the eyes she and Adrien shared, assuming they were prosaic and un-noteworthy, like my own bland brown eyes. But now that he was so close, I saw that they were complex; a galaxy of rich gold and blue. In photos, they were reduced to a homogeneous dark green, like a pal-

228 / amy taylor

ette of paints mixed together. But in real life they were beautiful.

Despite my apprehension, Adrien's presence was overtly professional and comfortable. I began to relax into my role as client.

"Okay, so what are we doing today?" he asked.

I self-consciously combed my fingers through my shoulder-length hair and explained the cut I wanted, pointing to where it needed some layers and using my fingers as scissors to demonstrate. He nodded happily and offered suggestions here and there. I was an easy client.

While he washed my hair, I lay perfectly still with my eyes closed, trying not to dwell on the absurd reality that Emily's twin brother was massaging conditioner into my head.

Afterward Adrien wrapped my hair in a towel, and I walked back to my seat. He then removed the towel, took a comb out of his black leather tool belt and began to hunt for my middle parting.

"Have you got much planned for the weekend?" he asked.

"Not really," I answered. "I'm new to Melbourne so I'm still figuring it all out."

"Oh—where are you from?"

"Perth."

"I swear half the people I know are from Perth. It's like, Perth, are you okay?" He laughed. "What made you move?"

I saw it then, the perfect segue, as if all the neural pathways and synapses in my brain were working together efficiently for the first time ever.

"Well, actually, someone close to me passed away," I said, shocking myself by delivering the lie perfectly, employing a subtly solemn tone while alluding to a subdued echo of grief in my averted eyes.

"Oh my god, I'm so sorry." He'd paused cutting, making eye contact with me in the mirror with one hand placed on his chest. "I'm so sorry."

"No, no, it's okay. But that's why I moved. I just had to get out of Perth."

I made a bet then that if I stayed silent Adrien might swing the conversation to himself. He'd gone back to cutting my hair, his face directly behind my head so that I could no longer see him in the mirror.

"I know exactly what you mean." His tone had shifted to something quieter and more serious. "I actually lost my sister just over a year ago."

I couldn't believe that the conversation had arrived at the topic of Emily and had required only the smallest tug of a string. I implored myself to remain calm.

"That's horrible. I'm sorry to hear that."

"So, yeah." He sighed and shook his head. "I understand that feeling of needing to leave. It's a lot better for me now, but it was so hard at first when I kept running into people who knew her. I really considered moving to Sydney at one point."

"That makes sense," I said. "I'm sure Emily had lots of friends."

Her name slipped out of my mouth and my heart lurched after it. He hadn't mentioned her name. I felt color rush to my cheeks. I couldn't see his face. An excruciating pause followed.

"Yeah," he continued, sliding the stool round to my left side without taking his eyes off my hair. He hadn't seemed to notice my slip. "She had so many friends. It was touching to see how many people loved her, but when they all started reaching out to me I found it really tough. I don't mean to be dramatic, but it was almost like I couldn't go out anywhere without bumping into someone."

He paused to wipe his scissors on the towel he'd placed over his knee. I felt uncomfortably warm. There was little airflow under the plastic poncho. I shifted my shoulders slightly to air out my damp armpits.

"I even ran into her ex twice," he explained darkly.

The evasive prefix of "ex" dangled in the air like a vaguely placed modifier. Had there been someone else? Some dislikable ex prior to Evan?

"You didn't like him?" I queried smoothly, surprising myself once again.

He leaned back a little to assess my hair, narrowing his eyes before running the comb through it again.

"She called back." The receptionist with the orange hair interrupted us, a phone pressed to her chest. Adrien swiveled to face her. "She can come in tomorrow at eleven or three?"

"Okay, tell her to come in at three," he answered.

She nodded and walked away, and he swiveled back to me, recommencing his combing. "Sorry, what was I saying?"

I was unsure how to remind him without sounding overly invested.

"Oh yeah, her ex, Evan. Well, they broke up and Em was devastated."

"Oh," I said, the sound tumbling out of my mouth.

It was an appropriate response for an impersonal outsider to make, although this time the delivery was owed to the fact that my mind was whirring rapidly. I stared blank-faced at Adrien, like a slowly buffering video, and he continued on.

"We spent a lot of time with each other after they broke up and now I'm really glad we had that time together because a couple of months later we lost her." He paused for a moment, having reached an emotional escalation that he clearly wanted to halt.

I gave him a moment, feeling like I needed one myself. All of this new information was jarring. It was as if we were discussing someone I didn't know, like I truly was listening to my hairdresser overshare about his sister's ex-partner—someone I couldn't care less about—rather than a man who, until recently, had a drawer full of my things at his apartment.

He rolled the stool around and focused on the back of my head.

"Anyway, so yeah, it was pretty tempting to move away and avoid everyone." He went on, snipping at the ends of my hair. "I can see why you made that decision."

"So why didn't you end up moving?" I asked.

"Well, I waited for a couple of months and the grief eased a little. Eventually I didn't feel like I had to run away anymore. I also met Marcus, my partner, and I couldn't ask him to move. He's been really supportive. Now I'm glad I didn't leave. I'm still working through it, but I'm starting to find that I like being reminded of her now." He had paused cutting and was looking at me through the mirror.

"Sorry," he said, his tone shifting, as if he was waking from a spell. "I feel like I've just been talking your ear off, how embarrassing. Enough about me." He flapped a hand in the air to swat the conversation away. "So, where are you living?"

//

Later, that night, I sat on the couch and opened Emily's account. I'd come to know it so well that I could probably recite the order of at least the first twenty posts, many of which were of Evan. It now struck me as odd that she hadn't deleted those photos, given the breakup. Adrien said that Emily had been "devastated" and this seemed to suggest that Evan had ended the relationship. This was a notion I wanted to embrace; to frolic and roll around in a field of daisies with. I'd falsely created a narrative in which Evan was unable to give me the entirety of himself because he was still grieving the loss of the love of his life, but the prefix of "ex" alluded to a distance, a fading of feelings into tepidness and an expanse of unoccupied space. I could now get rid of that narrative and begin anew with a different one, one in which Evan's girl-friend hadn't died, his ex-girlfriend had.

The very last photo Emily had ever posted was of Evan and her. Evan looked dotingly down at Emily and she smiled back at him with dimples creasing her cheeks. Emily had posted it almost exactly two months before the accident. I had noticed that Emily posted relatively regularly—the photos on her grid were separated by dates roughly a fortnight apart—and so it was surprising that this photo was not followed by any others, even though she'd lived for nearly eight weeks after. I wondered if she'd taken a break from social media, not an unusual thing to do. This would also explain why she'd left the images of Evan up, and how they came to remain there permanently. And how I, an outsider, had taken their presence to mean something they didn't.

I'd made a grave error in blindly building on the foundation of my own conjectures and insecurities. All the logic I'd once had was now slinking like a cat back through a hole in a fence and out of sight. This whole mess was my fault, I knew that, but the layer I now added to my condemnation was this: I'd sabotaged my relationship with Evan for absolutely no reason. I'd done exactly what I'd pledged not to do when I'd originally decided to avoid searching for him online; I'd suffocated our relationship with my preconceived notions.

I desperately wanted to speak to Evan, so I began drafting a message. I knew that if he refused to open the message, it would still light up his home screen, and even if he pretended he hadn't, I knew he would see it. The only problem was I had no idea what to say; I'd apologized already and it hadn't been enough. Offering up another limp "I'm sorry" was unlikely to draw out a reaction.

I imagined Evan in his kitchen, going about his evening— another evening of ignoring me—without the faintest idea of what had transpired in my life over the last few days: much crying, many revelations, a haircut.

Suddenly the animated ellipsis appeared at the bottom of our message thread. Evan was typing a message to me. I quickly left the thread to be sure that he wouldn't find me lingering there and waited, watching the three dots dance underneath his name. I breathed shallow and fast, my heart palpitating. Then the ellipsis disappeared. I held my breath and waited, expecting a message to come through, but nothing arrived. He'd changed his mind.

chapter thirty-five

"You look like shit," Soph said as I sat down across the table from her.

"Thanks, I got my hair cut," I replied.

"No, your hair looks phenomenal. But honestly . . ." Concern arrived suddenly on her face. "You look sick. Are you actually sick?"

After I'd informed everyone that I was working from home for the seventh workday in a row, Soph had messaged me to ask if I wanted to get a drink that evening. We'd met at a bar on Lygon Street; a long, thin space with small separate rooms like a house. There was a Nick Cave album playing, his voice crooning through the rooms like a forlorn phantom.

I dismissed her concern. "I'm fine. I've just got low iron." The perfect excuse for someone who wants to be perpetually tired and pallid in peace. A man wearing heavy-sounding boots interrupted us to take my order. I ordered a glass of wine he recommended and felt Soph's eyes lingering on me, taking in the way I wore my mental instability plainly in my harassed appearance. The bartender left, his boots clunking loudly against the wooden floor, and I looked back at Soph.

"Ooh, table service," I said, aiming to steer the conversation away from any remaining solicitude.

She ignored me. "Honestly, are you okay?"

"I'm okay—really. I just needed a break from the office."

Her relief was palpable. She had done her duty as concerned friend and was now more than happy to move on to less vulnerable topics.

"Tell me about it. It's like the *Titanic* in there," she said, shaking her head. "I walked into the bathroom the other day and saw Ash emptying the last of the free tampons into her handbag."

She reached for her wineglass and, as she took a sip, her phone vibrated on the table. She glanced at it, and then— clearly deeming the message more interesting than our conversation—picked it up. I wondered, as I watched her, whether I should tell her about the situation between Evan and me. I'd spent hours poring over the details, like a detective who'd let a case get too personal; obsessing over gaps in the story and refusing to let go of dead-end leads.

I'd dissected every conversation I could recall having with Evan, now viewing the details under the transformative beacon of new context, only to find any new assessment pointless given that he was still ignoring me. I understood that, by having only the voices of my own limited mind to converse with, I had likely created a distorted perception. What I wanted was to speak my thoughts out loud to someone else, to be awarded the clarity I knew that could offer. I imagined Soph could be the right person for this. She would not dispense advice from the heights of her loving, stable, and well-adjusted relationship, like Beverly would; Soph was in the trenches with me. I was certain she would laugh and sympathize with me in equal measure, to both acknowledge my mood and lighten it.

She might even have some suggestions about how I could navigate through the mess, how I might win back Evan's favor. She could support me; that is, after all, what friends are for, and I'd done the same for her countless times. How many times had I helped her analyze the messages she was sure had been ciphered? How many times had I willingly stepped into her fantasy, helping to brace her feelings by going along with the idea that some disinterested man was capable of cryptic restraint, or double meaning? Surely, in my time of need she would come to my aid.

I settled the matter in my mind. I would fill her in entirely. I would only have to do it once and then she could be my constant confidante. The bartender returned with my glass of wine. I drank half of it in one prolonged sip and then I began.

"So I—"

"Oh my god, look at this guy I matched with," she interrupted. "He's been messaging me." She was holding her phone out to show me a video of an incredibly veiny man lifting a large dumbbell.

"He's a personal trainer. We're meeting up on Saturday night. He told me to message him if I'm bored, but I told him I have plans so he doesn't think I'm just sitting at home waiting. *Honestly,* Ana"—she grabbed ahold of my arm for dramatic effect—"I might die if I don't get to sleep with him."

I nodded and began responding appropriately, but in my mind I had already started the lonely journey back to my couch.

//

Later I walked home from the bar, a decision that felt more like a rebellion against my fears than an act of bravery, because the self-loathing I was currently wallowing in had removed any desire for self-protection. I genuinely didn't care anymore.

I turned off Lygon Street, leaving behind the other groups of pedestrians and the rattling trams, and began walking down a darker and quieter residential street.

I looked inquisitively through any obliging and warmly lit front window, most of which belonged to share houses where privacy was viewed as inconsequential. What I saw was an endless repetition of the same basic bedroom: an overfilled clothes rail, an unmade bed, and a dusty succulent on the mantel next to a framed print or mirror.

When I accidentally made intimate eye contact with a woman who was using her laptop in bed, I returned, shame-faced, to focusing on the footpath.

It was then that I saw a man ahead of me. His presence reminded me of the man who had followed me on my morning run. I found myself walking faster and closing the distance between myself and the man. I wanted to know how it felt to be the one who dealt fear rather than experienced it. The man paid no attention to me as I quickened my pace. When I was close enough that my footsteps alerted him, he turned and glanced over his shoulder at me before turning back indifferently, clearly deciding that I wasn't a concern to him.

In the same way the runner had, I continued to gain on the man, all the while watching to see if he would react at all, but he didn't seem to care. I coughed as if to alert him, and he then took a sharp turn, crossing over to the other side of the street. I guessed that he too felt the weight of the situation and maybe he saw himself as the one required to alleviate it, not because he was fearful of me but because he didn't want to find himself as an unwitting predator. I followed him across the street, just as the runner had done to me. The man glanced back then, the streetlight illuminating his face. His brow was curved in confusion, or maybe annoyance. I continued to tail him, even as he subtly picked up his pace. Soon, I was near enough to him that our bodies radiated and prickled with the awkwardness of our proximity. I could even smell his cologne: leather and vanilla; abrasive and cloying. Unexpectedly he peeled away, placing his foot against a letter box and making an unconvincing show of fixing his shoelace.

He side-eyed me as I walked past. "What the hell?" I heard him mumble.

CHAPTER Thirty-Six

Lauren exhaled smoke out of the corner of her mouth and squinted in the bright sunlight.

"I don't know, I think I really like him," she said, shifting on the bench and looking out across the park, where a group of dog owners congregated, chatting among themselves and tossing the occasional ball. She was talking about Josh, who she'd been sleeping with ever since New Year's Eve nearly a month ago. When I'd arranged to meet with Lauren I'd expected her to already know about the current situation between Evan and me, but when she didn't mention it, I was caught off guard. Was she aware but pretending otherwise? Or had Evan genuinely not told her? I tried to plan how to raise the subject.

"You say that like there's something wrong with liking him," I said.

She glanced at me and released an exasperated laugh. "Sometimes I feel like I have to justify being attracted to a man," she said, dropping her cigarette and crushing it with her boot. "I mean, the sex is good, but I'm kind of disgusted by him."

I'd read an article about this recently; the increasing dismay many felt in response to the current condition of straight relationships and the desire to disidentify from heterosexuality. I'd found the article fascinating and for a moment I considered mentioning it, until I remembered it would be unfair to steer the conversation toward a broader, more societal perspective, when Lauren clearly wanted to air her specific and personal grievances.

"Disgusted?" I asked.

"Okay, well for a start he made this big thing out of offering to cook me dinner. Then, when I get there he's microwaving a jar of pasta sauce, which he then poured over pasta that must have sat in boiling water for about half an hour. It was bad."

I found the idea of someone serving this to Lauren, a woman who treated the food she ate the same way she treated the clothing she wore—as an expression of who she was—unfortunate.

"I just felt really bitter and resentful about it. I had him over to mine the weekend before. I made slow-cooked beef tacos, I even sourced dried guajillo chiles online for the salsa de cacahuate and then he, in return, offers me jar sauce and overcooked packet pasta. I just wonder if I'm expecting too much. Or am I just giving too much, you know? Am I being unreasonable by expecting my effort to be repaid?

"And—the thing is he's really sweet," she continued. "He's just sort of young. But he's not actually young—he's thirty. It just sometimes feels like he's twenty-two or something. Like he stopped evolving in his early twenties."

"So what are you going to do?"

She shrugged. "Keep sleeping with him. Teach him what al dente means. Train him with positive reinforcement. Mold him into an evolved partner."

"That sounds like a lot of labor."

"Then he will inevitably stop responding to me."

"Well, at least the next girl he invites over for dinner won't have to eat overcooked pasta and jar sauce," I joked, hoping to appeal to her allegiance to the sisterhood.

"Yeah, well, you're welcome, next girl, whoever you are."

She sighed, slumping in her seat and looking down at her boots.

"Dating at this age sucks," she whined. "I scroll through and think: I wonder what's wrong with you? Can't wait to find out!"

I frowned as she spoke.

"I'm only twenty-nine! I shouldn't feel like this."

I wanted to walk her back from this ledge and console her, but I knew that any reassuring words would seem condescending and disingenuous. I knew what it was like; dating was like being exposed to an endless conveyor belt of incompatible partners. The vigilant filtering was exhausting, and on bad days it was soul destroying. But given the lack of options, it was also a necessary evil, a bucking proverbial horse that you must climb back on time and time again. And, anyway, a relationship was not an island of respite from the rough seas of singledom; it was a challenge all of its own. It was the intensely exposing, at times mortifying, experience of letting someone closer and closer to your most vulnerable parts, while you hoped they weren't secretly planning to hurt you. What was the point in trying to reassure Lauren that things would get easier, if I didn't even believe it? We fell into silence as we watched a golden retriever return a tennis ball to its owner.

"Did you and George ever have a thing?" I asked.

She turned to face me, her eyes narrowed. "Did Evan tell you?"

"No, I swear he didn't tell me anything. I just picked up on something. There's tension between you two."

Her eyes searched me for a sign that I was being genuine. She must have found it. "Yes, George and I have hooked up a few times," she admitted, before leaping to clarify. "But not lately, obviously. Not since Hannah."

"I knew it!" I said. "Did you ever date?"

"No." Lauren scoffed. "It would never work out. George is only interested in the idea of me being secretly in love with him. That's our whole thing. That's the *allure* of it."

I was taken aback by the sudden display of acuity and the small glimpse of heartache she had shown me. I thought about the way the two of them so easily spiraled into bickering and saw it now as the obvious and unavoidable result of their suppressed romantic feelings. I didn't entirely believe that George was only interested in the flattery that would come from Lauren's admission of feelings. I'd glanced at him a handful of times as he watched her from across a table; his expression seemed to indicate deeper, more complex feelings beneath.

"I think he genuinely has feelings for you," I said.

"Maybe." Her indifference signaled that she'd long ago accepted their fate.

"Do you still have feelings for him?"

"Yeah," she admitted. "But I know him so well. If we

admitted our feelings and started dating, we'd just become a couple like any other couple. The mystery would be gone; the game would be over. Eventually he would lose interest and then I'd lose my best friend."

I was silent for a moment as I considered what she'd said. "The alternative being that you both say nothing and continue to hide your feelings forever?"

Lauren frowned, squinting into the distance. "I suppose."

I imagined this dynamic persisting for years to come. One of them suddenly finding themselves single and attempting, in a moment of loneliness, to step over the line and demand a reciprocation of feelings from the other—who at that inconvenient moment was comfortable and unwilling to make the necessary sacrifices. Vice versa, forever.

How would they cope when the other got married, or moved across the world for someone else, or had a child? How would they feel when the doors that could lead to them being together began to permanently shut? Would it not be better if one of them just admitted the way they felt, imploded the whole thing, and broke the cycle sooner rather than later?

"Don't you want to try it though? Wouldn't it just be easier to say how you feel and clear the air? George is smart enough to understand the nuance of it. I don't think it necessarily means you can't be friends again if it doesn't work."

"I'm too scared to do that," she concluded. "I just can't."

Her face took on a pensive expression and I dropped the subject.

"How are you and Evan going?" she asked finally.

"Not good," I said. "He didn't tell you?"

"Tell me what?"

"Well, I think we broke up," I admitted.

A vision of Evan telling me he wanted to be alone replayed and my heart lurched as if it were happening again in real time.

"What? Why? What happened?"

"It had something to do with Emily. He said he needs to be alone and I haven't heard from him since."

Lauren looked concerned. "I would offer to talk to him for you," she said, "but he has, historically speaking, had a real issue with me getting involved."

I wondered if this was referring to some other event between Emily and Evan, where Lauren had conducted an intercession and it hadn't gone well.

"That's okay, I don't think it would help. In fact, I don't think he'd like that I'm talking to you about him at all. Can I ask you something though?"

"Yeah, of course."

"What happened between him and Emily? Why did they break up?"

"He hasn't told you what happened?" She seemed surprised.

I shook my head.

"To be honest, the whole thing was pretty fucked-up. I can kind of see why he might have avoided the subject."

"What happened?" I asked again.

"Well, the first thing that happened was Evan told me he wanted to break up with Emily. I think they'd been together for about four years by then. He said he hadn't been in love with her for a while, but it was complicated, given they lived together.

"So, I counseled him about it. I tried to encourage him to just start a conversation with her and tell her how he was feeling. I'm sure you've figured this out by now, but Evan finds it hard to communicate on a deep level about how he feels."

I nodded.

"But I guess the idea of having that conversation was just too much for him, he couldn't do it. He became a bit self-destructive after that. In the end, months after our conversation, the whole thing blew up when Emily found out he was cheating on her."

"He cheated on her?"

"Yeah, with her best friend."

I stared at Lauren with my mouth open, the realizations falling too quickly for me to catch and make full use of them.

"He cheated on Emily with Nadia?"

"Oh, you know her?" Lauren asked.

"I've met her a few times."

"Yep, it was Nadia. Look, I love Evan with all of my heart, but it really wasn't his finest hour. The whole thing was a mess."

I imagined Evan and Nadia together and then quickly discarded the painful image. I recalled Nadia in the bathroom at the gallery when she asked about Evan; the way her eyes narrowed when we spoke about Emily. It was obvious now that I wasn't being sensitive when I felt she didn't like me. I'd assumed it was because of the complicated feelings she'd had watching me move into the space Emily had previously occupied. But now I wondered if her strange behavior was due to her feelings for Evan.

"How did Emily find out?" I asked. "Did they tell her?"

"No, I think she went through his messages. Anyway, she moved out of the apartment and the relationship was over. She was devastated, understandably. Then a few months later the accident happened."

Lauren blanched at the words, or maybe the memories, or both, and I realized that in the process of extracting information I'd selfishly forgotten that Lauren had lost a friend.

"You must miss her," I said.

"I do," she replied candidly. "Although now that we're talking about her I'm realizing that I don't really think about her much anymore. It's really sad that people are just slowly forgotten."

She paused for a moment before continuing. "So then after all of Emily's friends found out about Evan and Nadia they hated him, and when the accident happened before any of it was resolved, it was sort of set in stone, you know, that Evan was this monster who was never going to be forgiven. He was too anxious to even go to the funeral." She shook her head. "There was this incident at the pub a couple of weeks after the accident, one of Emily's friends, Hamish, just walked up to Evan and punched him. Right there in front of everyone."

"*Punched him?*"

"Yeah, nearly broke his nose. His anxiety got really bad after that and we had to stop going to certain places."

I thought about Evan's reaction after Josh's New Year's Eve party, his frustration at me for not backing down from trying to help that woman; his fear of an altercation. I thought about the list of date venues he'd created and saw it now as an attempt to be in control of where we went. I recalled his surprise when we bumped into Nadia.

"Wait, so he and Nadia never ended up dating?" I asked.

"No," she said. "The fallout was bad. To be honest, I think Evan was just being destructive and acting out. I don't think there were deep feelings involved."

"He still talks to Nadia," I said.

"Really?"

"Yeah."

"That makes sense, I guess. She's probably the only person who knew Emily well and would still talk to him. He never talked about Emily with you?"

"No," I admitted. "I tried to talk about her a couple of times, but he would just shut down. One time he basically kicked me out of his apartment."

Lauren sighed. "There are still a lot of unresolved emotions there. I think he still feels really guilty." She paused contemplatively. "Maybe he thinks that if you knew what had happened you would look at him differently."

"I wouldn't though."

She opened her tote bag and began searching for her tobacco pouch.

"Well, I guess he doesn't know that," she concluded.

//

That afternoon, at exactly 4:27 P.M., while I was doing last night's dishes and listening to a podcast about the damaging effects of blue light, the drought ended. The clouds parted and a message fell from the sky:

> *What if I apologized for being a*
> *complete dickhead, told you I*
> *missed you and asked you to come*
> *over. What would you do?*

It was so unexpected that I actually gasped. I stood in my kitchen and stared at the message in disbelief. It was as if I could feel the dopamine as it flooded my system, covering my every thought in the protective blanket of optimism and hope.

I sat down on the couch, typing, deleting, typing again. I crafted a whole paragraph that told him how sorry I was for prying and being insensitive. Then I subdued the impulse, deleting it all and replying:

Be there at 6:30 x

thirty-seven

After I responded to Evan, I set to concealing any evidence from the last two weeks of self-neglect, scrubbing and then moisturizing my body ritualistically as if it was about to be offered up as a sacrifice. I washed my hair and put on makeup, all the while practically intoxicated with excitement and anticipation. As my hair dried, I coaxed it into neat curls by twirling it with my fingers like Adrien had taught me and stood before my wardrobe to choose what to wear. I decided on a short white dress that was shirred and tight around my waist; milkmaid chic. I packed a bag, pulled my boots on, and left my apartment.

I crossed the train tracks under a blushing sky. The air was still and warm, reminding me of Perth and of balmy evenings spent with my ex in the courtyard of our favorite bar, and of our tipsy journeys home; the air perfumed by the manicured and flower-heavy front yards of Mount Lawley. Those were good memories, and I was learning to view them in isolation, protecting them, as Beverly had suggested, from being tainted by the bad memories that came later. At the time I'd been happy, and Beverly was right, I shouldn't let that happiness be recast as something else.

I stopped at a wine store on Sydney Road to buy a bottle. I chose something orange and organic. It cost forty dollars; I felt like celebrating. The staff member who helped me decipher the wall of options asked me what the occasion was and I told him that it was a celebration because I had not been broken up with after all. He looked at me strangely, but I didn't care. Nothing mattered because Evan and I were going to be fine. I now understood why there were parts of him that he wouldn't reveal to me: He was ashamed. Lauren was right that Evan was most likely concealing these truths because he didn't want me to see him differently or think of him as an irredeemably terrible human; the way he might think of himself.

Yes, Evan had chosen to do something widely considered to be morally wrong, something that had hurt another person, but I didn't think he was a monster. He was just another flawed human being living in a sometimes lonely and scary world. He'd made a mistake; he didn't deserve to be condemned forever.

The way forward was clear. I would wait for Evan to tell me what happened in his own words, when he was ready; the wait would pose no issues for me, now that I knew that any delay was not due to his enduring and preponderant love for Emily. Then, eventually, with it all out in the open, I would help to absolve him of the guilt and shame that became fixed in the wake of Emily's death.

But when Evan opened his door for me, he did so without smiling. A return to normalcy was obviously not going to happen without some effort.

"Hi," he said, his face composed. He was wearing his running clothes, his cheeks still harboring a fading flush.

"Hi," I replied, casting a smile out like an olive branch, only for it to be ignored. I quickly rearranged my face into a more penitent expression.

Evan didn't move to hug me. Instead, he walked to the couch and sat down. I placed the wine and my bag on the table and followed his lead.

"I'm sorry about what happened after the gallery opening," he began, his eyes directed downward, our bodies tense. "I really didn't mean to react like that. I shouldn't have said all those things and I shouldn't have made you leave—" He paused, pulling at some fluff on the arm of the couch and flicking it away. "I don't know if you've noticed but it's not easy for me to talk about Emily."

He gave me a sheepish glance, his lips curling in on each other and his mouth pulling into a tight smile.

"Now that you say that, I had noticed," I said, offering a small smile back. "I owe you an apology too. I never wanted to force you to talk about what happened. I was trying to show you that you *could* talk about it. I wanted to be supportive."

"It's okay, I know you were trying to help. I just felt like whenever you tried to talk to me about her, it wasn't the right time. I didn't know how to explain that." He paused, swallowing. "It was easier for me to stop the conversation."

"I understand," I said. "But I found it confusing, it felt like you were holding me at arm's length, or retreating somewhere. I didn't really know how you felt about me. It's been hard for me to be constantly guessing."

"You don't know how I felt?" he replied, raising his eyebrows in disbelief. "Ana, I've *never* known how you feel about me. You aren't exactly an open book." He paused as if deliberating on whether to make another admission. "Sometimes I wouldn't message you for days because I wanted to see if you would message me first for once. It was petty of me, I know, but I didn't know how else to get an indication that you were as serious about me as I was about you."

"You were waiting for me to message you?"

"Yeah."

"I thought that was you pulling away. I took that as a signal that you needed space from me."

"Not at all. Honestly, I was hoping you'd say you missed me or something. I don't know." He rubbed his hand over his face as if embarrassed by this admission. "I'd wait for as long as I could and then I'd give in and message you and everything would return to normal. It felt like I was always the one who instigated everything, like I was far more interested in you than you were in me."

It seemed preposterous to me that Evan would have no idea how I felt. In my mind, it seemed necessary that I put restraints on my actions to conceal the strength of my emotions. I was afraid that if he glimpsed the depths of my feelings, he would be repulsed and would either flee or become drunk with power and cruel.

I went back in my memory, attempting to place the lens of Evan's experience over my own. What evidence did he have to draw from? The many times I almost messaged him. The time I almost said "I love you" but decided not to. Unless he was a clairvoyant, the information at his disposal was limited. He was right; I always waited for him to message me. I hung back and let him make plans. Based on my actions alone, how could he not conclude that my interest in him was vague at best?

"So, we've been sitting around unsure of how each other felt this entire time," I said.

"I guess so."

"That was silly of us."

Evan released a halfhearted and weary huff of laughter.

"I thought maybe you needed things to move slowly because of—" I hesitated. "Well, because you'd lost Emily so recently. You wouldn't talk about her, so I assumed that you were still grieving. I guess I read it all wrong."

Evan nodded, his eyes cast down at his shoes.

"I should have been more up-front with you," he admitted. "Emily and I broke up a while before the accident happened and yeah, she meant a lot to me for almost five years of my life and I did love her, but we were acquaintances at best when she died."

I watched him with interest as he explained. It was strangely powerful to be in the unique place of having all of the facts and being able to see which he was willing to divulge. Prior to this I would hang on to every word he shared, but now it was as if I could see the workings of his mind reflected in his expression, in the way he paused and the words he chose to avoid.

"I was going through a really rough time and then you lined up next to me at that bar and, I don't know, you were talking about robots or something." He smiled. "All I could remember thinking was that everything was instantly better. I have so much fun with you, and I liked that you didn't know about everything that had happened. I could just be myself, external to all that. You were an outsider, but I mean that in the best way."

His words shifted the conversation's attention onto me, and I felt as if I were wincing in the spotlight.

"I wanted to keep things the way they were for a while. Before we had to, you know, start unpacking each other's baggage." He glanced at me, casually rubbing a finger over his bottom lip. Then he dropped his hand and a slow smile spread across his face. "I think I'm in love with you, Ana, in case that needs to be clarified."

I grinned back at him, giving in to a flight of affection. "I think I'm in love with you too, just so we're both clear," I said.

Still smiling, he shook his head, as if at our shared stupidity for having ever argued in the first place. Then he leaned in and kissed me.

"Let's just put this all behind us?" he suggested a moment later.

I nodded in mute agreement and he pulled me on top of him.

I kissed him back eagerly, tugging at his T-shirt and the waistband of his shorts. Then he was behind me, my body pressed against the arm of the couch. His movements just a little too forceful to feel good. I acquiesced, enacting an exaggerated enjoyment and regressing back to performance, as if to confirm to him that he'd made the right decision in allowing me back into his life; as if to reward him for explaining his feelings. I tried to ignore the fact that Evan had never before been so rough and absent, but the fact asserted itself with each thrust.

Afterward, Evan went to have a shower and I followed him to the bathroom, imagining that I would join him like I usually did, but as he stepped into the shower, he glanced at me out of the corner of his eye before pulling the shower curtain shut. The gesture was heavy with poetic symbolism, which seemed to say I was not invited to join him.

I returned to the couch and sat motionless, staring at the coffee table. I was trying to figure out why I didn't feel only relief and joy. I'd been given exactly what I wanted: his return, an admission of love. But there was a feeling, originating from somewhere deep in my body, a somatic sense of unease; an inexplicable wariness. I'd been given what I wanted, but on receiving it I had discovered how fragile it was. How much sacrifice the responsibility of its ownership entailed.

Evan's phone rattled and lit up on the coffee table. I glanced at it, seeing the blue Cefalù sky and ocean broken in the middle by two messages from Nadia:

Can I come see you? Please?

I want to talk about this.

I frowned as another message arrived: *I really don't want this to be over.*

A sense of dread, like a tide, began to rise within me. I leaned forward and picked the phone up, opening the message thread.

Immediately I was confronted by clear evidence that Nadia and Evan talked often. I scrolled backward through previous hours and then days. I found bland messages like *How's your day going?* jarringly interspersed with sexting, *I'm so wet;* the context of the conversations lost in the speed at which I was reading. I froze when I came across a naked image of Nadia from a fortnight ago, before Evan had told me he needed a break. In the photo Nadia posed provocatively in a mirror, her nipples small and hard; *I wish you were here right now*, Evan had replied.

I wanted to be the one going home with you tonight, she'd sent him after the gallery opening.

Soon x, he'd replied.

My stomach climbed toward my throat, and I moved one hand to my mouth as my eyes jumped feverishly around the screen. I watched message after message slide downward, the evidence mounting as time reached further back. He was sleeping with Nadia again and he had been since the anniversary of Emily's death in November.

The echoey click of Evan's shampoo bottle reminded me that he would soon finish in the shower and return, probably to ask what I felt like eating for dinner. I knew that there wasn't a reality in which I would be able to pretend I hadn't seen those messages. I had no desire to confront him either. He would not be able to explain the messages away; they were conclusive. I had only one desire: to leave his apartment and never speak to him again.

The sound of the shower being turned off triggered me to action. I left Evan's phone open to the message thread with Nadia, so he would see exactly what I had seen. Then I collected my bag. I heard the ring of Evan pulling a towel off the rack as I shut the door behind me.

I cried the entire walk home.

thirty-eight

"There is only one thing that determines who you bring into your life and that's your vibrations," the podcast host explained, as I peered over the edge of the bath and attempted to locate my phone. "When you vibrate at a low frequency you will continue to attract partners who treat you poorly, but it doesn't have to be like that, in fact when we—"

The sound cut out when my fingers finally connected with the pause button after much blind tapping. My tolerance had deserted me. I'd grown increasingly suspicious that the word "vibration" was just a label placed on nothing in an attempt to make it more tangible. Once it was named, I was supposed to believe that this nothingness could be used as a mechanism to control the world around me, to control how others treated me. A pointless exercise.

A week had passed since I'd discovered Evan had been sleeping with Nadia. After I left his apartment, he tried to call me twice; after that he sent me a message:

Where'd you go?

As if he hadn't understood what had happened. As if he hadn't been able to immediately figure it out. For days afterward he tried to call me. Messages arrived, confused at first:

I don't understand.

What happened?

I didn't buy it. I had no interest in his gambit, so instead I left him to continue addressing the void. Soon the messages began to plead:

Please can we talk?

I need to see you

Then, briefly, they became self-righteous:

This is really unfair of you Ana

I can't believe you won't even talk to me

Finally, by day four they turned bitter and resigned:

*You're seriously just going to ignore
me forever?*

This is bullshit

I hadn't received anything else since then.

When I got back to my apartment after leaving Evan's, I texted Beverly, *turns out Evan was sleeping with someone else. Just gonna be single forever xoxox.*

She immediately called me. "What an absolute *Barry*," she hissed.

After I told her what happened she told me she was buying flights.

"No—please," I interjected. I've always worked through

such moments of raw heartbreak best when I can receive support on my own terms. I just wanted to get through the messy part alone, to ugly cry on my couch in peace.

"Come over in a couple of weeks when I'm not so sad and boring," I beseeched her.

She agreed to come over as soon as I was ready, and I agreed to keep her informed. Since then she'd sent me a steady stream of memes and videos, and I'd kept her updated on my progress by sending her a photo of the first proper meal I made myself, a chickpea curry, to which she responded:

Proud of you xoxo

//

Predictably, I had found myself grappling with the post-breakup allure of transformation; the familiar sense that the conclusion of one chapter presented the opportunity to re-emerge into the next as someone different, better; the elusive version of myself who was perfect and therefore successful and loved unconditionally and never hurt. The temptation of change was never stronger than in the wake of a breakup, when rejection seemed to confirm that who I was required considerable revising. This delusion, I now understood, was further fed by concepts like "vibrations," which asked that I cast a critical eye over myself so thoroughly that I might find room for improvement even in my body's electromagnetic field.

When my ex broke up with me, I'd dived headlong into the comfort of transformation and clung to my desire to remove the parts of me that had been tainted by his rejection. This desire led me straight to the self-help shelves of every bookstore in my vicinity. I allowed myself to be drawn to theories that served my delusion; the more ambiguous the better. I wanted the kind of transformation that would be easy and fast. I wanted to read a sentence of wisdom that would dissolve my neuroses, or lift me above them so I could float painlessly. Of course, no profound but easily attainable transformation materialized.

When, as anticipated, I began to look for faults within myself that would explain Evan's behavior, I made a conscious effort to stop myself. Instead I attempted to acknowledge that what had transpired had very little to do with me. Nadia had been around before me and she and Evan had history, which gave me the sense that, rather than being deficient in some way, I'd just unwittingly become entangled in something larger than myself; something predestined. I was a casualty. An unfortunate obstacle between two destructive forces, just like Emily had been. I was able to think about Emily differently now. I saw clearly that she had represented more than Evan's ex. In some ways she represented the version of myself I envisioned when I imagined myself free of all my flaws: a person who was loved unconditionally. That was, of course, an image I'd built based on a foundation of assumptions. It was not the whole truth. I'd held Emily up as this idea of perfection, and yet, she'd also been rejected and hurt. That was evidence enough for me to conclude that none of this was personal. There was nothing, no carving of the self, no removal of perceived flaws, that would truly protect me from rejection.

I resolved, there in the bathtub, to adhere to this pledge of not transforming no matter how strongly I was drawn to its false escape. I would not strive toward some refined and filtered idea of a future that didn't exist. What I needed was radical self-acceptance; to meet myself exactly where I was, not where I thought I had to be. Otherwise I'd likely be in transit forever, waiting for the moment when I finally arrived at the belief that I was worthy of being loved.

I sank back into the bathtub, letting the water reach my chin. I was happy with my decision, my new plan. But then again, wasn't this just another pledge? The urge for transformation masquerading as something else: transformation in the form of not transforming. It was becoming too complicated. I had analyzed my thoughts into meaninglessness once again. I needed to stop putting so much pressure on myself. No, I needed to stop pressuring myself to stop pressuring myself.

I shut my eyes, attempting to tune out of my thoughts and into my fundamental physicality; the rushing of blood and the steady beat of my heart. I took deep, consistent breaths and tried to think of nothing. Even then I was aware of the irony that meditation was only appealing to me once my thoughts had become so cyclical that I longed for a break from myself.

My phone buzzed on the tiles. I reached over the ledge to pick it up. It was Beverly:

Um did you know your dad and Elke have an account for their coaching business?

Another message followed:

They have 30k followers!

She sent me a link.

I clicked it and saw she was right. My dad and Elke had an account, a surprising number of followers, and a bio that read:

Shane and Elke
Relationship and intimacy coaching
We help couples ignite together

Their feed was filled with videos of them sitting side by side on cushions addressing the camera. I tapped on one and my dad's voice filled the room.

"Hey everyone, Shane here. Welcome to our 'Thirty Days of Thoughts' series, where each day we pick a theme to discuss. Today Elke and I thought we would talk about honesty. We all know that honesty is important for intimacy—"

I exited the video and continued scrolling, stopping to occasionally watch another video or read a caption. The whole account felt like the answer to a question no one had asked, but then I remembered that's what practically every account was, and in this case there appeared to be a genuine audience that wanted to hear the answers. I was surprised to see that my dad had stage presence, a certain je ne sais quoi, something genuine and instantly likable. He spoke earnestly and it felt, as a viewer, like he was addressing me directly. I found a live Q&A video where the two of them had answered a series of questions their followers had apparently submitted to them.

"Thank you all for submitting your questions," Elke said. "We might have to do a part two. We received over a hundred."

My mouth dropped open. A hundred people wanted to ask my father and Elke a question about their life?

"Okay," she said, appearing to be reading the first question from her phone. "So, *How long have you lived in Indonesia?*"

They looked at each other.

"Well, I'll go first," she continued. "I moved here from Munich about twelve years ago."

"Thirteen years for me," my dad added.

"Okay—this is related, so let's jump to this one: *How did you find the courage to move to Bali?*" Elke asked.

A message from Beverly dropped down my screen:

Omg there's a video where they talk about mutual masturbation

I frowned, swiping the message away.

My dad began speaking, "I think—" He paused, as if sorting through his thoughts. "Well, there's a bit of backstory required here. I became a father really young—at eighteen, actually—and because of that I never had the same grace period to make mistakes like other young people do when they enter adulthood. That sort of trial-and-error stage of life was not available to me. I had to help support a family."

Elke was nodding and smiling encouragingly at him as he spoke.

"So I started a bricklaying business and I made a path for my life, which I followed for over a decade, but it was not the path that my soul truly desired. Over the years, I developed anxiety and depression and started drinking a lot. Honestly, I went to a dark place, and my wife at the time—the mother of my daughter—was going through something similar. We were fighting a lot. When she and I separated, I went on a surfing trip to Bali and after just a week here it felt like a weight had been lifted off me. I felt light, at peace, happy. I was present for the first time in a long time."

My father's past unhappiness was not a revelation to me. I had memories of my parents fighting—shouting and slamming doors, or not speaking for hours while I sat silently in between them—but to hear him disclose the depths of his un-happiness was enlightening. I sat up straight and turned the volume up higher so I could hear every word.

"That's how I found the courage to move. I knew I was a better person when I was here. I had to come back, stay for longer, and try to heal."

"Okay—what's the next one?" my father asked, looking over at Elke's phone. *"What is the hardest thing you've ever done?"*

"Hmm—for me it would be saying goodbye to my mother," Elke answered candidly. My father placed a hand on her back in support. "She passed away from pancreatic cancer when I was twenty-five. But I know she would be proud of the way I live now. She always encouraged me to follow my dreams and pursue a life I love."

She looked at my father expectantly. He placed his hands together in prayer, resting his chin on the tips of his fingers, his eyes pensively focused on the ceiling.

"For me it would be leaving my daughter behind when I moved to Bali," he said, dropping his hands back out of the frame. "That was by far the hardest decision of my life."

My mention was a surprise. I held my breath in anticipation of what he was going to say next.

"I had to choose between staying there in Australia with her," he continued, "or stepping away to figure out why I was so unhappy. It was a complicated thing to explain to a teen-ager, but I regret that I never tried. I never sat her down and explained why I did it. I never let her know that it was noth-ing to do with me not wanting to be around her or not loving her." He shook his head.

My throat began to constrict.

"I did it because I wanted her to know the best version of

me. I wanted her to have a father who set a good example. At the time I assumed she'd understand when she was older, but I could have explained it to her and I wish I had."

I pressed my teeth into my bottom lip, now viewing the video through an ambush of tears. It was true that my dad had never had a conversation with me about why he decided to move, and I had never pursued any answers. As a teenager I'd been afraid that I would be made to hear a list of all the reasons why living in Bali was better than being around me. As an adult, I'd stubbornly wanted to believe that his reasons no longer mattered.

"I learned from that experience that sometimes we hurt people in our pursuit of happiness," he continued, now crossing over the boundary of the question. "And I do believe that sometimes that's unavoidable. I don't think anyone should be held back from pursuing a life that makes them happy. But I also believe that good communication can spare feelings. It's in being vulnerable and sharing our deepest fears, our regrets, our desires and sadness, that we can leave less destruction in our wake."

I wiped my eyes. Even though it seemed I was not the intended audience for this confession, his words were relieving me of some burden.

"So true," Elke agreed. "Okay, next question: *How did you two meet?*"

She looked over at my dad. "It was at my yoga class, wasn't it?"

"Yeah, that's right." He nodded. "I was living here in Uluwatu and teaching surfing lessons when I heard about a new yoga class and I decided to go. There she was." He gazed back at Elke.

"The moment I saw Elke, I felt this insane energy radiating off her and I knew I just had to talk to her. So I hung back after the class, and we chatted for an hour. Instantly we had this incredible, divine connection, this deeply *sexual* connection. Our sexual energy—"

I winced, frantically tapping the screen in an attempt to exit the video.

Another message from Beverly dropped down the screen:

Are you watching these? I'M DYING.

//

Later that afternoon I was lying on the floor of my apartment and staring at the ceiling, watching as the light cast through the window morphed slowly to orange, when something Evan had said to me asserted itself once more, as if rising from the swirling inky sea of a Magic 8 Ball.

Evan had admitted that he'd inflicted silence on me because he hoped that, if pushed in such a way, I would come back to him, bringing with me some indication of how much he meant to me. He did this selfishly to assuage the fear he felt, but also because I had, in his mind, forced his hand with my behavior and tendency to withhold.

"It's in being vulnerable and sharing our deepest fears, our regrets, our desires and sadness, that we can leave less destruction in our wake." I could see the truth in my dad's words.

The lack of vulnerability and communication between Evan and me had caused destruction. There was no point in performing an audit on what was Evan's fault and what was mine. If I were to do that, to wash my hands of responsibility and to blame Evan and Nadia, I would steal from myself an opportunity to learn. The only things worth salvaging from the wreckage were lessons I could take into the future and the most valuable lessons were the ones that could inform me on my own behavior. The truth was that I had a tendency to withhold, to react to silence with stubborn complicity, which was arguably just another form of punishment through withdrawal: the act of reflecting silence back like a mirror. It was not unlike participating in some form of breath-holding competition.

My obsession with comparing myself to Emily had also shown that all of my efforts had not rid me of any fear. But rather, the more light I directed over the areas I wanted to uncover, the more shadows I created.

And, I admitted to myself, I avoided putting myself out there and being truly vulnerable because I was petrified of exposing myself to rejection. I knew why that was; I'd been hurt by the rejection I'd felt when my father decided to move away, the rejection I felt whenever my mother would sever our communication. It occurred to me then that if I dug at my mother's tendency to use silence to punish me, I would likely find the roots looked familiar.

All of these thoughts, of Evan, of my father, of my mother, of silence and punishment, rejection and love, were drawn to each other like magnets until they suddenly snapped into place.

Without moving from my back, I sent my arm out blindly beside me in search of my phone.

"Ana?" My mother answered on the third ring. I imagined her eyes narrowing and her lips drawing into a tight mauve-colored line.

"Hi, Mum."

"Good to know you're still alive. I haven't heard from you

in a while," she said. The words would usually set me on a defensive trajectory, but this time I allowed them to pass.

"How are you?" I asked. I could hear pan flutes in the background and the sound of her shaking out a towel. She was preparing for a client.

"Good—listen, I can't talk for long. I've got Linda coming for a Brazilian at four. But quick tell me, how's Melbourne?"

"Melbourne's good," I said.

"Is it? You sound a little flat."

"Well, I was dating a guy and then I found out he was sleeping with someone else."

I heard her stop fiddling with the towel.

"Oh, Ana. What happened?"

I told her everything, finally choosing to deny, at every turn, the constant urge to withhold my feelings and maintain a façade of doing well. I painfully extracted small vulnerable pieces of myself, like shards of glass from a wound, and offered them to her. Some pieces she acknowledged, others she discarded, but slowly I could hear in her voice as her usual defenses drew back and fell away. I continued on through this unknown territory, gathering the courage to say what I really wanted to.

"Mum," I began. "I'm sorry if it hurt you when I moved away, but I really haven't enjoyed the silence between us. Can we try to be better at this? I've missed you."

There was an awkward silence. She cleared her throat and then I heard her voice soften in a way that I never had before.

"Yes of course." She paused, taking a deep breath in. "I miss you too."

There was another pause. I remained silent, wary of making any sudden movements that might scare this timid moment away.

"Do you remember Barry?" she asked finally, her words signaling a return to the comfort of lighter topics. It felt as if we'd hiked to a summit and for a moment appreciated some vast and beautiful vista and now, having achieved our objective, were returning to the familiar path. I relaxed.

"Yes, unfortunately I do remember Barry."

"Did I ever tell you the story of what I did after I found out he was married?"

"I don't think so."

"Well, I went to his house and keyed his car."

"Mum." I laughed in surprise.

"I never told you this story?"

"Never."

"So, as I'm keying his car his wife, Wendy, comes out and catches me." I could hear that my mother was enjoying the act of entertaining me. She went on. "She says, 'What are you doing?' and I said, 'I'm keying his car.'"

I laughed again.

"Then she says, 'Barry's cleaning the pool, he'll be at least an hour.' And she asks if she can have a go. So I stood there and watched her carve *Prick* into the driver's side door. Anyway, now we're friends. We get coffee all the time. They got a divorce in the end."

She laughed and I heard the telling sound of a catch in her voice. I knew the sound well because I had the same affliction: the dreaded laugh-cry. For me laughter could often be a treacherous gateway to tears. It was like the door of my emotions opened and laughter came bustling through, unaware that other suppressed and opportunistic emotions had snuck out between its legs.

"You're insane." I laughed along with her, as tears slid silently down my cheeks.

thirty-nine

Alanis Morissette's album *Jagged Little Pill* was looping on repeat through my speaker. I was cleaning my apartment—in anticipation of Beverly's arrival—wiping down the stove and performing "All I Really Want" in my most earnest impersonation of Alanis's exasperated yodel. I had turned over a new leaf and found myself renewed. I'd glimpsed a clear and cloud-free horizon and kept my eye trained on it, holding myself steady through the turbulence until I reached it.

In other words, I had arrived at the one-month post-breakup mark.

My pledge for not transforming had been both a failure and a success. A success in the sense that I had not pursued change superficially, and a failure in the sense that, of course, change had happened anyway; I resigned from Gro after accepting a role at a user experience design agency. During my third interview I negotiated myself a wage higher than the one they were offering, following a script I'd found on the internet and at intervals discreetly wiping my sweaty palms on my pants. The office did not have a ping-pong table.

Soph had found a new role too, as were the requirements of our self-imposed "Resignation Pact." She left Gro a fortnight before I did. We celebrated her last day by getting sushi for lunch one last time. As a parting gift she tried to show me the Nudes Receivable album in her camera roll. I declined the present, swatting her phone out of my face and explaining that I wanted to be able to actually finish my tuna roll. It eventuated that our new offices were very close to each other. It would not be the last time we lunched together after all.

I hadn't heard from Evan for weeks, not since he clearly realized my decision to ignore him was not going to be retracted. I did hear from Lauren, though. She'd reached out a week or so after I'd stormed out of Evan's apartment:

I hope you're okay :(I know you
don't want to talk to Evan (fair
enough . . .) but I really hope we
can still be friends. I have so much
to fill you in on with Josh. For
example, he told me he only washes
his sheets when he does a "big
clean" and when I asked when he
does a "big clean" he said "when I
have a rent inspection." Let's catch
up soon? xx

We'd since been meeting for coffee nearly every weekend.

Beverly would be arriving in a few days. She'd booked tickets the moment I'd given her the all clear. She would stay with me for a week and we would drink wine and share my bed, talking late into the night, just like old times.

//

I was rinsing out the sponge when I heard a shuffling sound followed by a *clink* just outside the door.

Maria had still been placing food on my doorstep once a week. I'd been meaning to offer to do some more laundry for her, but I hadn't yet had the chance. I opened the door in the hopes of catching her, but it wasn't Maria. Instead, a man was crouched over in the act of fixing the foil that had come unstuck from the plate.

"Oh—sorry," he apologized, picking the plate back up and returning to his full height. He was thin with curly dark hair and the manufactured paleness of someone who spent most of their time indoors; an olive complexion that wasn't meeting its potential.

"You're not Maria," I said.

"No, I'm Alex," he explained, holding the plate out to me. "She asked me to drop this off for you."

"Thank you," I said, taking it and placing it on my kitchen counter. I quickly leaned over and paused my music before "You Oughta Know" began and I started involuntarily foaming at the mouth and hissing along with it.

"You're not Greek," Alex said.

"I know."

"Sorry—it's just that my yia-yia thinks you are."

"I thought she might. Can you keep a secret?"

"Of course. I'd rather not disappoint her anyway. She really likes you."

As he spoke, I realized that I recognized his face. He was

Alexander, the boy in the photo that Maria had shown me, only now he was an adult and no longer into wearing eyeliner.

"You're the boy in the photo with the My Chemical Romance T-shirt," I announced.

"Oh great, you saw it." He winced, color blooming on his cheeks. "I was such an overweight, angsty, emo teenager. No one understood the struggle of being a well-fed, constantly doted on Greek child."

"You were pretty cute." I laughed.

He grimaced but in a pleased sort of way and his eyes lingered on me; they were dark, almost black, and lined with thick eyelashes. I turned away from them and peeked under the foil of the plate he'd delivered. It held a pile of biscuits, each of them sprinkled with almond flakes.

"Your yia-yia's very sweet," I said.

"Don't be fooled, she always has an agenda," he warned.

"Oh, I believe that. She wants me to keep doing her laundry for her."

He laughed knowingly.

"She told me you baked her a cake?"

"I did. That was before I found out that she ran a bakery."

"Yeah, bold," he said as if he was genuinely impressed by my bravery. "I asked her if the cake was any good."

I looked back at him, waiting for the verdict. "And?"

He hesitated for a moment. "She said you're very beautiful."

"*Oof.*" I laughed. "Wow."

"Don't be offended, she has incredibly high standards. No one in the family has ever baked a cake that impressed her."

The mention of family reminded me of the conversation

Maria and I had when I helped her hang out her sheets a couple of months ago.

"You just moved back from London, right? Maria said it was to be closer to your nephew."

"Did she?" He laughed. "Well, I suppose that is partially true, but really it had more to do with a particularly bad bout of seasonal affective disorder. Good to know she holds me to such noble standards though."

I scoffed. "I haven't had a single conversation with Maria without her proudly mentioning you."

"Really?" he asked, looking amused.

I nodded.

"I've always had a suspicion that I was her favorite."

The conversation was organically drawing itself to a close, but I had an urge to keep talking to him, to hold him there in front of me a little while longer.

"Well, it was nice to meet you, Ana," he said, clearly having the same sense as me.

"Yeah, you too."

He hovered in the doorway, as if mulling over some complex equation.

"Do you want to join us for dinner? If you don't have plans," he asked finally.

"Oh, no, I'd feel rude."

"You wouldn't be rude at all. There's going to be way too much food and, honestly, my yia-yia would love for you to join us. She actually told me to knock and ask, but I didn't want to interrupt your"—he glanced at the speaker—"performance."

I closed my eyes and felt my face flush. When I opened them again, I saw him grinning at me with genuine pleasure.

"I love Alanis," he admitted.

"Do you?" I replied skeptically.

"Yeah." He nodded. "No one ever believes me when I say that, but it's true. I have two older sisters, that album was one of the soundtracks to my childhood. So what about dinner? Can I give Maria some good news?"

I imagined sitting around a table with Maria and her family, sharing food and wine and talking. An involuntary grin began to spread across my face.

"Okay, yeah. That'd be fun."

"Great," he said casually, his tone betrayed by his beaming smile.

"Ah, I might just have a shower first. I've been cleaning and—"

"Oh, yeah, of course. Sorry, I'll go," he said, stepping back from the door. "See you soon, Ana."

I said goodbye and closed the door, waiting a beat before rolling up the blinds on the kitchen window just enough so that I could watch as he walked away. He was still smiling, his grin reaching the very sides of his face. I could tell just by looking at the back of his head.

I picked up my phone, navigating to the search bar and lingering there. I could look Alex up. His father was Maria's son and I knew Maria's last name from the handful of times I'd collected her mail from her letter box and delivered it to her door. I considered the option, my cursor blinking at me in anticipation like a ticking clock.

ACKNOWLEDGMENTS

It's difficult to adequately acknowledge everyone who has been involved in the process of turning an idea into a novel. There are sources—chance interactions, overheard conversations between strangers, previously mundane-seeming memories—that don't lend themselves to the task of writing an acknowledgment page. So, I'll stick to the ones that do:

To my agent, Benjamin Paz, thank you for your constant wisdom and guidance and for being such a fast reader. I'm infinitely grateful for that "cold call."

To the team: Clio Seraphim and Whitney Frick at The Dial Press, Jane Palfreyman and Genevieve Buzo at Allen & Unwin, Andrianna deLone at CAA, and all the many others who work alongside them (especially Christa Munns, Deonie Fiford, and Pamela Dunne). I am so lucky to have so many talented and passionate people working with me. Gen gets a special mention here for coming up with the most perfect title for this book. Thank you, thank you, thank you.

To anyone else at Curtis Brown Australia, The Dial Press,

CAA, and Allen & Unwin who has even so much as sent a singular email about me or my book—thank you!

Gratitude will always be owed to Chris, without whom—and I'm not being dramatic—this book would not exist. Your unwavering belief in me is the reason I'm the person I am today. Thank you for reading twenty-eight drafts of this novel, you never have to read it again now.

Thank you to Sue and Graham Gladman, who read the first ever version of this book and encouraged me to keep going.

To Emily Bitto, thank you for the encouragement and delicate handling of a very fragile early draft. (Thanks also to *Kill Your Darlings* for facilitating this connection.)

To Louisa Trainer, thank you for sharing your yia-yia with me.

To family, blood and otherwise: Mum and Dad, Steve and Jan, Sue and Graham (again), Laura and Patrick, Brennen and Shannan and Amy. Thank you for the constant support and love.

To Celeste Holm, Jasmine Smith, Jayden Pileggi, Rachel Brown, Benjamin Quartermaine, Dylan Hughes, Holly Crane, Louisa Trainer (again), and Simon Webster—thank you for the messages, pep talks, and hugs.

Lastly, thank you to anyone and everyone who picks this book up. In a world where there are so many apps and streaming services vying for our time, the fact that you chose to spend yours reading my book will never cease to amaze me. Thank you.

ABOUT THE AUTHOR

Amy Taylor is a writer based in Melbourne (Narrm). *Search History* is her debut novel, and she is currently working on her next book.

Instagram: @amy_ester_

The Dial Press, an imprint of Random House, publishes books driven by the heart.

Follow us on Instagram:
@THEDIALPRESS

Discover other Dial Press books and sign up for our e-newsletter:

thedialpress.com